Island of

Hope

Praise for Award-Winning, *Island of Miracles*
"A beautiful account of the love and healing support of community!"
Chandi Owen, Author

"I can already see the Hallmark Channel movie!"
Anne, Goodreads

Praise for Award-Winning, *Island of Promise*
"[Amy] draws you in to the lives of her characters…she paints the picture so eloquently it's almost like you are there.
Cindy, Amazon

"I love Amy Schisler's books. I cried tears of both sadness and joy while reading this. I read this book in a day!"
Mitzi Mead, Goodreads

Praise for *The Devil's Fortune*
"The Devil's Fortune is a beautifully written, atmospheric tale chock-full of adventure and secrets. It gripped me throughout and left me feeling satisfied in the end. Highly recommended!"
Carissa Ann Lynch, USA Today bestselling author of MY SISTER IS MISSING

"Schisler once again delivers on her unique ability to combine rich history with a brilliantly layered cast of characters. The lines of what was, what is, and what is yet to be are beautifully weaved within this tale of pirates, treasures, secrets, faith and love. Destiny awaits!"
Alexa Jacobs, Author & President, Maryland Romance Writers

Praise for Award-Winning, *Whispering Vines*
"The heartbreaking, endearing, charming, and romantic scenes will surely inveigle you to keep reading."
Serious Reading Book Review

"Schisler's writing is a verbal masterpiece of art."
Alexa Jacobs, Author & President of Maryland Romance Writers

Also Available by Amy Schisler

Novels
A Place to Call Home
Picture Me
Whispering Vines
Summer's Squall
The Devil's Fortune

Chincoteague Island Trilogy
Island of Miracles
Island of Promise
Island of Hope

Children's Books
Crabbing With Granddad
The Greatest Gift

Collaborations
Stations of the Cross Meditations for Moms (with Anne Kennedy, Susan Anthony, Chandi Owen, and Wendy Clark)

Island of

Hope

By Amy Schisler

Published by:
Chesapeake Sunrise Publishing
Amy Schisler
Bozman, MD
2019

To Nick.
For many years, you have been the son I never had. I am so delighted with all that you've done and what you've become. I love you as my own.
Semper Fi.

Family Trees
Kelly and Middleton Families

Trevor Kelly

Veronica Zollo Kelly

Walter Middleton

Mitzi Mead Middleton

Kayla Kelly (Reynolds) Middleton

Aaron Kelly

Zachary Middleton

Katherine Middleton Kelly

Edward Middleton (Adopted)

Todd Middleton (Adopted)

Miren Kelly

Baby Kelly

Nicholas Gilmour Black

Taylor Corrine Murray

I lived most of my childhood in one remote part of the world or another. The daughter of an anthropologist, I learned about marriage from the Matsé people in the Amazon. I learned about community from the Australian Indigenous Peoples. The Torres Strait Islanders taught me what it means to be family. The Métis and Inuit taught me about God. But it was on a tiny island off the coast of Virginia where I saw all of those things put into practice in my own life.

From *Discovering the World On a Barrier Island*
by Katherine Middleton Kelly

CHAPTER ONE

A smile broke out on Nick's face as he crossed the causeway. He could see the line of hotels that created the right-hand side of the skyline on the west coast of the island. Beyond the buildings was the small downtown, and on the other side of that, was the marshy shoreline. Once he reached the island, he would proceed to the downtown though the house he rented was on the opposite side, to the left of the hotels and tourist hotspots. His best friend, Zach, had asked Nick to stop by the community center before he went home.

Nick would rather head straight to his house. He and his friend, Zach, shared the home for a short time before Zach married the girl next door, literally, and moved in with her and her two sons. He was beat from the long ride from Richmond, and he longed for a nap and a cold beer, not necessarily in that order, but Zach had always been there for Nick; and if there was one good thing that could be said about Nick, it was that he was loyal, sometimes to a fault.

As he fiddled with the radio in search of a clearer station, a song broke through the crackle of the on-air static, and Nick's hand froze on the dial. The song was an old one, but one that he liked to play on his guitar. It was a favorite of Megan's, and the memory of their time together caused a lump to form in his throat.

He conjured her image in his mind. Megan had the darkest hair and deepest brown eyes he had ever seen. A man could get lost in the depths of those eyes, and not even Nick's Marine training could save him from drowning in them. But it had been months since he'd heard from her. Until this morning.

Just before Nick left the police academy, with his worn-out military-issued duffle bag in hand, he'd received a text from Megan. After blowing him off when he first left for the academy, letting his texts go unanswered and eventually not answering his calls, she had disappeared from his life. The text this morning was affirmation that things were over. Megan was involved in a sexual harassment case back in her hometown of Washington, DC, and she was leaving to go back there for the trial. He knew that much. Zach had kept him informed. But the text let Nick know that she had decided to stay in DC. Her grandmother was beginning to fail, and her brother was unreliable. Megan was gone, and Nick had to move on.

As he drove through the downtown, Nick looked around at the shops that lined the street. There were a lot more people in town than he was used to seeing, but it was mid-May, and the beachgoers were beginning to arrive. He turned the wheel and maneuvered his car into the parking lot of the community center. The lot was packed, and Nick wondered if there was an event being held in the main room. It seemed that there was always something happening on the island, from art shows to seafood festivals to veterans' celebrations. He wasn't sure why Zach wanted to meet him here at such a busy time of day, and he hoped whatever was going on wouldn't get in their way and put off his nap time.

Though the lot was full, the community center was eerily quiet as Nick entered the atrium. The glass doors to the main room revealed nothing but darkness, and he wondered where all of the people were. Maybe people were just parking in the lot and being shuttled elsewhere for an event. That happened sometimes, and Nick breathed a sigh of relief that he and Zach could get down to business and be finished—whatever the business was—so that he could get home. But where the heck was Zach?

Nick hesitated before opening the door to the community center. As he pushed it open, the lights switched on, and he was momentarily blinded, but he could hear the shouts of joy.

"Surprise!"

Nick gazed at the crowd of people gathered in the room and swallowed the lump in his throat. Marines don't cry, he told himself, but he was having a hard time holding back the waterworks. He shook his head as he took in the beautiful scene. Everyone he knew on the island was gathered under a large banner reading, *Congratulations, Officer Black*. The sight threatened to bring tears to his eyes.

Playing the part of the happy-go-lucky guy everyone believed him to be, Nick thanked his well-wishers. He went to Kayla, Zach's wife, and hugged her, trying not to notice the scarf she still wore to cover her chemo-induced baldness. He hugged Zach's sister, Kate, and marveled at the size of her belly. She was showing more than he expected. He shook the hands of all the others who had come to celebrate his graduation from the state police academy and his return to the island and gave Zach and Kayla's sons, Todd and EJ, high-fives. Nick resisted the urge to grab Todd and pull him into a very unmanly, tear-inducing hug. The little boy beamed up at him, and Nick felt a tug at his heart. Nick had played a small part in finding the boy after his kidnapping earlier that winter, and the boy would always hold a special place in Nick's heart.

"How many inches did you grow while I was gone, kid?" Nick tussled Todd's light brown hair. "You've got to stop growing on me."

"Mom says I might be taller than EJ someday." Todd's grin widened.

"She might be right," Nick told him.

"A toast," Zach called out, handing Nick a bottle of beer. "To the newest Chincoteague Island police officer, Nick Black."

"To Nick," said Paul, the island's chief of police, who raised his own bottle before taking a swig.

Downing a good deal of his bottle, Nick wiped his chin with the back of his hand and looked around. "If you're all here, who's minding the station?"

Paul laughed. "Chris and Steve are staying dry today."

Nick glanced at the two officers who held up bottles of water. He finished off his beer and looked at Zach. "That's one down, and many more to go. Let's get this party started."

Zach shook his head, and Nick laughed before heading to the makeshift bar to find another bottle.

Megan who?

He continued to smile, despite the emptiness he felt in his chest, as he downed another beer.

***

"What do you think?" Kate asked her brother. Zach looked across the room at Nick. The young officer threw his head back and laughed, regaling the other officers with stories of his time at the academy.

"He seems okay. It's not like they were together for that long before he left. He'll be fine."

"I wish I knew someone—"

"Don't go there," Zach warned. "When he finds the right one, everything will fall into place. You know that better than anyone."

Kate smiled as she shifted her gaze to Aaron. He was spooning ice cream into Miren's mouth, open with anticipation like a baby bird's beak, and the sight filled her with joy. "You're right. God will bring him the right person at the right time."

"What's the whispering about?" Kayla asked, coming up behind them.

Zach motioned to their friend. "Kate's conspiring."

"Am not," Kate protested. "It was just a thought."

Kayla looked from her husband to her sister-in-law, and her eyes twinkled. "Zach, give her a break. She just wants Nick to have what the rest of us have."

"So do I, but it will happen when it's supposed to happen."

"I guess I'm just feeling guilty because Megan is my friend. I mean, I never thought they were right for each other, but still…"

"As I recall, you were worried about this from the start." Zach reminded her. "I seem to remember a conversation—"

"Yes, I know. I said I was afraid she would break his heart. I should have stopped it back then."

Kayla gently touched Kate's arm. "You couldn't have. They're both adults."

Zach snickered. "I wouldn't call Nick an adult."

"Be nice," Kayla admonished him before turning to Kate. "They made the decision to date. You didn't push them together. Thankfully, it was short-lived, and Nick can now settle into his job and his new life here on the island without any distractions."

"I wouldn't bet on that," Zach said as he watched Nick.

Kate sighed. It was going to be an interesting summer.

***

Nick bagged the trash while his friends laughed and joked amongst themselves. He was happy for them, truly he was. They had all been through a lot, and each one overcame their struggles, but they didn't do it alone. The four of them had each other, and they had rock solid families who stood by them.

He tried hard not to be jealous, perhaps envious was a better word, though Nick supposed they were both really the same thing. He spent his own youth being kicked from one foster home to another, never feeling like he belonged anywhere. No doubt it was that feeling that led him to the Marines. He gained an instant family, a group of people who had to count on each other in every way imaginable, their very lives depending upon them looking out for one another. His time in the Marines was his happiest on earth until he came to Chincoteague. From the moment he arrived and temporarily moved in with Zach, he had become part of the Kelly family, and he actually felt like one of Ronnie and Trevor's own children.

"Hey, you okay?" Zach asked quietly.

Nick realized he had been standing over the bag of trash, lost in his thoughts, as everyone else was getting ready to leave. He shook his head and sighed.

"Yeah, man, I'm good. It's just…" He looked around at the room that had, not long before, been filled with people he considered his closest friends and family. "This kind of got to me, you know?" He looked at Zach. "Thank you."

Nick tried to smile, but his heart wasn't in it. He appreciated the party, more than Zach could ever know, but in the end, Zach and Kayla, Kate and Aaron, Ronnie and Trevor—they were a real family, and Nick, well, Nick was just Nick, the guy they took in.

"Sorry about Megan," Zach said, as if he could read Nick's thoughts.

"Whatever, man. You know me. I never wanted any of that stuff anyway." Even as he voiced the words, Nick knew he was lying. To Zach and to himself.

"I mean, honestly, do you really think I care if some chick thinks she's too good to stick around?" He made a tisking sound with his tongue. "Come on, I left so many women behind in Richmond, I can't even remember all of their names."

Zach gave Nick a long, hard look before nodding his head. "Whatever you say, Nick. We're heading out. Kayla's exhausted, and Kate needs to get home and put her feet up. Paul and Anne are going to finish cleaning and close up. They said you don't have to stay. Paul's your chief, so if he says to go, you should listen." Zach winked at Nick. "Go back to the house and relax.

You've only got one day off before you're on the job, and believe me, the summers are crazy around here. You won't be able to take a load off again until after Labor Day."

"Thanks, but I'll help them get things done here. I don't have anywhere else to be."

"Suit yourself. Will I see you at Ronnie and Trevor's on Sunday? Dinner's at one o'clock."

"You bet, Zach. See you then."

Nick reached for Zach's hand, but Zach pulled him into a man hug.

"I'm glad you're home," Zach said as they parted. "It wasn't the same without you."

"I'm glad to be home," he said, grinning. The little island was the closest thing to a home he'd ever had, and whether Megan was there or not, he sure was glad to be back.

***

"Nick seemed well." Aaron rubbed Kate's feet while Miren played with blocks on the floor beside them. "Don't you think?"

With her back against the sofa and a pillow behind her for comfort, Kate leaned her head back and closed her eyes. She was so tired, worn out from the party, the pregnancy, and the worry she kept deep inside about being able to carry the baby to term. She blew out her breath and looked at Aaron.

"He did. I'm sorry that Megan broke his heart, but Zach thinks Nick will bounce back and be just fine. I hope the same can be said for Megan. She has a lot on her plate with the trial and her grandmother's health."

"She's tough. Otherwise, she wouldn't have made it this far."

"You're right. She's going to be just fine. I just wish she and Nick hadn't gotten together to begin with." Kate shrugged. "I feel terrible about it now, but I'm hoping to make it up to him."

"Don't even think about it." Aaron said. "You are not going to go poking your nose into Nick's love life."

Kate leaned her head back and closed her eyes with a sigh. "You sound just like Zach." She shifted so Aaron would switch to her other foot. His massages were sheer bliss.

Aaron laughed. "Good. Then I'm not alone. I mean it, Kate. Let it go. Nick will find someone."

"I know. I'll stay out of it," Kate said, resisting a moan of sheer pleasure as he turned her tired, swollen feet into moldable clay.

"Look, Nick's a big boy. He's got a good head on his shoulders, when he uses it, and he can decide who he wants to date. Maybe it's best for him to take some time to get a feel for his job, to get more involved in the island. If he's going to stick around, he should expand his friend group, stop hanging out with all of us old people."

"Speak for yourself." Kate shot Aaron a look and leaned back against the couch.

"Nick's young. He's what, twenty-three? He needs to find his place on the island and in the world. Until he does, he won't be ready for a relationship. From what I understand, he had a pretty crappy upbringing. He has a chance to rewrite his story, change his fate, and pursue his happiness without being held back by anyone or anything. Let him figure out who he is and what he wants in life and in a woman."

Kate looked at her husband, her mouth agape. "How are you so good at that?"

"At what?"

"At reading people and knowing exactly what they want and need. You did it with me. You do it with Kayla."

"Kayla's my twin. She doesn't count."

"You did it with Zach. You knew he was a sniper within minutes of meeting him.

"I wouldn't say minutes."

"Still, how are you so good at it?"

"After Craig died on my watch, on my command to board the ship, the guilt ate me up. I closed myself off from getting close to anyone, until you came along anyway. I knew he'd signed up for the job. He knew, as a member of the military, that there's always a chance something could happen. We all know that. Still, I blamed myself for not being the one down in the hold of that ship, for not seeing the man with the gun, for not stopping the shot somehow. Sure, we took the whole crew in the end, and we stopped a major drug shipment from coming into the US, but I lost a man, a friend. I spent years asking myself what I could have done differently."

"What does that have to do with being able to read people?"

"I spent a long time alone. Outside of work and family, I kept a distance from everyone, even Paul, and he's my oldest friend. I just didn't know what else to do." Aaron shrugged and continued. "It was my mom and Kayla who finally reached me. They insisted that I start going to things—cookouts at Paul's, festivals and events on the island, church. When Father Darryl was transferred here, I started seeing him. He was my age, and he certainly knew how it was to feel apart from everyone around him. He helped me get over my guilt and be open to life. Not long after that, you came along."

"I don't know what Zach would have done without his frequent talks with Father Darryl. Maybe Nick—"

"Kate." Aaron squeezed her foot, and she looked at him.

"I know, I know. I won't butt in." She sighed. "You missed your calling, Commander. You should have gone into psychology."

Aaron grinned. "It's in my genes. After all, Ronnie is my mom."

Kate believed him. If ever there were to be a Patron Saint of Good Advice, Ronnie would be the person the Vatican would choose for the position.

Feeling a rush of emotions, Kate rose to her knees and leaned down to kiss her husband. As she bent for the kiss, she was met with two chubby hands plowing into her protruding stomach.

"Me hug, too," Miren said.

Kate leaned back, and Aaron scooped up their daughter, bringing her in for a group hug.

"I'm so lucky," Kate whispered, feeling Aaron's arm around her and Miren in his lap.

"I'm the lucky one," Aaron said. Kate didn't argue with him. They were all blessed to have each other.

***

"Welcome home," Ronnie said as she enveloped Nick in a hug. "I made your favorite—spaghetti. With extra garlic bread."

Nick bit his lips, trying not to let his emotions get the better of him. Nobody had ever made him his favorite anything.

"Thanks, Ronnie. That means a lot to me."

Nick said hello to the rest of the family, keenly aware that someone was missing.

"I'm so glad you came," Kate said as she hugged him. "It hasn't been the same without you."

Nick's stomach filled with good vibrations at the sound of her words. "Thanks. I know it's not true, but it means a lot to hear it."

"It's true," Kate insisted. "We're all happy you're home."

Nick knew Kate was sincere, and the warm feelings in his stomach spread throughout his entire body. He was home, and there was no place he'd rather be.

"Dinner is ready, everyone," Ronnie called from the dining room.

Nick waited for everyone else to sit, trying to figure out where he belonged. He had always sat next to Megan, and the room seemed empty without her.

"Nick, sit by me," Todd called, and Nick went to the boy's side. The conversation was never dull when Todd was involved.

After Trevor led them in the blessing, the food was passed around the table, and conversation bubbled like an uncorked bottle of champagne.

Nick was filled in on the few changes to the Sunday dinner routine at Ronnie and Trevor's that had been adopted since he left for the academy. He learned that the families now took turns making dessert. The number of people at the dinner table kept growing, and nobody wanted Ronnie to take on all of the work by herself each week. To be fair, with summer approaching, everyone would soon begin taking turns hosting cookouts, crab feasts, and other dinners at their own homes.

"Don't worry, nobody's going to ask you to host a meal and actually cook," Zach told him as he passed the garlic bread.

"Hey, even I can order pizza."

"Pizza!" Ronnie said with a laugh. "The boys would be thrilled."

"Nick's making pizza?" Todd beamed up at his idol. "I'm in!"

"Hey, buddy, you can come over for pizza any time."

Todd grinned, and Nick felt contentment wash over him.

Despite the changes, dinner felt just like old times to Nick. Almost. If only he had someone to share it with.

When we lived among the Indigenous Peoples of the Australian Outback, I saw what it truly means to be a family. Family is much more than a group of people who share a common bloodline. It's a group of people who accept each other, support each other, and love each other, no matter where they came from, who they are, or what they've done. Not until I found myself on Chincoteague, did I truly understand the importance of it all.

From *Discovering the World On a Barrier Island*
by Katherine Middleton Kelly

CHAPTER TWO

The morning sun was warm on Taylor's back as she rode into the small corral. Her blonde hair hung in a braid down her back, and a white straw cowboy hat was perched on her head. She stepped down from Stormy, so named after the last foal of Misty of Chincoteague, the famed pony of the island and in literature. Like Misty's foal, Stormy had been born during a terrible storm. The first Stormy was born during the Ash Wednesday Storm of 1962, while Taylor's Stormy was born during Hurricane Tara, which hit the island two years ago.

"How'd she do?" Pete Murray asked his daughter. He clapped his horse on the rear and sent her out to pasture and walked to Taylor. He reached up to help her remove the saddle and carried it to the barn as Taylor answered.

"Perfect. She's the easiest foal I've ever handled. She has such a gentle nature." Taylor rubbed down the pony with a large soapy sponge. Stormy swished her tail at a fly but made no other movement. "She's just so agreeable and trusting."

Pete returned to Taylor's side and took another sponge from the bucket. "Well, you were there the night she was born. She knows you. She trusts that you will take care of her."

Taylor smiled. "I know. That's why I wanted her so badly at the auction the following year. I spent all those months making sure she knew I was still there." Taylor frowned. "I just wish I could have been the one to corral and lead her across the channel."

Pete sighed. "Taylor, we've been over this a hundred times. There has never been—"

"I know." Taylor cut him off and turned to face him. "There has never been a female Saltwater Cowboy. So what? Just because there has never been one, that doesn't mean it can't ever happen. Why won't they accept me?"

Pete shrugged. "It's not you, honey. It's just the way it is. The men—" He cleared his throat. "The people who drive the ponies across the channel for the auction come from the same families who have been corralling and driving the ponies for as long as the pony auction has been going on. The tradition has always been handed down to the boys in the family. It's just the way it's done."

Taylor shook her head, the same fury coursing through her veins that had been there since she was a little girl. "It's a ridiculous tradition. I've had my name on the list for years. I've manned the gates. I've kept watch over the pens. Heck, I've trained half the ponies that have been bought at the auction. I know more about horses than most of the young guys that have been accepted. Why am I overlooked every year?" She slammed the sponge into the bucket, and water splashed up on her, her father, and her pony. Stormy tossed her head back and nickered.

Taylor laid a gentle hand on the pony's neck and whispered to her. "It's okay, girl."

Without answering, Pete went to the side of the barn and turned on the spigot. He uncoiled the hose and pulled it toward Stormy. Taylor stepped out of the way and watched her father hose off the pony.

Taylor didn't demand an answer. She knew there wasn't one. Her father had lobbied hard for his daughter for the past nine years, since she was fourteen years old, but it made no difference. She sighed as she watched the horse revel in the spray. Stormy loved her baths. Unlike most of the other horses and ponies Taylor had worked with, Stormy allowed the water to dry on her back, aided by the hot sun, rather than roll in the dirt to hurry the process. Taylor sometimes thought that Stormy considered herself too prim and proper to roll on the ground. The thought made Taylor smile.

Pete finished rinsing the pony and turned toward the barn. "Time to get going. We've got a lot of work to do today. The Highsmith job is already behind schedule. We've got a lot to do to catch up. It's going to be a long day with a lot of heavy lifting. We need a good breakfast to get us going." He returned the hose to its holder on the side of the building while Taylor led Stormy and Big Red to their separate paddocks.

When she was done, her father went to her. "You'll get your chance, Taylor. I'll see to it myself."

She had her doubts, but she smiled at her father. He'd give her the moon if he could. She went to him and looped her arm around his as they headed toward the house.

"Thanks, Dad. I know you wish that was true as much as I do."

Before they reached the house, Pete stopped. Taylor felt his arm tense and his body go rigid. Before she could grasp what was happening, her father was on the ground. His eyes bulged, and his mouth opened. His hands went to his chest.

"Dad!" She went to the ground beside him and screamed for help. "Mom! Jenny! Help!" She reached into her back pocket and fumbled for her phone. She heard her mother and her younger sister running up behind her.

"Help, my father, he's... I think he's having a heart attack. Please, come fast."

***

Nick took a sip of his Coca-Cola, not the healthiest morning beverage, but his drink of choice. He looked out the window at the water beyond the marsh grasses behind the house he once shared with Zach before Zach and Kayla married and became their own happy family.

As he watched the waves roll in, Nick thought about dinner the previous night and how much he admired the lives and families his friends had. He often thought about his birth family though there wasn't much to think about. His mother gave him up when he was a toddler, perhaps when she realized that having a baby was too much for her. The closed adoption meant that he would probably never know anything about her or the rest of his blood relatives. He had no idea if his mother was a single mom or part of a struggling couple trying to make it in the world. Was he an only child, the oldest of subsequent siblings, or just the straw that broke the camel's back? He'd thought about getting a DNA test and looking for his family, but why open old wounds?

A seagull dove into the water as the toast popped up from the toaster. Nick made his way to the counter and wondered, not for the first time, what his mother was like—smart, loving, and gentle like Kate; wise, faith-filled, and artistic like Ronnie; or strong, devoted, and strict but fun-loving like Kayla. Was she like some of the foster mothers he had grown up with? The ones who abused him, or worse, the ones who didn't even know he existed?

Nick shook his head as he buttered the toast and added a smear of grape jelly. No, he refused to believe that his mother was cruel or hateful or negligent. He firmly believed that she had given him up because she loved him and wanted what was best for him. She wanted him to have a good family, he was certain of it.

A bowl of Froot Loops sat on the table, waiting for milk. Nick put the plate of toast next to the bowl and poured milk over the cereal. As he ate, he tried to conjure pictures of his earliest memories. Somewhere, in the faded photos that were tucked away in the recesses of his mind, there must be a picture of a smiling woman, looking down on him with love, telling him that everything was going to be all right. In the deepest part of his soul, Nick knew that he had been loved once and wanted. He knew that he had the capacity to return that love. He just had to stop making the same mistakes he always made and allow himself to believe that someone good and special could love him back.

Nick carried the empty plate and bowl to the sink. He told himself that he'd wash them later. He returned to the table and polished off the can of Coca-Cola. The house seemed so quiet, and Nick felt lonely living there without Zach. Maybe he needed a roommate. That was something to think about.

After brushing his teeth, Nick stared at his reflection in the bathroom mirror. He was used to seeing himself in uniform, and he knew he'd make a darned good police officer. For now, he'd concentrate on his first day on the job as an official police academy graduate. He'd work hard and make a good living, a comfortable enough living to provide for a family. He always said he didn't want that, and he may have fooled most people, but he couldn't lie to himself. Nick wanted a family more than anything in the world. A family who would look up to him and believe that he was a good man, a good husband and father, a good provider. He knew he had it in him if he tried hard enough.

***

Kayla and Zach returned to bed after getting the boys to school. They enjoyed the peace and quiet while lying in each other's arms.

"Are you sure you don't want to go on a longer honeymoon?" Zach asked for the hundredth time, knowing what her answer would be but feeling the need to ask anyway.

"Positive," Kayla answered. "I think the few days we have planned at the Woodloch are going to be perfect."

Zach raised himself up onto his elbow and propped his head in his hand. "I hope so. I feel bad that you didn't get a real wedding, and now we're not taking a real honeymoon."

"Zachary Daniel Middleton, what are you talking about?" Kayla sat up and pulled the sheet up to her collarbone, securing it under her arms. "I had the perfect wedding. We were married in our church, surrounded by family, wrapped in a cocoon of love. What could be better?"

Zach traced the line above the sheet, marveling at her beautiful, flawless skin above the scars she insisted on keeping hidden, even from him. He looked into her eyes. "We got married in secret, the morning of Ethan's funeral, the day before your breast surgery. I can't imagine it was your dream wedding."

Kayla frowned. "You know what, Zach, I had the proverbial dream wedding, and look how that turned out. Eddie kept secrets from me. He put himself in danger and got himself killed. My boys didn't have a father for years, and then you showed up just in time to save us all." She clasped his hand with both of hers, and he felt the warmth of her touch. "I don't care about another dream wedding. Heck, I don't even care about the reception. I just want to celebrate our happiness with our friends and family."

Zach opened his mouth to protest, but she let go of his hand and put a finger to his lips. "You listen to me, Zach. I love you. I want to spend the rest of our lives together, raising our boys, supporting our family, and being happy. I'm looking forward to our reception and to our getaway in Pennsylvania, but what I'm really looking forward to is our marriage. A wedding is an event, something that lasts for a day and is then over. The party ends, everyone goes home, and the humdrum begins. But it's that humdrum that I long for—the happily-ever-after with you. We're building something that lasts for more than a day. We are creating the foundation for years and years to come. That's all I care about."

Zach didn't think he could speak. Less than two years prior, he was in a desert, killing as many enemy targets as he could, making the Wikipedia list of top snipers in the world. Almost eight months ago, he thought that the woman he loved might die, not by his hand, but by a silent killer inside her cells. Now, he was lying in bed with that same woman and looking at a lifetime of happiness.

As he pulled Kayla to him, he prayed that all of the bad times were behind them. Zach believed Kayla when she said they were going to have a happily-ever-after, and he was going to spend the rest of his life making sure nothing stopped that from happening. He was the luckiest man in the world. He wished everyone could find a love like his and Kayla's, and he had God to thank for his good fortune.

***

Nick finished his new employee paperwork and wondered what the day might bring. He knew that the crime on the island consisted mostly of small stuff—DUI arrests, some underage partying, minor fender benders, and an occasional fist fight.

Nick chuckled. He'd had his share of fist fights. Throughout his life, Nick's hot temper had gotten him into trouble. It had led to beatings from various foster fathers. It had been the root cause of many breakups. It had gotten him kicked out of class and kicked off the job. He thought back to the fight he was in during his sophomore year of high school when he was arrested and sent to the county's Teen Court Program of the Juvenile Court Division. He was sentenced to thirty hours of community service and a three-month stint as a juror for other peer cases. Nick stayed involved with the program throughout high school, moving from a juror to an attorney and then to a judge. The program's mentor suggested that Nick look into the ROTC program at his school, and there, Nick found the place where he belonged.

With his thoughts still on the best days of his youth, Nick stood and stretched. His back ached from sitting, and he moved in such a way as to allow popping and cracking along his battered spine.

"Everything good, Nick?" Paul stopped in the hall and looked at the new officer.

"Just fine, Sir. Stretching my back for a minute."

"If you want to stretch your legs, I've got a job for you. I just got a call from the market. Some kids were caught shoplifting. They could use a good scare."

Nick laughed. "I can handle that. Been there myself."

Paul raised his brow. "Why does that not surprise me?"

Nick grabbed his hat and whistled as he grabbed his gear. He missed his days as part of a band of brothers—the routine, the focus, the feeling that he was making a difference in the world, and the camaraderie—that all ended when he fell off the back of a caravan and did irreparable harm to his back. If it weren't for the friendship he had struck up with Zach, recuperating in the clinic from an eye injury, Nick didn't know what he would have done.

Being part of the island's police force brought a lot of those feelings back. Nick knew he'd made the right decision. It was the next step on his long road to adulthood, and he was ready to put the car into drive and push down the accelerator, with or without a female companion.

"Nick, hold up," Paul called as Nick reached the front door of the department. "We just got a 911 call from the Murray place. Might be a heart attack. Always helps to have an officer on the scene when the ambulance arrives. You game?"

Nick shrugged. "Why not?"

***

Dad, please, wake up.

Taylor continued the internal plea as she and her mother administered CPR, each word punctuated by the thrust of her palms into her father's chest. In the distance, she heard the wail of a siren.

Jenny, younger than Taylor by six years, stood and craned her neck. "There's a police car coming." She waved to the driver and ran to the car as it came to a halt in the driveway.

"My dad—we think he's had a heart attack. My sister and my mom are doing CPR."

Taylor continued thrusting, only glancing up at the approaching officer. She didn't recognize him but didn't have time to think about that. She kept to her task but felt him drop to the ground beside her.

"Let me take over." The officer nudged her as the ambulance turned onto the lane.

"I've got it."

"Your breathing is labored, your face is beet-red, and you're not going to do him any good if you pass out."

As if to back him up, a stream of sweat ran into her eye, momentarily fogging her vision. She quickly moved aside, and he took over.

Taylor rolled back onto her heels and took a deep breath. She watched as her mother and the unfamiliar officer tried to revive her father. She pushed herself out of the way when the paramedics said they would take it from there. Her friend, Tori, a fellow classmate throughout school and now an island paramedic, cast a sympathetic look in her direction.

It seemed as if she were in a dream as she watched Tori and Jimmy work on her father. She heard their voices, but their words made no sense. Everything felt like it was moving in slow motion. She watched her mother climb into the back of the ambulance and felt Jenny take her hand.

"I'll drive you to the hospital," the stranger said.

Without thinking, she followed him to his car, but slowly, reality crept in.

"Wait. Mom's going to need her purse and the insurance info. Let me grab it."

Taylor rushed into the house and retrieved her mother's purse and her backpack from the hook in the kitchen. Taylor had never been a purse kind of girl. She hurried out the door and folded herself into the backseat of the patrol car. Her heart skipped a beat as the car leapt into drive and the *wee-woo* of the siren filled the air. Jenny laid her head on Taylor's shoulder, and Taylor tilted her head so that it rested on her sister's head.

As they veered around corners and sailed down streets, Taylor sniffed back a tear. Her last conversation with her father had been yet another rant over the situation her father hated as much as she did. She closed her eyes and wished she hadn't lost her temper with her father over something that was out of his control.

***

Nick concentrated on keeping up with the ambulance but glanced, every now and then, at the sisters in the backseat. Both were blonde and quite pretty. One looked like she was probably still in high school, but the other looked closer to his age. He knew they were distraught and was surprised they held it together. When he glanced again, he saw a tear slide down the face of the older sister. She blinked out another before using the back of her hand to wipe them away. He shifted his gaze to the younger girl. She shook with silent sobs, and he admired their self-control.

Though the sound of the siren screamed, Nick felt an uncomfortable silence envelop him. He'd never been in this type of situation. Should he remain silent? Should he make small talk? Ask if they were okay? He cleared his throat.

"Are, uh, are you two okay? Can I call anyone or do, uh, anything?"

As if startled to find him there, the older girl blinked several times as her gaze met his in the rearview mirror. He saw a wave of emotions roll across her face.

"Um, thanks," she managed. "I'm not sure what you can do."

"Taylor, should we call grandma?"

He saw the older one, Taylor he supposed, nod. "I'll call them." She leaned forward, reached behind her back, and pulled out a phone. Nick watched the road and assumed she was calling her grandparents.

"Gram, it's Taylor…Gram, we're on the way to the hospital. We think Dad had a heart attack…Yes, she's with him…No, Jenny and I are with, uh…" she hesitated and caught Nick's eye in the rearview mirror.

"Officer Black, Chincoteague Police."

She repeated the information, assured her grandmother they were okay, and said they would see her at the hospital. Again, Nick marveled at how well she kept herself together.

The thirty-minute drive felt like it took hours. When they pulled up into the emergency bay, Nick hustled from his seat and opened the back door. The girls quickly exited the car and began following the stretcher, carried by Tori and Jimmy. Their mother put a protective arm around the younger sister, Jenny was it? Before disappearing into the double glass doors, Taylor turned back.

"Thank you," she called. "For the ride and the support."

Nick stood by his car and watched the doors close behind them. He wished there was more he could do.

***

Taylor looked around the room at the many faces who had gathered to hear word about her father. He had been rushed into heart surgery, but the doctors had warned them that it was going to be touch and go. The damage was severe, and they shouldn't get their hopes up. Still…

"Hey, Taylor, how are you holding up?" She didn't need to look up at the face above the dark jeans and plaid shirt to know who was standing in front of her. She'd known that voice her entire life. She reached for his hand and tugged on it, signaling for him to sit in the chair beside her.

"Hi, Chad."

The two had grown up together, graduated together, dated on and off, and decided they would always be good friends. Chad worked at one of the marinas on the island and helped with the pony drives. Like Taylor, he was hoping to be selected as a Saltwater Cowboy someday. His chances seemed much better than hers.

"I'm sorry about your dad." He offered her a lopsided grin. With his bright green eyes, perfect head of hair, and chiseled muscles, he was the heartthrob of nearly every girl on the island. To Taylor, he was just Chad.

"Thanks. We're—" Taylor stood suddenly as the doors opened, and a middle-aged doctor in scrubs walked into their midst. She hurried to her mother's side and took Jenny's hand. Before he said a word, Taylor read the sympathy in his eyes, the crease in his brow, and the tension lines around his mouth. Her heart lurched.

"I'm sorry. We did all we could."

Donna Murray began to sink to the floor. Taylor quickly reached out to support her mother and tried to remain calm. Chad was immediately at her side. He took her mother in his arms and led her to a chair. Taylor mouthed a thank you and sat beside her mother. Jenny sobbed, and Chad put his arm around the sixteen-year-old and let her cry into his shirt.

Taylor's gaze passed from one face to another— firemen, Father Darryl and fellow parishioners from St. Andrew's, Pete's brothers from the American Legion, neighbors, and friends. Most were Saltwater Cowboys. Some were island newcomers, and others had lived there as long as her father had—a short fifty-one years. Taylor stood.

"Thank you, all, for coming. We appreciate you being here. We'll let you know when arrangements are made." She turned to Chad. "Can you drive us home?"

Chad nodded, but a nurse broke through the crowd, a clipboard in hand.

"Ms. Murray. I need you to sign a release for the body. Where would you like it to be sent?"

A sudden realization took hold, and Taylor felt like she couldn't breathe. All the air was sucked from her chest, her stomach revolted, and she bent over in grief as well as to stop the vomit she felt rising in her; sobs escaped her lips. When Chad tried to put his arms around her, she pushed him away. As she fled to the nearest restroom, she heard him say, "I'll take care of that" and was grateful that he was there to step in where she could not enter.

***

All Nick ever wanted was a family. He watched mothers dote on their children and fathers beam with pride, and he wished he had been one of the lucky ones. That evening, as he microwaved a frozen meal, he thought about the Murray girls and their relationship with their father. Was it good? Did they love him? Was he kind to them? Did they have the kind of upbringing that he never had?

His thoughts were interrupted by the vibration of his phone.

"Officer Black." He smiled at the words. He liked the way they sounded.

"Nick, it's Paul. I thought you'd want to know that I just got word that Pete Murray died in surgery."

Nick let out a long, sad breath. "Was he a good man?"

"The best. A good friend of Trevor's. Thanks for taking care of things at the house and for driving Taylor and Jenny to the hospital. I know it would have meant a lot to him."

"Happy to help."

When they hung up, Nick thought about Trevor and what his sudden death would do to Kayla and Aaron. Though he had never met Taylor and her family before that morning, he felt an obligation to watch out for them. He'd make a point of checking in on them in a day or two. It was the least he could do.

I arrived on the island as a frightened girl, unsure of where I was heading in life, but knowing that I had to escape the nightmare that was my past. The people of Chincoteague welcomed me with open arms. They became an extension of my family, a family I didn't know I needed until I became a part of it.

From *Discovering the World On a Barrier Island*
by Katherine Middleton Kelly

CHAPTER THREE

Zach agreed to meet Nick for lunch at the deli. He waved to Jane, the owner, as he slid into the booth. She nodded, and he heard her call back his usual—a Reuben on rye bread, pickle, and homemade chips.

"How was your first day?" Zach asked his lunchmate.

"Not great." He filled Zach in on the events of the previous morning.

"Oh, man, what a way to start," Zach said. "You okay? I'm sure it was a lot to deal with."

"Yeah. It was a lot to process, but I guess it's part of the job."

Zach nodded. "You order?"

Nick smiled. "I didn't have to. Jane always knows what I want. I never even have to tell her."

Zach nodded. "Yep. She's good at keeping track." He observed his buddy for a moment and became concerned. Nick looked forlorn. That was the only word Zach could think of when he looked at his friend.

His expression showed more than sadness. The droopy eyes, turned-down lips, and lack of all enthusiasm made Nick look downright broken-hearted.

"You okay?"

"No, man, I'm not okay."

"Megan?" Zach figured he'd cut right to the chase.

"I don't know." Nick said with a sigh. "I mean, sure, I miss her. It's weird to be here and know that she's gone, but I keep reminding myself of Ronnie's advice that everything happens for a reason."

"Then why the long face?"

"Those girls, I guess. Well, one was a girl. One was about my age. Anyway, I keep thinking about how it's going to be for them to not have a dad. I know what that's like. Even at their ages, it's not easy. And it's probably going to be harder for them because they had one for so long. From what I understand, he was a good man. It's just so f-, I mean messed up."

Zach suppressed a grin. Now that Nick was working on a family-friendly island resort, he was trying hard to clean up his language. Zach knew firsthand how difficult that could be after a stint in the military, especially for a guy who grew up on the street like Nick had.

"I'm sure they'll be fine. This place has a way of taking care of its own. Everyone will look out for them."

"I know, man. I just feel bad."

Zach looked up at the blonde twenty-something waitress, someone new, as she placed a glass of Coca-Cola in front of him. Nick was already nursing a glass.

"Anything else you gentlemen need? Jane's already put in your orders."

"I think that's it for now, thanks," Zach said. "New here?"

"Yes, I just started on Saturday."

"Are you a local?"

The waitress shrugged. "Is anyone?"

Zach nodded. "I know what you mean." He smiled as she walked away and turned back to Nick. "So, what else did you do on your first day?"

"A lot of paperwork. First day paperwork and then incident paperwork after I got back from the hospital, not much else. I was supposed to give a couple teenaged shoplifters a good talking to, but I got the Murray call instead. All in all, I guess it ended up being a pretty quiet day, all things considered."

"Don't complain. From what I remember from the few months I worked there, not all days are like that."

"Humph, I bet you're right. With summer just around the corner, I can only imagine what my days are going to be like."

The waitress placed Zach's Reuben and Nick's BLT on toast in front of them. "Here you go. Let me know if you need anything. My name's Holly."

"Thanks, Holly," Zach said. He bowed his head to pray, and Nick waited. While Nick was the one who first got Zach going back to church when they were both stationed in the Middle East, Nick didn't wear his religion on his sleeve, or anywhere else for that matter. His church attendance was sporadic at best, and Zach wondered if that was part of the problem.

Nick took a bite of his sandwich, and the men ate in silence for a few minutes. Zach was happy to wait for Nick to talk.

"So, how's the wedding planning?" Nick asked.

"Good. Not much left to plan."

"That's good. Paul says it's not a problem for me to have off, but I'll miss helping you set up the day before."

Zach grinned. "I'm sure that's breaking your heart."

Nick was quiet for a moment before saying quietly, "Hey, Zach, I need to tell you something."

Zach's sandwich stopped in front of his mouth as he eyed Nick. This sounded serious. "Okay, what's up?"

"Zach, remember that day we went surf fishing? It was right after I got here, and you were trying to decide whether or not to tell Kayla how you felt about her."

"Yeah," Zach said. "I remember." Though he wished he could forget that whole period of time when he was so busy wallowing in guilt and self-pity that he almost lost the love of his life.

"You told me then to stop chasing young college girls and start thinking about the kind of woman I'd want to come home to at night."

"Yeah," Zach said, dragging the word into two long syllables and waiting for Nick to say more.

"I told you that I didn't want a woman to come home to, that I was happy chasing after one girl and then another and not being serious with any of them."

"Yeah, I remember. What about it?" Zach already knew Nick was all talk.

"So, the thing is..." Nick hesitated. "I lied."

"What do you mean, you lied?"

"I lied to you about not wanting someone to come home to."

Zach blinked a couple times and then took a bite. He chewed slowly and swallowed, running his tongue along the top of his front teeth.

"Yeah, I know. So, what?"

Nick sat back on the cushioned bench in the booth. "What do you mean, you *know*?"

"Nick, I served with you, and I lived with you. I'm not an idiot. We've talked about our pasts, about our upbringings. I know you better than you think. I've told you before that you're full of it."

Nick opened his mouth to speak but didn't respond. He reached for a French fry and took a bite. Zach waited for Nick to say something, but when the former Marine stayed silent, Zach spoke up.

"Look, Nick, I know you had a rough childhood."

"That's an understatement."

"And I know that you try to put on this tough-guy, Marine, police officer façade."

"What the heck is a façade?"

"Don't play dumb with me," Zach said. "You, more than anyone I've ever known, wants someone to love, someone who will love you back with her whole heart, someone who will give you the family you never had. I get it. You had terrible examples of what parents should be, and even though you're scared out of your wits, you want to be what you never had."

Nick's jaw dropped. "How did you...how do you?"

Zach shrugged. "After a while, Ronnie rubs off on you, and you learn how to listen and what to say."

"Man." Nick blinked and shook his head.

"Anyway, back to your supposed lie. I know that you want a wife and kids. It's understandable. All men come to that realization at some point."

Nick looked away for a moment before looking back at Zach. "I guess so." He shook his head. "But what if it never happens? What if I'm not meant for happiness?"

Zach wiped his mouth with his napkin. "Nick, that's about the dumbest thing to ever come out of your mouth, and believe me, you've said some pretty dumb things." Zach drained his soda and smiled. "It will happen. Give it time. You're young. Enjoy the summer. Get used to the job. See where God leads you."

"Is it really that simple?"

"It's really that simple. Trust me. Like you, I had to learn it the hard way. It's part of the process. Just enjoy life as it is now. Everything else will happen when it's supposed to happen."

Nick seemed to mull that over while he took the last bite of his sandwich. "I can do that. I can wait and see what comes along."

"That's good."

Nick nodded slowly. "Thanks, Zach. Appreciate the advice. Lunch is on me."

"I assumed it was," Zach said as he stood to leave. "Now, I suggest you get back to work before Paul sends the cavalry out looking for you."

As Zach left the deli, he wondered if he should have said more—encouraged Nick to go back to church or suggested he talk to Father Darryl. Zach shook his head. The Spirit hadn't prompted him to go there, so perhaps that was a conversation for another day.

***

When she stepped out, from the dark-paneled funeral home, Taylor blinked several times, allowing her eyes to adjust to the bright sunlight. She reached into the side pocket of her backpack and retrieved her sunglasses. Squaring her shoulders, she turned and headed toward St. Andrew's, just down the street. She glanced at her watch to make sure she wouldn't be too late for her appointment with Father Darryl.

When he made the appointments for her, Chad had tried to gauge how much time she would need at the funeral home, but the decisions had been even more agonizing than she imagined, and time slipped away from her. Luckily, Chad had been right on target with his estimation. According to her watch, she had fifteen minutes before Father was expecting her.

Lost in her thoughts about the prayer cards, casket, military honors, and all of the other decisions that were thrown at her in the past couple hours, Taylor failed to hear the vehicle slow down and pull up to the curb just ahead of her.

"Taylor?"

She looked toward the police car and wrinkled her brow. Did she know this person? She bit her bottom lip before realization dawned.

"Oh, Officer, um, uh…"

"Black," he supplied, opening the car door. "Nick Black. I thought that was you and wanted to stop and see if you're okay. I mean, if your family is holding up okay. I mean…" He looked away and sighed. "I'm sorry. I'm new at this. I just wanted to see if you needed anything."

Taylor was surprised to find herself smiling. "Thank you, Officer."

"Please," he said, moving away from his car and onto the sidewalk. "It's Nick."

"Okay, then, Nick. Thank you for asking. It's going to be rough for a while, but we'll find a way to bounce back." She hoped she sounded more confident than she felt. How do you bounce back from losing the most important person in your life?

"Do you need a ride somewhere?"

Taylor exhaled a small laugh. "No, but thank you. I'm just leaving the funeral home and heading to the church." She motioned to the church. "There's so much to do. I never realized…" She stopped, unable to expand on her thoughts. Everything was so overwhelming.

"Are you making the arrangements alone?" He looked around as if trying to spot another person rushing to her side.

She shrugged. "Yeah, just me. Mama was supposed to come, but she, well, she wasn't ready to get out of bed this morning. I guess it's a lot for her to handle."

Nick walked a little closer to her. "I would think it's a lot for anyone to handle."

Taylor bit back a cry. "I think you're right. My grandparents are flying in today, but they live in South Carolina now. Mama's parents are divorced and remarried. She doesn't really talk to them much." Why was she sharing so much? He didn't ask for her family history. She chalked it up to nerves and overwrought emotions.

"Your sister?"

"School." She lifted her shoulders and let them drop. "She has finals soon. I told her they would understand if she wanted to stay home and would probably even waive her finals, but she wants to get into a good pre-med program, so her grades mean a lot to her. She didn't want to miss any classes."

"How old is she?"

"Sixteen. She's only a sophomore, but she has her whole life mapped out."

"What do you do?"

"I work with my d—" Taylor's voice cracked, and she sucked in her breath to stop herself from breaking down in the middle of the sidewalk. "I'm sorry. I really have to go. I don't want to be late."

Without saying goodbye or waiting for a response, she fled toward the sanctuary of St. Andrews.

***

Nick watched Taylor flee to the church. He wished there was something he could do to help her. He'd experienced the death of friends, and he mourned for the men lost and the families they had back home. But this was different. These people were now his neighbors, and he felt an obligation to look after them. Maybe it was just the fact that he was there, that he tried to revive the guy with his own hands. Whatever it was, Nick felt the need to do something.

On his drive back to the station, he thought about Taylor. From what he gathered, she worked with her dad. Nick wondered what kind of business he owned. Was there some way he could help out there? He'd have to ask Paul, or perhaps Trevor, what he could do. It might be just what he needed to fill the void in his life.

He looked at the families going in and out of the shops—the early birds already beginning their summer. It was almost Memorial Day, and the town was already starting to swell with extra inhabitants. Nick parked the cruiser and got out for a stroll down the main street.

As he made his way to the local doughnut shop, he smiled and said hello to the people he knew. The last thing he needed was extra sugar and calories, but he'd always had a sweet tooth, especially when something was bothering him.

"Good morning, Diane." He smiled at the shop's owner behind the counter.

"Nick, you're back. Welcome home." The woman smiled back at him.

Nick felt a warm gush in his gut at her greeting. Home—a foreign concept to him for so many years. Yet he knew from the first weekend he was on the island, when Zach, Kayla, and the boys showed him around and introduced him to their family, that this was a place he could truly make his home.

Nick marveled at the list of doughnuts, all with names indicative of the island. Marsh Mint was a mint-chocolate chip doughnut with chocolate frosting. Sandy Shore was a cake doughnut dusted with sugar and cinnamon, and Chocolate Waves had a marble interior and rich milk chocolate frosting. There were dozens of selections with catchy names and original flavors. Nick had tried just about all of them.

"I've got your favorite, fresh off the cooling rack," Diane said. She turned to the rack and used a sheet of pastry paper to pick up a doughnut. She handed him a

Pony Pork doughnut, a glaze-covered creation baked with brown sugar and bacon.

None of the women who had a hand in raising him ever knew his favorite kind of anything, but here was this woman he barely knew, handing him the sweet concoction he loved the best. *Why couldn't she or Ronnie have been my mom?*

"You're a doll, Diane. Thank you. What do I owe you?" He reached for the doughnut with one hand and his wallet with the other.

"Nick, how many times do I have to tell you that your money is no good in here. Now get out of here and keep on making this island safe for me and my customers."

"One of these days, you're going to realize how much money you've lost to me."

"Nonsense. You just keep coming back with that smile of yours, and we'll call it even. And bring that pretty young thing with you next time. I haven't seen her in a while."

"Will do," Nick said hastily, hiding his faltering smile by taking a bite of the doughnut. He waved goodbye and hustled his way out of the shop.

Somehow, the doughnut tasted even better than he remembered it. He finished it, licked his fingers, and threw the paper wrapping away just as he saw Kayla's friend, Tammi, leaving the bank.

"Nick, how's it going?" She flashed him a genuine smile.

"Going just great." He smiled at Tammi. "And yourself?"

"Doing fine." Tammi cocked her head and put her hand on her hip. "How's the new job going?"

"It's good. Quiet so far."

"That's good to hear. You look good, like you're enjoying life."

Nick smiled. Tammi made him feel special. Actually, she had a way about her that made everyone feel special. "I am, Tammi. I am. And I'm enjoying it even more having run into you." Nick grinned at her and batted his eyes.

Tammi shook her head and headed toward the market, her laugh drifting behind her. "You are a helpless flirt, Nick Black." She pointed to the sky. "You'd better get inside before the rain starts. It's going to be an ugly day once that system rolls in."

"Will do, Tammi. You take care."

He walked back to his car and headed to the station. He was enjoying life. Now, he wanted to find a way to help the Murray family enjoy life again, too.

My father's parents died when I was very young. I don't remember much about them or their funerals, but I do remember the funerals and mourning rituals I observed when we lived amongst the Aboriginals of Australia. There was such a finality when it came to death. When a person was gone, he was gone. Mourning was short, and families and communities moved on in peace, knowing their lives must continue uninterrupted. As a child, I didn't understand how people could just forget their loved ones and go on with their lives so easily. As an adult, I've come to believe that it's a necessary tool of survival.

From *Discovering the World On a Barrier Island*
by Katherine Middleton Kelly

CHAPTER FOUR

By Thursday, Taylor was beginning to get used to her father's absence. At least, that's what she told herself as she stood in the doorway to his office. She wasn't sure she would ever get used to his missing plate at dinner or his empty chair during Jeopardy, her parents' favorite time of the day. She smiled, remembering how her parents would try to beat each other to the answers.

She entered the room and walked to his desk. She fingered the cherry wood and stopped to pick up the framed family photo, prominently centered on the desk. To the right of the picture was her father's laptop. It was still open to the calendar, a list of color-coded boxes signifying which jobs were simple mowing, which ones involved light planting, which ones would need heavy-duty machinery, and which ones were planning meetings with people searching for design ideas or hoping to carry out elaborate yard makeovers.

Taylor scanned the walls and the plethora of framed documents that adorned them. There was his honorable discharge from the Air Force and his citation from the president, thanking him for his service during the first Iraq War. There was his college degree in landscape architecture, earned using his own hard-earned cash rather than the GI Bill money that he saved for his children. There were also several framed awards from outdoor magazines for Best Landscape Design and Most Original Backyard Gardens, among others.

"Hey, Taylor, you ready?" Jenny stood in the doorway in the black dress their mother had purchased for her the day before.

"Sure. Is mama ready?"

"She's going out to the car."

Taylor nodded. She looked around the room once more before following her sister out of the room that would never again feel the same.

***

Out on patrol, Nick found himself thinking about Taylor and her family and the funeral being held that day. He wouldn't have gone, even if he had been off, but he wished he could think of some way to show his support for the family.

Up ahead, Nick saw a motor vehicle swerve onto the side of the road, nearly hitting a mailbox. He turned on the siren and lights and pulled out onto the road. He had discovered that the most common task of a police officer on the island was arresting drivers under the influence of alcohol.

After coming to stop behind the car, Nick approached with caution. From behind the wheel, a young man, not much older than EJ, looked penitently at Nick.

"License and registration."

"Officer, I'm sorry. I should have been paying more attention." The young man's hands shook as he reached for the registration.

"You been drinking, smoking pot, anything like that today?" Nick read the name and address, a local kid.

"No, sir. I was, uh, I was texting my boss to tell him I was running late." The boy's face turned crimson.

"That's a serious admission, son. You could have hit that mailbox back there, could have ended up in a ditch, could have hit a tree, or worse, an oncoming car."

"Yes, sir, I know, sir. I'm really sorry."

Nick looked at the name on the license again. "Justin, I'm going to do you a favor."

The boy looked up at Nick with hope in his eyes.

"In fact, I'm going to do you two favors."

The boy nodded.

"First, I'm just going to write you a warning. Second, I'm going to call your mom."

The boy's face fell. "You are?"

"Yes, I am." Nick took a small notebook and pen from his pocket. "Write her name and number on this."

With trembling hands, the boy accepted the notebook and wrote down his mother's name and phone number.

"Hang tight," Nick said, taking back the notepad. "I'll be right back."

Several minutes later, Nick handed the license and registration back to the kid along with a warning. "No ticket, but I have a feeling you won't be socializing much in the next couple weeks."

"Was she real mad?"

Nick looked at the kid, remembering what it was like being his age. Nick knew, at that age, one small screw-up can change the course of your entire life, for good or for bad. "She was more worried than anything. Imagine how she felt hearing the words, 'Ma'am, this is Officer Black, and I'm with your son.' What kind of thoughts do you think ran through her head?"

Justin looked away. "I guess she was pretty scared at first."

"Imagine how she would have felt if I had shown up at her door and said to her, "Ma'am, I'm sorry. Your son was in an accident and didn't survive'."

The boy winced then turned toward Nick. "It won't happen again, sir. I promise."

Nick watched Justin cautiously drive away. His might not be the most important job in law enforcement, but if he saved that kid's life, or the life of someone on the road with him, then the job was worth it.

Nick walked back to his car with a profound sense of pride. He had a purpose in life, be it small or great. He was here to make a difference. Whether it was aiding at the scene of a heart attack, or keeping the streets safe for drivers and pedestrians, he felt good about what he was doing.

After Nick turned the car around, he spotted a 'For Sale' sign on the side of the road. His eyes widened, and he smiled.

***

The church was standing-room-only when Taylor, Jenny, and Donna followed the casket down the aisle. Teachers, firemen, veterans, storekeepers, and long-time friends were all in attendance. Taylor spotted Chad and smiled. Her father had always hoped she would marry Chad, but he never pushed her and accepted her insistence that she and Chad would always be friends but no more. There was no spark between them and had never been, even when they dated. Taylor's chest heaved as she realized she was following her father down the same aisle where she hoped to walk beside him on her wedding day. That moment would never come.

They sat through the Mass and listened to the homily, but Taylor hardly heard what was said. When her 'Uncle Trevor' stood up to deliver the eulogy, she smiled. Though Trevor was a few years older than her father, they had grown up on the island together. Her father idolized the man and loved telling stories about how he used to try to get Trevor's attention whenever the older boy had been at Pete's house.

"When I was a boy, my best friend was James Murray. Most of you remember James. He, like his brother, Pete, was loved by everyone. He was one of the good guys and did his best to try to keep me out of trouble. He was the only one who knew the truth about my dad." Uncle Trevor paused and looked down at the paper on the lectern. Taylor knew it was hard for him to talk about his own upbringing, and she hoped she hadn't caused him any pain by asking him to speak today.

He looked back up and continued. "James always took the high road, and I, well, let's just say I took the first road out of town." Taylor smiled and the congregation chuckled. "There were many things I admired about James, but the biggest was his love for his little brother, Pete. Pete was never a nuisance, never the baby brother, never just an annoying kid to James, and I grew to love Pete as much as his brother did.

"When word reached me that we had lost James back in '91 to an Iraqi land mine, my first thoughts were of Pete. I was on ship off the Alaskan coast and counted the days until I could get to a phone on the mainland. Service was spotty at best, but the good Lord allowed me to reach the family. Pete was home on leave, and his first words to me were, 'You're the only brother I have now.' And I took those words to heart." Uncle Trevor looked directly at Taylor. "Pete became the brother I never had, and his girls became like family to me." Taylor wiped a tear from her cheek and smiled at Trevor.

"Pete was an honorable man, an upstanding airman, a devoted husband, a loving father, and a loyal friend. I remember the time…"

Uncle Trevor made everyone laugh. He made them cry. He touched hearts, and Taylor felt good that she had chosen him to pay tribute to her father.

When they walked down the path toward the open grave, the light rain began to clear, and a bright rainbow arched over the cemetery. Everyone looked at one another, assured that Pete was smiling down on them. Taylor tried her hardest to hold back her tears as she laid a single, long-stemmed rose on her father's grave.

"Goodbye Daddy," she whispered. "I'm going to make you proud. I promise."

***

"Anybody home?" Nick called as he gently pushed open the kitchen door on Friday morning.

"In the office," Zach called back.

Nick made his way around the kitchen table to Zach and Kayla's office. He stood in the doorway and assessed the room. It was originally a dining room, but Kayla's father helped her convert it into an office. Now the room had one wall lined with bookshelves that held everything from classic cookbooks to classic literature, and three desks, each customized for its user. Zach and Kayla shared a partner's desk that Ronnie recently found in an antique shop. The double-wide oak desk allowed two people, usually attorneys, to work across from each other with drawers and filing cabinets framing the chair opening on each side of the desk. Of the other two desks, one offered a bare space for EJ's laptop and a shelf of required reading. The other had all of the necessary school tools, from crayons to scissors to #2 pencils, for a fourth grader.

Nick wondered how it must feel to work alongside your wife all day in a well-kept, cozy office where you planned meals and wrote cookbooks.

"How's the wedding planning going?"

"Busy," Zach responded, his brow creased as he read his computer screen.

Kayla sighed. "Don't mind him. He's trying to decipher the publisher's contract for the cookbook. I told him to call his father since he's been through this, but he says he can figure out all the fine print on his own."

Nick leaned against the door jamb and crossed his arms. "When does it hit the shelves?"

"Hopefully by next October. It can take nine months to a year for a book to be published, but I'd love to see it out in time for Christmas. Cookbooks are still very popular presents despite the plethora of recipes on the internet." Kayla smiled at Nick.

"What are you working on?"

"Wedding details, of course." She smiled. "I can't believe it's just over a week away. I'm just making sure we haven't forgotten anything."

"With you and Ronnie in charge? Not possible."

Kayla's smile widened. "Very true." She paused and looked him up and down. "So, what brings you over?"

"I'm buying a boat."

Zach's head swiveled toward Nick. "A boat?"

"Yeah." Nick uncrossed his arms and straddled EJ's desk chair. He rested his arms across the back of the chair. "I saw a 'for sale' sign on a boat the other day and went by this morning to take a look. It seems to be solid and doesn't need too much work. I texted Aaron and asked him to check it out, and he went over on his way to work as well. Says it's a good deal."

Zach leaned back in his chair. "Do you have any idea how to drive a boat? And where are you going to keep it?"

"I can dock it out back." He gestured toward the pier behind the house next door.

"Nick, have you taken a good look at that dock? It's falling apart, and the marsh has risen so much, that you'd practically have to swim to it."

"Yeah, but I can fix it, and I plan to extend it beyond the marsh."

"That's a huge endeavor, and you don't know which end of the hammer to hold." Zach's eyes narrowed in disapproval.

"I can figure out how to build a pier. Give me some credit. I'm not an idiot." Nick shook his head and looked toward Kayla. "I do know how to hold a hammer."

Kayla smiled. "I'm sure you do, Nick."

"Why on earth did you buy a boat?" Zach asked.

Nick rolled his eyes. "Because I like to fish. Why do you think?"

"I mean," Zach said in the same tone he used when thirteen-year-old EJ asked to do something out of the question. "What made you decide to up and buy a boat? Isn't that something you should take your time with, hunt around for a bit, and then make an informed decision?"

Nick shrugged. "I saw the ad, knew I had the money in the bank, and figured I could have some fun with it this summer."

"Isn't that a bit hasty? What if you have an emergency and need the money? You're starting a new job. How much time will you have to fish?" Zach narrowed his eyes at Nick. "Wait a minute, is this about—"

"It's about me wanting a f…" He looked at Kayla and felt the heat rise to his cheeks then looked at Zach. "It's about me wanting a boat. You got a problem with that?"

"Zach," Kayla said gently. "Nick is a grown man. He can make his own decisions about what he purchases."

"Thank you, Kayla." Nick gave Kayla a warm smile but fixed a glare on Zach. "First of all, I still have plenty of money in the bank in case of an emergency. Second, I'll have just as much time as anybody else who works a full-time job. Third, it has nothing to do with anyone or anything. And fourth, to go back to your earlier question, I do know how to operate a boat." Nick refused to look away from Zach. Darn it, he wanted a boat. Period. There was no underlying reason other than he liked the idea of having a boat.

"Glad to hear it." Zach sighed, shaking his head as a smile began to form on his face. "So, how soon do we take it for a test run?"

Nick laughed. "I knew you'd come around. I'm picking it up after work on Sunday. It needs some work, like I said, and I need to fix that dock, but I figure I'll have it in the water by the Fourth of July."

Zach's smile disappeared. "The Fourth of July? Summer's practically over by then."

Nick shrugged. "*This* summer. But I can fish all year, depending upon the season, and there's always next year. But you know…" Nick grinned, knowing he was going to win this argument. "It will be in the water a lot faster if I can get a little help from a friend, someone with enough free time to work on the pier while I'm on duty."

"You had him at fishing," Kayla said, her eyes twinkling. Nick felt his face redden again as she looked at him with affection. She might be married to his best friend, but he was kind of in love with her just the same. Any man with a beating heart would be. She was going to make the most beautiful bride. Nick looked back at Zach.

"So, I gotta run, but two weeks from tomorrow? Nine a.m.? I'm off that day." Nick stood and looked back at Kayla. "I mean, if that's okay. I know you'll be newly married and all."

Kayla waved the thought away and grinned. "It will feel like we've been married for months by then."

Zach rolled his eyes. "I'll be there. And after this week, I'm finished with track in the afternoons. And I can help on Saturdays after EJ and I have our morning run."

Kayla started to protest, no doubt realizing Zach was committing all his spare time to helping Nick.

"Great idea," Nick cut her off. "It would be a good bonding experience for you and EJ—fixing up a fishing boat. Don't you think so, Kayla?"

"You're just looking for cheap labor," Zach told him.

"Maybe," Nick said. "But you gotta admit, I'm right. Catch ya later."

Nick turned and headed back toward the kitchen door. When he got to his car, he realized he forgot to ask Kayla what the name of Taylor's family business was. He knew the funeral had taken place, and he assumed that the family was trying to find a new normal. Whatever the business was, by Monday, Taylor would probably be back at work. By then, Nick hoped to have figured out how he was going to help her and her family move on.

***

Friday's sun was sinking low behind the house where the women gathered. The gentle rhythm of the canal, sloshing against the dock, and the reeds swaying in the breeze, added to the tranquil aura around Ronnie and Trevor's home. Inside, Kayla inspected her handiwork on the tiny glass bottle of honey. The bottle read, 'Love as Sweet as Honey, Zach and Kayla.' She was so happy she could burst and felt an intoxicating joy consume her. She closed her eyes and soaked up the happiness that flowed amid the endless chatter of the women as they glued labels to the little jars.

Ronnie's large dining room was filled with laughter, balloons and crepe paper, and the heady scent of her special recipe, Girls' Night Out Margaritas. It was the third Friday in May, and Zach and Kayla's wedding reception was just a week away. Kayla was grateful to be spending the evening with her closest friends, adhering labels to the fancy glass jars that were filled with locally collected, golden honey. Though she had been very insistent that she did not want or need a bridal shower, her mother and friends conspired to make the evening of wedding preparation as festive as possible. Kayla knew they were right. This was just what they all needed.

"These are such a great idea," Tammi said as she unpeeled a label and placed it carefully on a bottle. "Wedding favors can be so impractical."

"And what better way to highlight Marian's award-winning honey than at the biggest wedding of the year?" Anne smiled, holding up a jar and looking at their good friend, Marian. "I love the way the honey glistens in the sunlight."

"Kayla, why is there no date on the bottle?" Kate held a bottle up so that they could all see the label.

"Well, we're going to have two wedding dates," Kayla told her. "I couldn't put the date of the reception and ignore our actual wedding date."

"Of course." Kate nodded. "That makes total sense."

"I know it's been months already, but I still can't get over you not telling us about the wedding." Debbie shook her head. "I'm supposed to be your oldest and closest friend, yet I had to find out about it from your mother the next day when she called to say you were out of surgery."

"Well, there was a lot going on," Kayla said quietly before stealing a quick glance at Tammi and hoped her friend didn't harbor any ill will about the wedding that took place just hours before her son's funeral.

"I think it was a beautiful thing for you and Zach to do." Tammi's voice shook as she spoke, and Kayla noticed a slight tremble of the fingers that held an unlabeled jar. "We live in a world full of hate. True love should never be taken for granted. No matter what else is happening, we must always welcome and celebrate love."

Kayla watched as Kate reached over and grasped Tammi's hand. The two had become very close, and it made Kayla feel good for both of them. She noticed everyone's eyes were misty. She glanced at Taylor Murray sitting to her right. Under any other circumstance, Kayla would probably not have invited the much-younger woman to her so-called bridal shower, but once she knew it was taking place, she felt compelled to include her. After all, Kayla had always seen Taylor and Jenny as the little sisters she never had, which made them family, and family looked out for one another.

Kayla leaned over and whispered to Taylor. "Hey, how are you holding up? You know, I'm always here if you want to talk."

Taylor offered a weak smile. "I'm okay. It's hard, but Mama needs me to be strong." She shrugged, placing the bottle she was holding on the table.

"That doesn't mean that you can't fall apart, you know. You're allowed."

Taylor gave a genuine smile this time. "I know. Thanks." She glanced over at her mother. "I just don't know how she's going to get through this."

Kayla patted the young woman's hand. "You'll all get through it together, and remember, we're here whenever you need us."

"Thanks, Kayla. I appreciate that. I'm really happy to be here, thank you for inviting us."

"You're family, Taylor. You're always welcome here."

***

"How are things with you? Everything good with Zach and the boys? How about Aaron and his wife and baby?" Taylor listened, truly interested as Kayla told her about Zach coaching track, Todd becoming obsessed with fishing, and Miren's latest milestone.

"She's growing so fast," Taylor said. "And Aaron and Kate seem really happy."

Kayla's whole face radiated warmth and love as she spoke about Aaron and Kate. Taylor tried to listen, but her thoughts drifted. It seemed that every little thing reminded her that she no longer had a father.

"So, now that Zach is the new track coach, he's hoping EJ will join his team next year when he starts high school. And…Taylor? You look like you're a million miles away. Am I overloading you with information?"

Taylor winced. "I'm sorry. I was listening. Zach's coaching track. That's nice." Taylor knew she shouldn't bring down Kayla's mood or ruin her shower. "I think I should check on Mama."

"I understand. Go, check on Donna. Let me know if she needs anything."

Taylor found her mother in the kitchen with Ronnie. Each of them had a margarita in hand. Taylor rarely saw her mother drink more than a glass of wine, but nobody could resist one of Aunt Ronnie's margaritas.

"Taylor, honey," Ronnie said, going to Taylor and wrapping her in a hug. "My heart aches over the loss of your dad. He was such an amazing man. If you ever need anything, don't hesitate to call us."

Ronnie's words warmed Taylor's heart. She was so tired of hearing, "I'm sorry for your loss," and "How are you holding up?" and "Time heals all wounds." While she knew those people had the best of intentions, she didn't know how to respond. With Aunt Ronnie, Taylor knew that every word was from the heart.

"Thank you. I'm sure Mama will appreciate having you nearby if she needs anything."

Aunt Ronnie studied her for a moment. "Taylor, it's okay for you to need someone, too."

Taylor felt a lump form in her throat. "I know. Thank you." She turned toward her mother. "Mom, I'm tired. Is it okay if I go? Since Jenny drove here from practice, she can drive you home. That is, if it's okay with you."

"Of course, Taylor. But are you sure you want to go? It's so lonely at home." Her mother looked away, and Taylor felt her heart break a little more. "I might drive to the beach for a bit, take a walk. Is that okay?"

"Sure, honey," Donna said. "Just stay away from the ponies. It's going to be dark soon, and I don't want something happening to you when nobody's around."

"I know, Mom. I'll be careful." Taylor gave her mother and Aunt Ronnie hugs and went to find her sister. Jenny shot her a look of disdain for leaving her there to drive their mother home, but she didn't argue. Taylor knew her sister would rather have been out with friends, but their mother insisted they all go to the party together. Now, Taylor was leaving, and she knew Jenny would resent her abandoning them, but Jenny would get over it.

She said her goodbyes to the other women and thanked Kayla again for the invitation and told her to give her a call if she needed any help to get ready for the big day. Anne told Taylor that she and Paul were having a picnic on Sunday and that she was welcome to attend. Taylor thanked her but didn't commit. She appreciated the invitation, and the ladies were all very sweet, but Taylor was much younger than the rest of them. If she wanted to go out and have fun, she had plenty of friends she could call.

Once outside, Taylor walked to her truck, a Chevy that was just what she needed to hook her horse trailer to or haul around landscaping materials.

"Leaving so soon?" Trevor called from the garden in the center of the front yard.

"Afraid so. You're working late."

"Thought I'd take advantage of the sunlight that's left. There's too much estrogen inside."

Taylor laughed and gestured to the gardens where bleeding hearts, peonies, and bearded irises bloomed.

"Your yard looks nice." She knew how much time and effort it took to get a yard to look nice. Trevor's looked like a pro had done it, but he had done it all himself. If he ever had a question, he called her father who… "Dad would tell you it looks wonderful. Just like he would have done it." She blinked at the sky to gain her composure. "I'm sorry. It hits me sometimes."

"Of course, it does, honey. And it's okay. You're allowed to cry." Trevor stood and removed his gardening gloves. "It's going to take some time, Taylor. And there will always be things that make you think of your dad, but someday, you'll realize that you're able to think about him without crying. It won't happen right away, but it will happen."

Taylor nodded. "Thank you, Uncle Trevor. I'll remember that." As Taylor started her car, she wondered how much of Trevor's advice was taken from his own experience after the death of his mother. He was a teenager when she died, around Jenny's age. He had lost his mother, his best friend, and later, his father. If anyone knew about grief, it was Trevor.

Taylor drove through the downtown. There was a line of cars pulling into the campground, a sure sign that the tourist season had begun. The parking lot at the little hotel near the Chamber of Commerce was full, and dozens of people walked the streets, enjoying the warm night. Though summer hadn't officially begun, the line in front of the ice cream parlor was wrapped around the building.

Taylor passed the Chincoteague Museum where the famed pony, Misty, now resided and continued down the road toward the bridge that connected Chincoteague with the national seashore of

Assateague. It was where the Chincoteague ponies roamed and one of the few places she truly felt at home. She passed several grazing ponies as she drove along the marsh beds and looked carefully at each one, always trying to spot Stormy's baby brother.

The lot on Assateague was almost empty when Taylor pulled in and got out of her car. In a few weeks, the beach on the national seashore would be packed seven days a week and most nights until dark, but tonight, only a few people walked along the shoreline, amid the crashing waves. Taylor was glad that there weren't many people around. She wanted to be alone.

She stopped to gaze at a military ship out on the horizon. How she wished she could swim out there, climb aboard the ship, and beg the crew to take her far, far away. Away from her sadness, away from her heartache, away from life without her father. Sadly, she knew life didn't work that way. There would always be a hole where her father once was.

She closed her eyes and took a long, deep breath of the salty air. She could hear the waves as they rolled onto the shore and the gulls that called overhead. When she opened her eyes, she saw three ponies walking in the nearby beach grass as a tourist shot pictures of them with her phone, in the faint light of the retreating day.

She watched the ponies and ached to be one of the ones to drive them across the channel and lead them to their new homes. She had worked as, what she liked to call, a pony liaison for many families over the years, helping them to learn to care for their new family members. She partnered with the local 4-H to create care packages for the families, containing body brushes, curry and mane combs, hoof picks, and feed. She had worked alongside her father, foaling ponies, tagging them, and keeping watch over the herd. She knew more about the ponies than some of the men did. Why was she never chosen to ride with them? If only her father were still there to fight for her.

Life is hard whether it's lived in a remote jungle or in a big city or on a small island. In so many of the places where I lived as a child, there was a sense of community in which everyone cared for the needs of each other. Our culture doesn't do enough of that. There aren't enough people who truly want the best for others or who put other's needs in front of their own. It's one of the things that sets apart small communities the most.

From *Discovering the World On a Barrier Island*
by Katherine Middleton Kelly

CHAPTER FIVE

"Paul, can I ask you a question?" Nick stood in the doorway to Paul's office at the start of his shift on Saturday.

"Sure, Nick, come on in. What's up?"

Nick took a seat in the wooden chair across from the desk. "That man who died, Mr. Murray?"

"Yeah, what about him?"

"What did he do? I think I heard he owned a business or something."

"He was a landscaper, though to call him that would be like calling Emeril a cook. He was a master. He designed some of the most high-profile gardens and yards in the state. He's the one who redid the land around the governor's mansion in Richmond a few years back. He won all kinds of awards."

"Wow, an operation like that, he must have had a ton of employees."

"He did. Here and in other locations around both Maryland and Virginia.

"What's going to happen to them now that he's gone?"

Paul looked thoughtful for a moment. "I would assume Taylor will run the business now. He's been grooming her for years."

"Is she as good as he was?"

"I couldn't answer that. Trevor probably could. He's her Godfather."

"Trevor? I had no idea the families were that close. I mean, I knew they were friends, but I didn't know he was her Godfather."

"Trevor and Pete's brother were best friends. James died in Iraq back in the first Gulf War. I guess Trevor and Pete bonded over that."

"Hmm. I guess they'll all be at the wedding. I mean, if it's not too soon for them to be celebrating."

"I doubt they'd miss it even under the circumstances."

Nick stood to leave. "Thanks, Paul."

"Nick, why the interest in Pete?"

Nick looked around Paul's office. He stared at the framed picture of Paul, Anne, Ben, and Lizzie for a long moment before he spoke.

"I don't know. I guess, because I was there, I kind of feel like I should do something to help them out."

"Nick, let me give you a piece of advice. Don't get emotionally involved with any of the victims you deal with. It's not healthy."

"I'll keep that in mind," Nick said as he left the office. He knew Paul was right. They had been told the same thing at the academy. But knowing it was good advice and following it were two very different things.

***

"Taylor, what are you doing out here?"

Taylor looked up to see Jenny standing inside the greenhouse watching her. Jenny's brow was furrowed, and her mouth was pinched in a perplexed stare.

"I've got to separate these Hosta plants. They're too overgrown." She went back to wrestling with the plant.

Jenny slowly approached Taylor. "Taylor," she said quietly. "I don't want to go on Monday. I'd rather go to school. Is that okay?"

Taylor stopped what she was doing and cocked her head to the side. She traced her top teeth with her tongue, a habit she'd had since she was twelve and wore braces. "I don't think you have to go. I'll ask Martin." Martin had been her father's attorney ever since he started his business twenty years prior. "Are you sure you don't want to be there, though? These are dad's wishes for his family. Aren't you curious?"

Jenny shrugged. "Not really. I already know that Daddy left you the business and Stormy. I mean, she's already yours, but I'm sure he made sure that his investment in her goes to you. He never really intended for you to pay that half back, and you know it."

Taylor nodded. "I know. He wanted me to have that pony as much as I did. He would have sold the house to buy it, but he didn't want me spending my whole savings to buy her. But, Jenny, I'm sure he left you something."

"I'm sure he did. Mama will get the house and the land that isn't owned by the business. I'm sure that he will make sure I'm compensated to make up for not getting 'stuff'." She used air quotes as she spoke. "But it doesn't matter to me either way. Daddy isn't coming back and knowing that you're getting the business or that my college and med school are paid for, isn't going to change that."

Sympathy tinged with guilt engulfed Taylor, and she longed to go to her sister and hug her, but Jenny would have pushed her away. She didn't like to show her emotions and detested appearing weak or incapable.

"I'm sorry, Jen. If Daddy did leave me the business, I'm happy to—"

Jenny held up her hand. "Stop. Don't say you'll split it with me or make me a partner or anything like that. I don't want that, and you know it. You're the one who always wanted to follow in Daddy's footsteps, not me. I'm okay with all of that, have been for years. I just don't care about what's in the will."

Taylor took a deep breath then released it. "Fair enough. You go to school; Mom and I will go meet with Martin. When you get home from lacrosse practice, I'll let you know what happened."

Jenny nodded. "Sounds good." She stood as if to go but gazed at the Hosta for a moment, her mouth twisted as she pondered something. "Hey, Taylor, you're going to shred the roots if you're not careful. Do you want some help?"

Taylor smiled. "I'd love some help." Though Jenny had no desire to pursue a career in landscaping, she knew as much about plants as Taylor did, and they always knew they could count on each other for help.

***

Aaron sat behind Kate in the tandem kayak in their favorite cove just after sunset on Saturday. It had been tricky getting Kate into the boat, but they managed without ending up in the water. Aaron admired his wife more than anyone he had ever known. She had a big heart, a fierce determination to take care of others, and a will to keep going no matter what she faced.

"I'm so glad we did this. I miss being out here with you," Kate said as they sat in the secluded cove.

"Me, too," Aaron said. "We're so busy all the time. We need to make more time to do things like this, especially with the baby coming."

"Agreed."

Kate and Aaron sat idle in the boat, watching the way the moonlight shimmered on the water, and Aaron thought about how blessed he was.

After a few minutes of silence, Kate spoke quietly, as though talking any louder would ruin the tranquility of the night. "The funeral was nice."

"It was. I guess this is the first chance we've had to talk since Thursday. Thanks for going."

"Of course. Trevor thought of Pete as family. Why wouldn't I?"

Aaron shrugged. "I don't know. You never really had a chance to get to know him. He was a great guy."

"I gathered that from Trevor's eulogy. It was really beautiful."

"I honestly don't know how he got through it without crying."

"Oh, come on, Trevor knows how to keep a straight face and emotions in check. He must have been quite the rear admiral in his day."

"From what I hear, he was."

Kate sighed. "It's sad and kind of scary. Pete was pretty young. It frightens me to think that I could lose you so suddenly long before I'm ready.

Kate's head moved back and forth, and Aaron wished he could lean up and put his arms around her without sending them both into the water. "Don't worry about that, Princess. I'm not going anywhere."

"Every night I pray that we can have long and happy lives together. Do you think your Aunt Donna prayed for that, too?"

Aaron swallowed. What could he say? "I'm sure most people who love each other pray for that,

Princess. Only God knows what his plan is, though, and we have to trust that."

Kate blew out a long breath, and Aaron felt the kayak rock back and forth as she shook her head. "What, in his plan, could call for a wonderful husband and father to be taken from his family at the age of fifty-one? They hadn't even gotten to the good years yet—grandchildren, retirement, rocking on the front porch."

Even without being able to see her face, he knew the expression she wore. Her lips were tight, her eyes introspective, and a tiny wrinkle creased between her blonde eyebrows.

"Let's talk about something happy," Aaron said. "Tell me a story from one of your childhood adventures."

After a moment, Aaron heard Kate release a contented sigh. "Did I ever tell you about the time Zach and I kayaked on a bioluminescent bay?" The tone of her voice was full of nostalgia rather than worry, and Aaron knew he had said the right thing.

"I don't think so," he answered, genuinely interested in the tale she was about to share.

"We were living near Australia, on Moa Island in the Torres Strait. I was about ten at the time, maybe eleven. It was right before we moved back to the States. I'm not sure why we were in American Samoa, but we were." She stopped speaking for a moment, and Aaron pictured her frowning, trying to recall why they took the trip. "Anyway, while we were in Samoa, Zach and I met this guy who offered to take us kayaking in this bay that he said glowed in the dark. Of course, we thought he was crazy, but my dad told us he was legit, so we went."

"It glowed in the dark?"

"It actually did. It was amazing. We went on the night of a new moon, so the only lights around were the twinkling stars. As soon as we got out into the bay, Zach told me to look at where the paddle was hitting the water. Every time the paddle went into the water, the ripples around it lit up with this bright blue light. It was one of the most amazing things I've ever seen."

Aaron watched Kate tip her paddle into the water as she talked about the glow as if she might conjure up the lights right then and there.

"What caused the glow?" Aaron asked

"It was caused by the glow of millions of tiny bioluminescent fish. And I mean tiny. The guy we were with told us it's the same kind of glow as a lightning bug, only blue instead of yellow. Every time the water moved, the fish glowed."

"That sounds amazing."

"It was. But what was really amazing was the shark."

"The shark?"

"Yeah, a baby reef shark. Apparently, reef sharks are very curious and like to investigate whatever is nearby. One of them swam right up beside the kayak, and the entire outline of its body glowed this iridescent blue. It was the coolest thing I've ever seen."

Aaron could hear the smile in her voice and wished he could see her face. He loved to watch her when she talked about her nomadic childhood with the indigenous peoples of the world and the adventures she and Zach shared.

"I'm not sure how I'd feel about a shark, baby or not, investigating my kayak."

Kate laughed, and the sound of her delight made Aaron's heart swell. "Trust me, we were totally safe. Reef sharks wouldn't hurt anyone. In fact, they're often more afraid of you than you would be of them."

"I'm not so sure about that," Aaron said. Only Kate would laugh off a shark. He knew there were other things she feared far more than that, carrying the baby to term being at the top of the list. He picked up his paddle and held it over the water. "Ready to head back?"

"Just another minute or two," she said, her voice almost pleading. "This might be the last time I can get into a kayak for a while."

Aaron understood. Nights like this were a rare gift. He laid his paddle across his lap. They would wait a little longer. He would do whatever it took to make his wife happy. He thought of Taylor and hoped she would be able to find some kind of happiness to relieve some of her pain.

For some reason, an image of Nick appeared before him.

***

Taylor nervously fingered the strap on the backpack in her lap. She and her mother, Donna, sat in the reception room at Hollis, Bolte, and Green on Monday morning. Taylor had never attended the reading of a will before, and she was nervous for some unknown reason.

It's not as if Daddy had some offshore account or a secret love child we will suddenly hear about.

She sighed and looked at her watch for the tenth time.

"We're early," her mother reminded her. "Martin is a very busy attorney. He'll call us in when he's ready."

As she said the words, a door opened, and Martin appeared with another middle-aged man. They shook hands and said goodbye before Martin turned to Donna, his arms outstretched. Donna stood and gave him a brief hug.

"Donna, again, I'm so sorry."

"Thank you, Martin. You've always been a good friend to us."

"Well, I hope to make this as easy as possible." He looked at Taylor. "Are you ready to come in?"

Taylor nodded and stood, following Martin and her mother into the office.

Unlike the sparse reception room with generic prints on the wall, Martin's office had many personal touches. His college and law degrees hung on the wall along with paintings (originals, Taylor assumed) of

hunting scenes around the Delmarva Peninsula.
Taylor's father and Martin had hunted together many
times, but it wasn't something Taylor or Jenny had any
interest in. Several framed photos showed Martin
posing with prominent state and national politicians
from both sides of the aisle, and Taylor wondered, not
for the first time, how well-connected he was. It always
struck her as odd for an estates and trusts attorney to
be that chummy with higher-ups.

"Please, take a seat." He gestured to two high-back
red leather chairs. Donna and Taylor took their seats,
and Martin walked to the other side of his desk to sit in
his chair. He picked up a file and fingered through the
contents for a moment before he put it back down and
looked at Donna. "I think most of what's in the will
won't be any surprise to you. You and Pete came
together, so you know what goes to whom as far as the
business and land are concerned, but I will read it out
loud as a formality."

Donna nodded, and Taylor took a deep breath.
Hearing her father's will was not something she
thought she would be doing for many years to come.

Martin cleared his throat.

"I, Peter Francis Murray, of sound mind and body,
bequeath to my loving wife, Donna Jo Murray, our
house and all possessions therein unless stipulated
below." He paused. "Do you want me to list the
exceptions?"

"No, thank you, I know what they are. Unless
there's something he added…"

Martin cleared his throat again, cast a nervous glance at Taylor, and swallowed before shaking his head. "No, no changes to that list."

Taylor sat up straighter. Did that mean there were changes farther down?

"A trust fund will be set up for my daughter, Jennifer Delaney Murray, to cover all college and medical school expenses." He looked at Taylor then continued. "Murray Landscape and Design, and all its holdings, will become the sole property of Taylor Corrine Murray." He cleared his throat again and reached for a glass of water. He took a long drink before reading more. "Also, to Taylor Murray, I leave my place as a Chincoteague Island Pony Penning Saltwater Cowboy."

Taylor felt as if the air had been sucked from her lungs. Her father left her his spot on the team? Was that even allowed? Did that mean…?

"I'm sorry," she said with a quivering voice. "Can you please read that last part again?"

She listened carefully, trying to digest what that meant. "I don't understand. Is that legal? Are they obligated to follow his wishes?"

"Yes, well, that's something that remains to be seen."

Taylor's head was spinning. Her father had either left her the greatest gift she could ever have asked for, or the biggest can of worms the island had ever seen opened.

***

Nick had the day off and had a good idea as to how he wanted to spend it. He woke up, downed a can of Coca-Cola with a microwaved breakfast sandwich, and headed to the remotest part of the small island. He had only been there once before, but the route wasn't a hard one to follow. When he pulled up the drive, he was struck for the first time by the sight of the house in front of him. With all the excitement of his first call on his first day, he hadn't paid much attention to the property, especially once he saw Taylor and her family on the ground outside the fenced-in area where the pony was.

The entire property was enclosed with a long, wooden fence, and Nick wondered if it had once been a farm of some sort. He whistled as he drove closer to the massive, white, three-story house. It had balconies that ran along the exterior of both upper floors and a wrap-around porch that encircled the first floor. Running from the house, through the marsh, was a long pier, not unlike the one he intended to build on his own property, but a large boathouse sat at the end of this pier, overlooking the water. To the right of the house was a series of immense greenhouses and multiple barns that probably held landscaping equipment. To the left of the house, there was a barn with a fenced-in yard where a pony stood, eyeing him with a curious stare. A larger, red horse stood in another fenced area, paying him no mind.

Nobody came out to greet him; no dogs barked as he parked and exited the car. There didn't seem to be anyone home or in any of the greenhouses. He walked to the impressive-looking house and rang the bell, but there was no answer.

"May I help you?"

Nick turned toward the man's voice. A tall, lean and muscled man, wearing work boots and a ball cap, approached him. Nick walked down the steps to meet him.

"I'm looking for Taylor Murray, or anyone with the business I suppose."

"Are you a client? We don't usually see clients here at the property."

"No, sir, I'm…uh…" What was he? Not really a friend, so what then? "I'm the police officer who responded to the 911 call last week. I wanted to stop by and see if there was something I could do to help. I'm happy to lend a hand if they need it."

The man looked him up and down before shaking his head. "Much appreciated, I'm sure, but we've got plenty of help. Most of the employees are out on jobs today." As if realizing his manners, or deciding that Nick was no threat, the man stepped closer and offered his hand. "Cal Winters. I work for the Murrays, run a lot of the day-to-day operations so they can concentrate on design."

Nick shook his hand. "Nice to meet you. Officer, uh, Nick Black. I don't really know any of the family and don't know much about the business, or any landscaping business, but I wanted to let them know that I'm happy to help if they ever need anything."

"Like I said, it's much appreciated. I think we've got everything under control. Would you like me to tell Taylor that you stopped by?"

"Um, sure, that would be good." Nick knew that meant it was time to go. He headed to his car but stopped before getting in. He gazed at the house and looked once more around the property. It looked like Taylor and the rest of the family would do just fine without Pete around. Yep, they would do just fine.

***

"Are you okay?" Donna asked as Taylor drove them back to the ranch. "You haven't said a word since we left Martin's."

"I'm not sure," Taylor answered honestly. "I'm thrilled, confused, scared—"

"Scared of what?"

"Maybe scared isn't the right word. I'm just not sure what to do about, about…"

"It meant a lot to your father that you be a part of it all. He knew how much you wanted it."

Taylor took her eyes off the road to glance at her mother. "Did you know?"

Donna shook her head. "I suspected he might try to do something like this, but I always thought this day would be so far into the future, that…" She looked at the window, and Taylor knew she was trying to stop herself from crying. Donna turned back to Taylor. "I never imagined it would be so soon."

Taylor inhaled deeply and loosened the death grip she had on the steering wheel. "Well, I guess the first thing I need to do is contact Will Cheney and see what he says. My name's on the wait list, has been for years. Traditionally, when someone dies, their spot goes to their son. I don't see why this would be any different." Even as she said the words, she wondered if they were true. Nobody had ever pushed the issue before. Things were just done a certain way, and nobody really questioned them. Maybe it was time somebody did.

***

Nick stood on the broken-down dock and pictured the boat bobbing and weaving in the water. There was a lot to do to get the dock ready before he could bring the boat home, and it seemed that he had more time in his day than he anticipated. He might as well get to work.

As he measured and calculated and thought about how he was going to fix the dock and add an extended pier, he pictured the pier he had seen that morning. Nick didn't have the means to build a boathouse or a lift to keep his boat elevated above the water, and he never would on a police officer's salary, but that was okay. He was happy just having a boat.

He wondered what kind of boat was housed inside the boathouse at the Murray's place. Would Taylor laugh at his little fishing vessel? Did she like to fish? Would she say yes if he…

What was he thinking? He barely knew the woman. And her father had just passed away. What was wrong with him?

Nick let out a long breath and looked down at the broken planks. He turned and gazed back up at the house, noting the distance between the dock and the dry land. There was a lot of marsh to cover, and not a lot of days in the summer. If he was going to do this, he had to get his mind on the project at hand. Taylor Murray was way out of his league. He should just put her out of his mind right now.

He headed up to ask Zach if he could borrow his truck, determined to put all thoughts other than his dock and boat out of his mind. But as his boots made loud sucking noises, when they sunk in and were tugged out of the marsh on his walk back toward the house, an image of Taylor floated across his brain.

It's funny when you think about the things people are afraid of. I've been up close with sharks, crocodiles, and hippos. I lived in African villages where we were warned not to go into the forest because of black mambo snakes and hungry jaguars. I watched people die from spider bites in the Australian Outback. I experienced tsunami warnings and violent hurricanes. Never, at any of those times, was I afraid. When my ex-husband became abusive and then began stalking me, I learned what fear is. My fear wasn't caused by an animal or a weather forecast. My fear was caused by another human being. How sad is that? And how lucky am I to know that now, no matter what I face, I can face it head-on with courage and with the support of a whole community of people who love me and have my back? I pray that everyone is blessed to find that someday.

From *Discovering the World On a Barrier Island*
by Katherine Middleton Kelly

CHAPTER SIX

Kayla watched Zach in the mirror as he walked up behind her and bent to kiss the side of her bare neck.

"You're so beautiful," he told her, wrapping his arms around her bare stomach. She imagined how the peach fuzz on her head felt against his forehead.

Kayla smiled at the reflection of the man behind her. "I need to finish getting dressed. Mom wants me to go to the house to go over the checklist for the reception one more time and then I have some errands to run before the boys get out of school."

Zach gently turned her to face him. "Baby, I'm worried about you. You're doing too much. It hasn't been that long since you finished the radiation and—"

"Stop," Kayla commanded, shaking her head and biting her lips together. "I don't want to go over this again. I've told you, after four months of chemo, the radiation was a piece of cake." She firmly set her features and looked at him with determination. "We decided to do this in May, and it's May. I want to celebrate. It's been a long time since my family and friends have been able to do that. After everything we all went through, how can you ask me—"

"Kayla." Zach quietly said her name as he tightened his hold on her, and she fought the urge to melt into him. "I'm not asking you to postpone the reception. I know how much everyone is looking forward to it, especially your parents and the boys. I just want you to slow down." He pulled back and forced her to look at him. "We've started the business back up. You've thrown almost all of your energy into writing the cookbook. You threw a big party for Nick, insisting on cooking the food yourself."

"I had help," she protested.

"But you still handled the bulk of it."

He was right about that, so she didn't argue. "Okay, but it's what I do. I like cooking. I like cooking for other people. I love the business we started. I love providing the ingredients for healthy, easy meals for families. It's what we wanted—to create and run the business together. And I wanted to give Nick a party."

Zach took her hands in his. "Sweetheart, I know. I get it. You want everything to go on as normal. You want to work and help people and make everyone happy. But you have to take care of yourself."

Kayla pulled away and gently pushed him aside, reaching for the capris she had placed on the top of the stand by the shower.

"Zach, this is taking care of myself. I need to do these things. If I get tired, I take a nap. If I need to stop and start again later, I do. Why do we have to keep having this argument?" She pulled the capris on as he watched.

"It's not an argument. I just want you to be healthy. I love you."

Kayla stopped mid-reach, leaving her t-shirt on the stand. She looked up at Zach. She knew he wanted only the best for her, for them. She reached up, caressed his cheek, and smiled. "I love you, too. I promise, I won't overdo it. You can call mom and check up on me later. You know she won't lie. If she thinks I'm overdoing it, she'll let you know."

Zach looked at her for a moment before letting out a long sigh. "Fine. But I will call and check up on you."

Kayla laughed as she splayed her hand on his cheek, her fingers entwining themselves in his hair. He needed a trim before Saturday.

"Come here, soldier." She leaned up and kissed him. "Maybe I'll conserve some energy for later. After the boys are in bed."

Zach grabbed her waist and pulled her to him. "I'm going to hold you to that," he growled as he hungrily kissed her.

Pushing Zach away, Kayla picked up her shirt and pulled it over her head. She removed the auburn wig from its stand and placed it carefully on her head.

"What do you think?" she asked.

Zack surveyed her new look. "I like the color, but you're still beautiful without it."

Kayla smiled. She knew he meant every word.

***

"How's Nick doing?" Kate asked Kayla.

The two of them sat in two of Trevor's handmade Adirondack chairs on the back deck, sipping lemonade. Kate stretched her bare legs out in front of her, soaking up the warm sun rays.

"He seems to be doing well," Kayla told her. "Did I tell you he bought a boat?"

"Aaron told me. He said it was a really good deal."

"Nick said the same thing. That dock is a real eyesore though. There's no way it will hold a boat. He's got his work cut out for him."

"Well, he's single, doesn't socialize much, and works pretty reasonable hours. He should be able to get it fixed up."

"He asked Zach to help. They plan on fishing as much as they can once the dock is finished and the boat is in his possession."

"Poor Kayla," Kate teased. "You haven't even had the reception yet, and the honeymoon is over."

Kayla smiled. "It's okay. If Zach is happy, then I'm happy. The business is going well, we've got a nice advance on the cookbook, and he gets paid to coach. If he wants to spend his summer building a dock and then fishing, that's fine with me. If there's one thing we've all been reminded of lately, it's that life is short."

Kate shook her head. "Those poor girls. I can't imagine losing my father, and I'm more than ten years older than Taylor, and even older than Jenny. They're not married and don't have children. I can't help but think of all he missed out on."

"I know. I feel terrible for them, but don't feel bad for Uncle Pete. He's in a much better place. I bet he's already talking to St. Peter about redesigning the entrance to Heaven and planting elaborate gardens everywhere."

Kate smiled, lifted her glass to her lips, and took a long drink. "I bet you're right. I'm sure it's hard for his family to think like that right now, but he's smiling down on them and watching out for them as we speak."

"Well, look at you two. Time for a break?" Ronnie quietly closed the porch door behind her and took a seat on the wooden loveseat that completed the furniture set Trevor made for her on her previous birthday.

"Where's Miren?" Kate asked.

"With Trevor. He's going to watch her while we tend to the important matters of the day." She winked at her daughter-in-law.

"Mom, what's going on?" Kayla eyed her mother with suspicion. "You called us over here to help, but there's nothing to do. The favors are all finished and put in the back bedroom. The cookies are baked, decorated, and in the freezer. The tent won't go up until Friday morning, and we can't do the rest of the food until then either. Kate and I have gone over the whole checklist, and there's nothing to be done. Did Zach call you or something?"

"Zach? Why would he call me?"

Kate tried to hide her smile, but Kayla caught it. What did these two have in store for her today?

Kayla knew her mother was trying to throw her off. The bride looked from one woman to the other.

"Mom," Kayla moaned. "Just spill it, okay?"

Ronnie's eyes twinkled. "Grab your purses and come with me." She stood and went back into the house without another word.

Kayla turned to her sister-in-law. "You know what's going on, don't you?"

Kate shrugged. "Maybe. Maybe not." She stood and headed for the house, leaving Kayla to continue wondering.

Ronnie drove, and the three women went over the checklist again though they knew that everything that could be done ahead of time had been neatly crossed off the list. When Ronnie pulled into the parking lot of the island's most exclusive spa, Kayla squealed.

"Mom! You didn't."

Ronnie shook her head. "I didn't."

"Zach?"

"Nope," Kate answered.

"Then who?"

"Your father," Ronnie said, turning to her daughter. "He wanted the three of us to have a fun and relaxing girls' day out before the reception."

Kayla fought back tears. The last year had been tough for her. She knew everyone was worried about her, especially her father. She was his little girl, after all. Her thoughts turned to Taylor and Jenny and how much they must miss their own father. Poor girls, she thought again before remembering that this day was supposed to be about enjoying herself.

"Well, what are we waiting for?" Kayla asked. "I haven't been to a spa in years."

She was out of the car before either of the other two could open their doors. Kayla was going to make the most of every minute. After all, life was short.

***

Both Kate and Kayla's cars were in front of the house when Taylor pulled into the driveway of the wooded lot. She didn't see Aunt Ronnie's vehicle. With any luck, all three women were out together somewhere. Uncle Trevor's truck was parked near the garage. Taylor took a deep breath. She didn't know if this was a good idea, but what choice did she have? She needed to talk to someone, preferably a man and one who knew the island's history.

She put the truck into park and slowly made her way around to the garage door. Trevor had created a nice workshop for himself in the garage where he built outdoor furniture and could always be found there if he wasn't in the yard.

"Hello?" Taylor pushed open the door and peered inside.

Her Godfather stood by a chair, paintbrush in hand. He smiled when he saw Taylor. "Well, hello, Taylor.

What a nice surprise. Unfortunately, Ronnie and the girls are out for the day."

"That's okay. I was just driving around and, well, to be honest, I was hoping we could talk."

Trevor looked surprised. "Me? Of course. Let me clean this up first." He started toward the sink.

"No, please, keep painting. We can talk while you work." Taylor thought it might actually help to have Trevor stay busy while they talked. In fact... "Can I do something to help?"

"Oh, you don't have to do that."

"I know. I want to."

Perhaps he sensed her unease, or maybe he just liked the idea of having help. Either way, he rummaged around for another paint brush and handed it to her.

"Just do light, easy strokes, back and forth. Use enough paint to not streak, but not enough to drip." He demonstrated his technique.

"Okay, I can handle that."

For a while, neither spoke, though Taylor noticed her Godfather watching her quizzically a time or two.

"I don't think I ever asked what got you started making chairs?"

Uncle Trevor looked at her and smiled. "It was either that or go to marriage counseling."

"What?" Taylor was shocked. Were Uncle Trevor and Aunt Ronnie having marriage problems?

Trevor laughed. "Retirement finally got to me. I was bored out of my mind and driving Ronnie crazy. She kept bugging me to find a hobby. I have a friend, on the Western Shore, a retired Air Force Vet, who builds these chairs for a little extra income. Actually, your dad introduced us." His expression turned wistful for a moment, but he smiled and continued. "Anyway, I gave him a call, went to see him, and copied some of his patterns. It took me a few tries to get it right, and I'll never be as good as he is, but I enjoy it."

"Do you ever sell them?" It occurred to her that they would be a great addition to some of the landscapes they were working on.

"Sometimes, but not often. Your dad has asked me that before." He smiled. "But I like giving them away. Both of the kids have them on their back decks. And I gave Anne and Paul Parker a set for their twentieth anniversary. You've seen them here and there around the island. It makes me feel good to give people something they can use and appreciate."

Taylor still tucked away the information for the future. He hadn't said he *never* sells them.

"Aaron and Kayla are lucky to have you. Kate and Zach, too," she added quietly.

"You were lucky, too, Taylor. Your dad was a one-of-a-kind guy." He looked up and gazed at her. "And he's not really gone, honey. He's still here with us, praying for us every moment of every day."

Taylor stopped painting and looked at Trevor. "I know, but…"

"It's not the same. I know. Believe me, I understand."

"Uncle Trevor, can I ask you something?"

"Of course, honey, you can ask me anything."

"I—" She faltered, unsure of how to phrase her question. "My dad. He left me something." She looked away and stared out the windows. "Did your dad ever do anything that made you question everything? Including the things you always thought you wanted?"

Trevor was quiet for a moment. In the silence, they heard a rustling noise coming from the baby monitor on Trevor's workbench. Trevor reached for Taylor's paintbrush.

"Taylor, I'm getting hungry. How about we go get Miren and then make us some lunch and sit on the back deck? We can talk out there."

Taylor handed over her brush. "I don't want you to go to any trouble."

"Who said it was trouble? I'm hungry, and I could use the company. Besides, it sounds like my work for the day is over."

Taylor smiled. "Okay. To be honest, I'm hungry, too. I can go get Miren while you clean up if that helps."

"Perfect," Trevor said. "I'll meet you in the kitchen."

While Trevor sliced some peaches and made bite-sized sandwiches for Miren, settled on the floor beside them, Taylor made the subs. They added some potato chips and pickles to their plates, and then poured themselves tall glasses of lemonade before going out onto the deck. Trevor and Miren sat across from Taylor at the picnic table. Trevor immediately bowed his head, and Taylor joined him in saying grace. Trevor got Miren settled and then took a couple bites of his sub. He washed them down with the lemonade and then began to speak.

"My dad was a mean, selfish SOB."

Taylor blinked several times. Had she heard him right? She knew his mother died when he was young, and his father died several years later. She knew he had a hard upbringing, but it sounded like there were things she didn't know. She looked at Miren, who happily slurped down a tiny piece of the peach, and then waited for Trevor to continue.

"He could find any excuse to beat the tar out of me. And my mother. His fist to her stomach is the reason I'm an only child." He let that sink in before he spoke again. "I thought about running away so many times, I lost count, but I couldn't leave my mom, even though I hated her at times because of it. Your grandparents and Uncle James took me in more times than I could count. Back then, of course, people didn't talk about things like that, and the island was so small... anyway, they helped me the best they could." He shook his head. "All I wanted was to get away from that man. Nothing else mattered. I could have gone down a bad road, nursing anger and self-pity, but instead, I studied hard, made a name for myself playing ball, and worked at a local greenhouse on weekends. I was determined to get a scholarship to some place that would take me far away from my dad. I didn't know how I was going to get my mom away from him, but I was gonna figure it out somehow."

Trevor stopped talking and took another bite of his sub. Taylor had so many questions, but she waited patiently for him to continue his story.

"At the beginning of my junior year, a recruiter from the Coast Guard came to my school. I'd never thought about going into the military, but something he said really hit me hard." He looked Taylor in the eyes. "He said, 'Everyone has something that pushes them, makes them become the person they were meant to be. There's no better place to put that determination into action than by protecting and serving your country.' I'm not sure I really understood all that his statement entailed, but I knew that I had been protecting my mom and myself my entire life. It's what I knew." He took a long drink before focusing his gaze on Taylor once again. "Sometimes we're dealt a bad lot in life. You got lucky. Your dad was one of the best men I've ever known. Whatever he did, whatever he intended, he thought it was for the best."

Taylor took a deep breath. "He willed me his spot as a Saltwater Cowboy." She swallowed and met Trevor's gaze. "It's what I've always wanted. It's a dream come true, but do I pursue it? Do I go down that road?"

"Choices like that aren't easy. They are life-altering choices. Take my mom. She never left my dad," Trevor said sadly. "Not until the day I buried her, after he beat her so badly we couldn't even have an open casket at her funeral." He shook his head. "My dad died in a prison fight before I ever got to thank him."

Taylor gasped. "Thank him? For killing your mom?"

"No," Trevor said firmly. "For showing me the kind of man I never wanted to be and for forcing me to take an uncharted road, to figure out what I wanted in life and go after it. You see, Taylor, in all bad, there's something good that we can take away and learn from or improve upon. Your dad is giving you an opportunity here. You can seize it and rise to the occasion, forging a path on an uncharted road, or you can let it go. Ronnie would tell you to pray for an answer. She would say that perhaps your father's death was meant to push you into going where you were meant to be. Your dad knew that you have the potential to be a great Saltwater, ah, Cowgirl." He grinned. "The question is, do *you* want to do that?"

"More than anything."

"Then, my dear child, you have to decide if you're willing to fight for it." He handed Miren one of his chips while Taylor thought about what she wanted to do.

"Uncle Trevor, do *you* think I should?"

He looked thoughtfully at her before nodding. "I think you'll be surprised. Just because something has always been a certain way doesn't mean it has to stay that way. I think you'll find that most of the men will agree with that."

"And the ones who don't?"

"You'll have to prove them wrong."

***

"How was the spa?" Trevor met the women at the door when they returned and gave Ronnie a kiss on the cheek as she entered. "As promised, dinner is on the grill."

"You are the best," Ronnie told her husband. "The spa was wonderful. Just what we needed."

Kayla went to her father and hugged him. "Thank you, Dad. It was just what I needed."

"You're welcome, honey. I'm glad you all had fun." He released his daughter and said hello to Kate.

Kate hugged him before apologizing. "I hate to run, but I should get Miren home and start dinner myself."

"Same here," Kayla said, glancing at the clock. "Zach and the boys will be starving by the time it's ready."

Trevor hugged his daughter goodbye and turned to his daughter-in-law. "Kate, Miren was an angel, as usual."

"Thanks, Trevor. I really appreciate you watching her." She lifted the little girl from the highchair, hugged her in-laws, and waved goodbye as she followed Kayla from the house.

Once they were gone, Trevor asked Ronnie to join him out by the grill. "I had a visitor today." He kept his tone causal as he lifted the lid to check on the steaks.

"Oh?" Ronnie leaned back on the deck railing and stretched her arms out.

"Taylor."

Ronnie's relaxed stance changed as she stood straighter and looked at her husband. "Taylor? She came by to see you? Is everything okay with Donna?"

"Yes. She wanted to talk about her father, or rather, about something he left her in his will."

Ronnie left the railing and went closer to Trevor. "His will?"

Trevor slowly nodded. "He willed her his spot in the Pony Penning group."

"The Saltwater Cowboys? Can he do that?"

Trevor shrugged. "I don't know. She doesn't either. She's wrestling with the decision of pursuing it."

Ronnie pressed her lips together and looked off into the woods for a moment. "She should. It's not just about her. It's about all the women in her generation and beyond."

"It could get nasty."

"It could, but I think we should give them more credit than that. Most of them will be on her side, don't you think?"

"I do. It's the loud minority she's going to have to worry about."

***

Taylor hefted a large shrub from the truck as she thought back to the previous day and her discussion with Uncle Trevor. She used all her strength to maneuver the bush into place beside the library steps.

"Need help with that?"

She looked up to see a familiar police officer standing beside her. She stood and smiled.

"We keep running into each other." She cocked her head to the side. "Unless you're following me."

"Following you? I'm supposed to stop stalkers not become one."

She laughed. "Oh, really? Is that why you showed up at the house yesterday morning?"

She watched the color rise to his face and felt a twitch in her stomach. He was kind of cute.

"I just stopped by to see if you needed anything. I mean, if your family needed anything. I figured it was the least I could do."

"Cal told me. Thank you. That was very kind."

Nick gestured toward the shrub. "That looks heavy. Do you normally do the heavy stuff yourself?"

Taylor grinned and shrugged. "Sometimes. Did you think that, because I'm a female, I'm not capable of heavy lifting?"

Nick waved his arms in front of him. "No way. I didn't say that. I just meant..." His face grew a shade redder, and Taylor laughed.

"I'm just kidding." She suddenly wondered what the other men on the island thought. She could out-bench press many of them, so why couldn't she ride beside them? "Anyway, I like doing the small jobs like this. It gives me time to work alone and think. When I'm with a whole crew, it's hard to find any peace and quiet. Sometimes, I need a day with my thoughts."

"And this is one of those days?"

She sighed and offered a weary smile. "It is."

"Anything you'd like to talk about? I'm willing to listen."

She eyed him and thought, *what a nice guy.*

"Maybe sometime. I think I'd like that. For now, though..." She pointed to the back of her truck. "I've got a few more things to take care of."

"No problem. I've got to get back to the station. I guess I'll see you at the wedding this weekend?"

Taylor smiled and nodded. "I'll be there."

They said goodbye, and she watched Nick walk away. She'd spent her entire life on the island, and while she loved it, she'd never really connected with any guys on the island, other than Chad. It might be nice to go out with someone she hadn't known since kindergarten.

Once, when we lived in a small village in South America, I witnessed the wedding between a young couple. It was my first wedding, and I was drawn, not only to the faces of the bride and groom, but to the faces of everyone in attendance. There was so much love radiating from each person that it was as if the entire canopy of the forest was filled with a palpable emotion that could be captured and bottled. When I married Aaron, in the little church on Chincoteague Island, I felt that same feeling, as if the church was filled with so much love that it could lift us all up into Heaven like a giant helium balloon.

From *Discovering the World On a Barrier Island*
by Katherine Middleton Kelly

CHAPTER SEVEN

It was all-hands-on-deck Friday morning at the Kelly house. Though Nick was at the station, Zach, Aaron, Trevor, and Zach's father, Walter, were at work, erecting the rental tent. It took all four men the better part of an hour to raise the canvas. Taylor, Jenny, and Donna joined the other women as they watched through the windows and laughed at the spectacle of the standing and falling of the poles while the men figured out the logistics. Even with the spring breeze, all of the men were drenched with sweat by the time the last support rope was tied.

Jenny leaned over to her sister. "If Daddy were here, they would have had it up within a half hour, tops."

"You're right," Taylor whispered. It was the first time she'd been able to think about her dad and smile without becoming teary-eyed.

"Okay, ladies, back to work," Ronnie ordered.

Within minutes, vegetables and fruits were being sliced and arranged on trays, several hams were roasting, and potatoes were being peeled for the potato salad. Peeling potatoes was actually comforting to Taylor, something she had done many times on family holidays when she helped her grandmother make homemade mashed potatoes.

"How's it going?" Ronnie asked Taylor. She assumed that Ronnie wasn't talking about peeling vegetables.

Taylor smiled. "Every day gets a little easier."

Aunt Ronnie looked at her with sympathy. She put her arm around Taylor and pulled her in for a quick hug. "It does, and it will continue to do so." Ronnie stood by hesitantly, and Taylor wondered if Uncle Trevor told her about the will.

"Did Uncle Trevor mention…?"

"He did."

"And?"

"And I think you should do what's best for you."

Taylor frowned. "That's not really an answer."

"I guess it's not." Aunt Ronnie heaved a long sigh. "If it were me, and I was your age with your talent, I would do it."

"You would?"

"I would. And I think the guys will surprise you."

Taylor nodded thoughtfully. "Thanks, Aunt Ronnie. I'm thinking I just might."

Aunt Ronnie leaned over and put her arm back around Taylor, giving her a little squeeze. "We're all going to be rooting for you."

Taylor turned her eyes to Aunt Ronnie and smiled. "Thank you. That means a lot to me."

"How's it going in here?" Trevor picked up a cucumber slice and popped it into his mouth as he surveyed the process with the food.

"Just fine, Dad. We don't need any more cooks in the kitchen." Kayla smiled as she poured the water from the potatoes that had just finished boiling.

"Who says I want to cook?"

"We don't need any taste testers either," Aunt Ronnie told him. She motioned to the backyard with a smirk on her face. "I see you finally got the tent up."

"Do I detect an air of superiority in there somewhere?" Trevor narrowed his gaze at his wife.

"Not at all," Ronnie said. "Far be it from me to criticize your tent-raising skills. How long did it take you guys to get it to stand?"

"Oh, Ronnie," Mitzi Middleton, Kate and Zach's mother, interceded for Trevor. "I'm sure it's harder than it looks. I know that it's much more complicated than any tent Walter and I erected in our days of living in the wilds."

"Mom," Kate said with a laugh. "We never lived in a tent."

Taylor watched the two families interact and thought about her own family. She cast an eye toward her mother and saw Donna turn away to wipe a tear from her cheek. They would never again have those seemingly small, insignificant encounters with her father—the light teasing, the family jokes, the loving looks that passed between her parents and the gagging sounds she and Jenny made when they saw 'the look.'

Taylor felt like she was about to burst into tears. She laid down the potato peeler and walked from the kitchen, careful not to draw attention to herself. Without anyone noticing, she scurried through the open door to the back porch and headed toward the pier. She needed some time to collect herself.

"Hey." She heard Jenny come up behind her on the dock. "It was getting a little stuffy in there."

Taylor put her arm around her sister. "It was."

They stood in silence for several minutes, watching the sun hover over the canal.

"Taylor, do you think we'll ever laugh like that again?"

An unbidden memory from earlier that week popped into Taylor's mind—the laugh that Nick elicited from her outside the library.

"I think so, Jenny. Someday."

***

At four in the afternoon, Kayla stood outside and surveyed their work. The food was prepared, the tables and chairs were set up, the dance floor was laid, and thousands of white lights were strung above it all, as if God had filled the tent with all the stars of the heavens

just for the special couple. Ronnie had gone to pick up
the boys and some pizza. Kayla, EJ, and Todd were
spending the night there rather than going back to their
own house. Though they had been married for months,
Kayla insisted on keeping with tradition. She didn't
want to see Zach until they renewed their vows the
following day.

Kayla walked through the tent and down to the end
of the yard. A wooden divider ran along the grass.
About two feet below, on the other side of the divider,
was the canal. Kayla and Aaron spent many
afternoons, as children, paddling their kayaks in the
canal where their mother could keep an eye on them. It
seemed just like yesterday, they were splashing each
other with water. She loved this place—the house, the
yard and canal behind it, the island itself. She was so
happy that she and the boys had returned home after
Eddie's death. Nothing bad could touch her here. Even
cancer had turned out to have no power over her island
paradise.

Though she didn't hear his footsteps on the grass,
Kayla sensed Zach as he came up behind her. He
wrapped his arms around her waist and gently pulled
her backwards so that her back leaned against him. She
closed her eyes and took in his scent—body soap,
sweat, and beer. Not the most romantic of scents, but
the combination, along with the salty water and the
fragrance of the flowers in the nearby garden, offered
her a strange yet comforting feeling of contentment.

"Ready?" Zach whispered the word into her neck.

"More than ready. I can't wait to celebrate with everyone we love." A sense of sadness washed over her. "Well, almost everyone."

Always able to read her mind, Zach said, "It's okay to miss Eddie if that's what you're thinking. You loved him, and it's natural that you'd be thinking about him today."

"I did love him. We all did. We just thought we'd have more time." Kayla sighed. "I never want to make that mistake again."

"We'll cherish every second we have together."

Kayla nodded. "I think we've done a pretty good job of that since the cancer. We're just constantly reminded that everything can end in an instant, aren't we?"

Zach squeezed her, and she let herself melt into him. "I love you so much, Zachary Daniel Middleton."

"Not half as much as I love you, Kayla Elizabeth Middleton."

After a few minutes, Zach spoke. "Nick told me he ran into Taylor the other day."

Kayla's eyes opened. "Oh, really? And?"

"I don't know. Something about the way he looked when he mentioned her. Should I tell him to back off?"

Kayla watched a blue heron glide just above the canal until it was out of sight. "No. Let's see where it leads. God works in mysterious ways."

"Think she can handle him?"

Kayla chuckled. "I think the real question is, can he handle her?"

***

Nick stood nervously beside the other men as they flanked Zach on the altar. Though the renewal of vows was merely ceremonial, Zach and Kayla had asked their closest friends to stand with them. Nick hadn't been at the first ceremony. He'd been too busy trying to track down the kidnapper who had killed Tammi's son and would, a few weeks later, abduct Todd.

Today, he stood at the front of the rank and file, ahead of Aaron and Paul. He knew that the bride's side would be heavier. Kayla's lifelong friend, Debbie, would be at her side along with Kate, Tammi, and Anne. Nick wondered about the other women Kayla was close to and found himself scanning the pews. Before he could find the person in question, the music started, and the congregation stood.

Nick smiled as the women processed down the aisle. Each wore a knee-length green dress with white lace over it and carried a single light-green rose. Kayla told them that green roses symbolize life, growth, and the renewal of life and energy. Those were the things she wanted this day to represent—the sanctity of life, the growth of her and Zach's love, their renewal of love to each other, and the life-giving power and energy of God. Nick thought the flowers were kind of ugly and looked fake, like they had been dyed by some artificial means, but who was he to say so?

When Kayla entered the church, and the congregation stood, Nick found his vision roving away from the bride. His eyes stopped on the blonde-haired woman in a blue and white flowered dress. Beside her, stood a teenager in a pink and white striped dress. He could see their profiles. Both women and their mother smiled, but as he watched, their mother—Donna?—dabbed her eyes with a tissue. As Kayla passed their pew, the woman turned toward the front, and Taylor caught his eye. He smiled, and she smiled back. It took everything in him to look away and focus on the bride.

Throughout the rest of the hour-long nuptial Mass, Nick had to force himself not to look at Taylor. He wished he could see her expression when Aaron read from the Book of Ruth:

Wherever you go I will go,
wherever you lodge I will lodge.
Your people shall be my people
and your God, my God.
Where you die I will die,
and there be buried.
May the LORD do thus to me, and more, if even death
separates me from you!

He wondered if it reminded her of her parents and the love they shared and wished he could relay a message of sympathy.

He wanted to glance her way during the vows to see her gaze as it fell on the happy couple.

Instead, Nick kept his focus on his best friend and his wife. Their eyes never left each other's. They were alone on the altar, despite the priest and altar servers. Their world encompassed them and them alone, and Nick silently thanked God that they had the opportunity to share their love with their family and friends. When they said their vows the first time, they had no idea what the next day would bring, what Kayla would wake up to when the anesthesia wore off. They only knew that they loved each other enough to take the chance and be together. Nick longed for that kind of love. He'd searched for it his entire life. Each time he thought he found it, it slipped through his fingers.

As he thought about unrequited love, he experienced the sudden sensation of being watched. Though he'd been fighting it throughout the ceremony, he allowed his gaze to find Taylor. She was gazing back at him.

***

Taylor stood by the outdoor bar, waiting patiently for the bartender to hand her a drink. As she waited, she turned to watch the festivities. The sun was sinking behind the trees, and the twinkling lights cast a magical glow that infused the atmosphere with the promise of love and new beginnings. She was so happy for Zach and Kayla and for the boys. They were the perfect family, and she looked at them with admiration and a bit of envy as the four of them danced together in a happy circle of love.

"It's a beautiful sight, isn't it?"

Taylor turned and smiled at Nick. "It is. They look really happy together."

"Zach's crazy in love with Kayla. He told me he knew she was the one the first night he saw her."

Smiling, Taylor accepted her beer from the bartender.

"A girl after my own heart," Nick said, his hand over his heart. He looked at the bartender. "I'll have the same, please."

"Do you really think he meant it? Zach, I mean. Do you think he meant it when he said he'd loved her since he first saw her?"

"There's one thing I know for sure about Zach. He never lies and never exaggerates."

Nick accepted his beer, and they began walking aimlessly toward the canal.

"I've always wondered if love at first sight is a real thing," Taylor said.

"All at once everything is different, now that I see you."

Taylor came to an abrupt halt. "Excuse me?"

Nick's face reddened. "Sorry, I didn't say that. I mean, I did, but it wasn't me. It was Rapunzel. You know, in *Tangled*?"

Taylor looked at Nick for a moment and wondered if he was for real. Before she could help herself, she began to chuckle and then laugh. The laugh grew until she was so giddy, she didn't think she could stop. She covered her mouth with her hand and tried to stop herself.

"I'm so sorry. It's just that…I mean…I've never heard a grown man quote a Disney movie, but it was so, so appropriate!"

"I find that every life lesson you need to know can be learned from Disney movies."

Taylor felt her smile deepen, and she shook her head. "You might be onto something, Nick."

He looked back toward the tent where the music and dancing were in full swing and turned to Taylor. "In that case, how about a little piece of advice from the gargoyle in the *Hunchback of Notre Dame*, 'Life's not a spectator sport. If watchin' is all you're gonna do, then you're gonna watch your life go by without ya'." He held out his hand to her. "Care to dance?"

Taylor didn't hesitate. "I'd love to."

***

Nick needed to catch his breath after the fourth fast song. He motioned toward the bar, and Taylor followed him. He ordered two more beers and drank half of his in one swallow.

"I can't remember the last time I danced. It might have been my junior prom," Nick said.

"You haven't gone to any weddings since then? I feel like I have one every month."

Nick shook his head. "Nah. Zach's really my only friend, so this is the first." He gave her a lopsided smile. "I probably shouldn't admit that."

"There's nobody from college you stayed in touch with?"

Nick felt a pang in his gut and looked away. He took another long pull of his beer. He kept his gaze on the distant sky as he answered. "I didn't go to college. Joined the Marines the day I turned eighteen. Got my GED before I headed to boot camp." He shrugged. "It seemed like the right thing to do at the time."

"I think that's brave," Taylor said quietly.

He turned back to face her. "You do?"

She nodded. "My dad did the same thing, only he joined the Air Force."

Nick felt his mouth curve into a tight bow. "Did he ever regret it? Not going to college?"

Taylor started to walk toward the dock, and Nick followed. "He went eventually. He worked hard, established his business and found that he had a talent for design. He could have used the GI Bill to pay for it, but he saved it for me or Jenny to use. It took him a long time, but we all went to his graduation." She smiled and put her hand on his shoulder as she lifted her foot and took off one shoe and then the other. It was the sexiest move Nick had ever witnessed, and she wasn't even trying. She sat on the edge of the dock, and Nick joined her.

"We were so proud of him. I was just a kid, but I remember thinking to myself, 'that's my dad up there.' I thought he was the smartest person in the world."

"I've heard he was a great guy."

"He was."

They sat in silence and gazed across the canal where the evening sky was painted with red, orange, pink, and purple brushstrokes. The last of the rays set the marshy water on fire.

"It looks like one of Aunt Ronnie's paintings."

"It does. Kate has an amazing one hanging in her house. Ronnie painted a sunset in some secret cove Kate and Aaron like to go to."

Taylor smiled. "It's not so secret. We used to go there when we were little and had more time for things like kayaking and tadpole chasing."

"You don't have time to chase tadpoles anymore?"

"Afraid not. I'm pretty busy six days a week with the business and most evenings I'm either with Stormy or helping people break and train their ponies."

"Stormy. Is that your horse? The one in the corral at your house?"

"Yeah, but she's not a horse. We used to have horses on the ranch, lots of them, but most of the barns are used for the landscaping business now. The only animals we have now are Stormy and my dad's horse, Big Red. He's a horse, but Stormy is a bona fide Chincoteague pony. I wanted one my whole life. Two years ago, I helped my Dad with her birth." She looked at Nick. "The firemen keep careful track of the ponies and try to be there when they give birth. That way, they can track the herd better and be there in case of any complications. Anyway, when Hurricane Tara blew through a couple years ago, I was home on fall break. My dad volunteered to go out with the vet and check on the ponies. My mom had a fit when he said I could go, too, but I was twenty-one. What could she do?" Taylor shrugged.

Nick liked the sound of her voice. He thought he could listen to her all night.

"So, dad and Dr. Trainor and I went out to Assateague, and we found a pony going into labor. The wind and rain were fierce, but she was so scared. I held her head and talked to her while they took care of things at the other end. As soon as I saw the foal, I knew I had to have her. Dad didn't want me spending my hard-earned money on her. The ponies are quite expensive, you know. So, he told me he'd pay for half. It was supposed to be a loan, but he forgave it in his will."

She took a deep breath and let it out. Her face glowed in the twilight, and Nick wanted to reach out and touch her cheek but refrained. They barely knew each other, and though that had never stopped him before, this felt...different.

"Can you keep a secret, Nick?"

Caught off guard by the question, Nick swallowed, uncertain of what she might say. "Sure. Like I said, I only have one friend." He grinned, but Taylor's somber expression didn't change.

"My dad left me his spot as a Saltwater Cowboy."

Nick blinked. He wasn't sure what that meant. "Is that a baseball team or something?"

Taylor looked at him, her brow creased. "You don't know much about the island, do you?"

"I guess not."

Taylor explained about the wild ponies that lived on nearby Assateague, how they were owned and cared for by the Chincoteague Fire Department, and how they were auctioned off every year with the proceeds going to the Fire Department.

"Is it a big deal, then, to be a member?"

Taylor sniffed. "You have no idea."

"Well, then, congratulations. That's good news, isn't it?"

"It would be if I were a man."

Nick didn't understand. "A man?"

"Yeah, no woman has ever been a Saltwater Cowboy, hence the name, *Cowboy*. I've had my name on the wait list for nine years."

"Then, you'll be the first, right?"

"I wish it were that simple. Even if you're on the list, that doesn't mean you'll get picked when a spot opens. There are only two ways to get a spot—you either earn it through years of dedicated volunteering, or you inherit it. I've done both."

"Then what's the problem?"

"I wish I knew. Like I said, no woman has ever been chosen. It's just not something that's ever been done."

"You know, Cinderella once said 'Just because it's what's done, doesn't mean it's what should be done'."

That brought a smile to her face. "You're something else, you know that?"

"Hey, I told you my philosophy." He held his hands up and shrugged. "So, what are you going to do?"

Taylor held Nick's gaze for a long moment. Her voice was steady when she answered. "I'm going to make it happen."

***

Taylor climbed into bed and yawned. A light knock sounded on her door. "Come in."

Jenny pushed open the door, entered, and closed it behind her. She sat on the edge of Taylor's bed and then made her way to the extra pillow on the other side. "Did you have a good time at the wedding?"

"I did. How about you?"

Jenny stared at the ceiling. "I did. It was different without Dad, but I had a good time. I'm glad EJ and Lizzie were there. I mean, they're younger, but they're cool."

"I saw you with Billy Hill." Taylor often wondered about their friendship. Was he to Jenny what Chad had always been to her, or was there something more?

Jenny shrugged. "Yeah, he's a good guy. Just a friend, though."

"That's okay. You'll meet plenty of boys in college."

Jenny was quiet as she stared ahead. Taylor watched the shadow of the rotating fan moving across her face in the lamplight.

"I saw you laughing tonight. Really laughing. You looked happy."

Taylor smiled. "Yeah. That police officer who drove us to the hospital? His name is Nick. He says Zach's his best friend. They seem like the least likely of besties, but I guess it works for them."

"You spent a lot of time with him tonight. You danced and sat on the dock and then danced some more. It was nice. To see you happy, I mean."

"It was nice to be happy."

"You haven't been happy for a long time." Jenny finally looked at her sister. "Since way before Dad died."

Perceptive as always, Taylor thought, but she didn't admit that Jenny was right. "What makes you say that?"

"Taylor, I live here. You haven't been the same since you came back from school. Do you not like living at home?"

Taylor thought about it. "No, it's not that. I just…" What was it? She thought back to something she said to Nick. "All of my friends are getting married. They all met someone at school or right after graduation. I'm back here on the island with all the same guys I've known my whole life. I guess, it's just a little depressing."

"Chad's in love with you, you know."

Taylor scoffed. "Give me a break. He's in love with every girl."

"No, he's not. He just dates every girl because you won't go out with him."

Taylor sat up straighter. "I don't think that's true."

Jenny yawned before pushing herself up and standing by the bed. "Suit yourself. For what it's worth, he's not good enough for you, and Dad never liked him anyway."

The statement surprised Taylor, but Jenny always had her finger on the pulse of everything.

Taylor watched her sister cross the room to the door. The door was almost all the way closed when she stopped and poked her head back into the room. "That police officer, Nick? Would Dad have liked him?"

Taylor didn't have to think about it. With a smile, she said, "Yeah, Dad would have liked him."

"Good," Jenny said before closing the door.

I've always been fascinated by the idea of a Vision Quest. Many cultures around the world, including Native American peoples, send their young men on a vision quest around the age of thirteen. When we were in Ecuador, we talked to some of the boys after they returned from their journeys. Each boy described his personal experience in the forest after being given a hallucinogen. Most of the boys proved their courage and had their true callings revealed to them by the spirit of the forest. I remember one young man who surprised us all. After he had been gone for three days, his family assumed the worst. Had he shown fear and run away, unable to face his village again? Had he been unable to find food and starved deep in the forest? Had he been mauled by a wild animal? When the boy finally returned, a triumphant glow emanated from him. He had shown courage in the face of his greatest fears, and we all knew he now possessed wisdom beyond everyone's imaginings.

From *Discovering the World On a Barrier Island*
by Katherine Middleton Kelly

CHAPTER EIGHT

"I'd like to see Will," Taylor said to Dina, the secretary to the president of the local bank and another friend from high school. They had already exchanged pleasantries, and Dina offered her condolences to Taylor.

"He's on a call right now, but he has a break in his schedule before his next meeting. I'll let him know you'd like to see him." She scribbled a note and took it to the man behind the closed door.

Taylor sat down and waited. She toyed with her phone, checking emails and scrolling through Instagram, while she waited. After what felt like an eternity, the door opened.

"Taylor, sweetheart, come in. What can I do for you today? Everything okay with the business?"

Taylor followed the older gentleman into the room. "Yes, everything is fine."

"And your mother?"

"She's doing as well as can be expected."

"And that grandmother of yours? She looked like she's still enjoying the sun and the golf courses in South Carolina." Will had always been sweet on Pete's mom, reminding everyone that she was the 'one that got away'."

"Gram's doing fine. They didn't stay long though. Mom insisted they get back to their lives. You know how it is with mothers-in-law." Taylor smiled.

Will laughed, his large belly shaking with each chortle. He offered a bottle of water, which she declined, and took a seat behind his desk.

"So, what brings you here today, Taylor?"

Without saying a word, Taylor opened the folder in her lap and handed the document over to Will. She had made a copy of the will and highlighted the part in question. She waited for him to respond. His bushy eyebrows raised as he read the bequeath, and he cleared his throat before he looked at Taylor.

"Well, this is, uh, quite an unusual circumstance, eh?"

"I'm not sure it's that unusual at all. Aren't half the cowboys sons and grandsons who inherited their spot?"

He sat back in his chair and exhaled, steepling his fingers beneath this chin. "Well, yes, but, you see, there is a protocol for this type of thing."

"I'm sure there is. Just tell me what we need to do. I'm happy to follow all the rules." Taylor smiled demurely at him, even batting her eyes a time or two.

"Well, I would have to, uh, talk this over with the other administrators."

"Mr. Cheney, Will, you and I both know that I have the qualifications, that I've worked with the ponies and the new owners. We know that I've been there for births and deaths and for every pony swim and penning since I was born. There are men on the team who aren't even from the island." Quietly, she added, "You know this is what my father wanted."

Will nodded. "I'll see what I can do."

Taylor knew he meant it. He was an honorable man. They shook hands, and Taylor stopped to say goodbye to Dina before leaving. As she walked to her car, she thought about Nick's quote from their talk on the dock, *Just because it's what's done, doesn't mean it's what should be done.*

***

Flies and mosquitoes filled the humid air as Taylor led Nick through the marsh in search of Angel. They dodged the slimy water as best they could, their boots making small sucking sounds as they trudged on the soft ground.

"She's the first pony we bought. I like to check on her now and then. She's foaled three times since we bought her."

"I don't understand why the pony is still on the island if you bought her."

"Every year, the auction has several ponies that are buybacks. Someone bids and purchases them, but the ponies stay here on the island and are cared for by the fire department. It protects the longevity of the herd and allows a good number of the ponies to always live in the wild."

"And your company buys them?"

"Every year. We like knowing that we're contributing to the welfare of the animals and the department but still allowing the ponies their freedom. Dad was a huge proponent of the program."

She stopped short and reached back for Nick's hand. She squeezed it hard, and he felt a surge go through him. Looking up, Nick saw at least a dozen ponies grazing in the marsh ahead. He instinctively knew that Taylor was telling him to be quiet and keep his distance. He had no intention of getting any closer. What if they decided to stampede? Could he and Taylor outrun them? He was sure Taylor could, but Nick had one too many beers since returning to the island.

Taylor took a step back so that she stood next to him. She leaned toward him and whispered. "The one with the black coat and white mane, that's Angel."

Nick nodded, but all he could think about was how close they were, how he could smell the floral scent of her shampoo and the peppermint gum on her breath. He felt a twinge in his stomach.

Taylor made an almost inaudible gasp and tugged on his hand. "Look," she whispered and pointed to an all-black pony standing several feet away from the rest of the herd. "There's Phantom! He's usually hiding."

He could feel her excitement pulsing from her. Or was it his own heartbeat, pulsing with the energy that flowed from her hand in his? He swallowed, unable to speak or think rationally. All he knew was that he would traipse through a hundred acres of marshland to find every pony on the island if she would let him keep holding her hand.

***

Nick was quiet as they climbed into her truck. Taylor wondered what he was thinking but felt funny asking. Something had happened back at the wildlife refuge, and she wasn't sure what it was. After they spotted the ponies, they walked in silence back through the marsh. A tingling sensation ran up her arm when she realized they were still holding hands. It felt good. Very good. It had been a long time since she'd held hands with a man other than her father. She thought back to what she had told her sister.

"My dad would have liked you." She didn't look at him as she put the truck in reverse. She suddenly felt shy.

"I think I would have liked him. Though, I have to admit, I know nothing about horses, or ponies, and even less about plants."

Taylor smiled. "But you're honorable and loyal and kind-hearted." She stole a look at him before pulling out of the lot. "Those are the things that would have mattered to him most."

"How do you know that? Maybe I'm some crazed psycho who has you fooled."

She laughed. "Maybe, but I doubt it. My Aunt Ronnie and Uncle Trevor would never have let you become a part of the family if that were the case. They're pretty perceptive people."

"I have to agree."

They both looked ahead for a few minutes, neither speaking until Nick asked, "So, what should our next adventure be?"

Taylor grinned and cast a sidelong look his way before returning her attention to the road. "I don't know. I guess that's up to you. I chose a pony hunt. What would you like to do?"

"How about dinner?"

Taylor blinked. She wasn't expecting that though she didn't know why. They had a great time at the wedding together, and the morning had been pleasant. Why shouldn't they go out on what she assumed would be a real date?

"I think I'd like that."

"I'm working tonight and tomorrow night but how about the next night?"

"This week might be tricky. I've got a major job going on in Pocomoke. I might not be back until late most nights."

"Doesn't the crew have to stop at five or something? Like a normal job?"

"Usually, yes, but we were already behind schedule because of the heavy spring rains and now..." She looked away for a moment. "Anyway, we would have been there today if the clients weren't having the driveway paved. Why they didn't wait until we're done is beyond me."

"Okay, so when's a good time for you?"

Taylor thought about it. "How about Friday night? I won't let my crew work late on a Friday. And I'm hoping we'll be wrapping up by then."

"Friday sounds good. I'm off Thursday and Friday this week, so no night shift to make me sleepy on our date."

Taylor laughed. "I sure hope I'm not such bad company that you're worried about falling asleep on our first date." She liked the sound of the words, 'first date.'

"I don't think you're bad company at all."

She felt the color rise in her cheeks. "You're not so bad yourself, Nick," she said quietly.

She came to a stop in his driveway. "Thanks for going with me this morning. I hope it wasn't torture for you. Between the bugs, the humidity, the smell of the marsh, and the mud, I guess it wasn't where most women would take someone on their first outing together."

"I didn't even notice."

Taylor looked at Nick. His smile was sincere, and his eyes conveyed more feeling than she was ready to acknowledge. They had just met, yet there was something there, a pull that she couldn't deny. She smiled at him, looking forward to getting to know him better.

"I'd better get going. I have some errands to run, and I know you need to rest before work. I'm looking forward to Friday."

"Me, too, Taylor. I'll pick you up if you don't mind riding in my car. It's not nearly as nice as your truck."

She detected a bit of embarrassment in his inflection and in the way he looked away as he spoke.

"Nick, cars are not my thing. My truck is a necessity for work. Other than that, it's just a way to get to one place or another."

He looked back at her and smiled. "I'll see you on Friday. Text me when you know what time works best."

She agreed and waited until he got to the steps of his house. He turned and waved, and she felt a flutter in her stomach. She turned up the radio and headed back toward the ranch, singing at the top of her lungs.

***

Golden beads of sunlight appeared among the ripples on the water beneath them as Zach and Nick hammered the new planks onto the dock. They worked to the rhythm of the music on Nick's playlist.

Zach and Kayla had spent three nights at a lakefront cabin in Pennsylvania, but they were home, and Zach was ready to help Nick get the boat in the water. Nick was grateful to be working the night shift this week, so he'd have time to work on the dock. His afternoon naps were just enough to get him through his shift as long as he had a steady supply of Coca-Cola.

"Aaron tells me the boat is in even better shape than he first thought," Zack said, talking over the beating of the hammers.

"Yeah, it's more than seaworthy. As soon as the dock is repaired, we can put her in the water."

"You've got a good plan for creating a pier over the marsh. I'm impressed."

Nick smiled. "I'm glad you approve."

He liked the feel of the hammer in his hand and the sun on his back. He would have been quite content if his stomach wasn't growling. He sat back on his heels and surveyed the progress they'd made after just a couple hours of work. They had a ways to go before the pier extended past the marsh and reached the dry grass, but they were getting there little by little.

"Hey, Zack, you hungry?"

Zach finished hammering his plank into place and stood. He stretched his back before slowly nodding.

"Come to think of it, I am getting hungry."

"How about we heat up that casserole you brought over and grab a couple beers? After that, I might have another hour or so in me before I need a nap."

"Sounds good," Zack said, moving his head from side to side so that his neck and upper back snapped and popped. Nick did the same.

"Man, we're getting old."

Zach leveled his gaze on his young friend but didn't comment. He just shook his head, turned, and walked toward the house, their boots sinking into the marsh beneath them with each step until they hit dry land.

Nick followed Zach toward the house with a large smile on his face. There was hardly a time in the past few days that Nick hadn't been smiling. As if Zach could read his mind, a trait he seemed to have mastered, Zach spoke up.

"So, I hear you and Taylor really hit it off at the wedding."

"You could say that," Nick answered. "We've been texting and talking on the phone every day since then. We spent the morning together at the Chincoteague Wildlife Refuge yesterday. Her company does some buyback thing at the pony auction so the ponies can stay on the island and roam free. She likes to check on them once in a while to make sure they're doing okay."

"I can think of much better ways to spend my morning than walking through the marsh looking for ponies."

"It wasn't so bad. I mean, there were bugs, and it was muddy and humid, but other than that…" Nick shrugged.

Zach regarded Nick skeptically, his mouth turned up on one side, and his brows arched. "Other than that, how was the play Mrs. Lincoln?"

Nick grinned and held the door open for Zach. "Okay, it wasn't a stroll in Central Park, but it's what she wanted to do. She said I get to pick the next thing we do."

Zach arched his brow. "The next thing? And that is?"

"Dinner. Friday night. Any suggestions?"

Nick reached into the refrigerator and handed Zach a beer, took one a Coke for himself, and removed the chicken casserole leftovers Zach carried over from next door earlier that morning. "What do I do with this?"

"Hand it over." Zach put his beer on the counter and took the glass dish. Nick watched as he removed the plastic wrap, added a bit of water, covered the dish with a paper towel, and put the dish in the microwave. He picked up his beer, opened it, leaned back against the counter, and looked at Nick. "Okay, so what kind of dinner?"

"What do you suggest? I want it to be nice, but not too fancy."

Zach nodded. "The Ropewalk. If it's not too hot, you can eat outside. The menu has everything from chips and slaw to seafood entrees. Make a reservation."

"Sounds good. Thanks."

When the microwave beeped, Zach opened the door, stuck his finger in the middle of the casserole, and closed the door, adding another couple of minutes. He turned back to Nick and tipped back his bottle.

"Be careful with her, Nick. She's just been dealt a massive blow. She doesn't need to be hurt again."

"I don't intend to hurt her," Nick said. "I like her. A lot. There's something about her. I don't know. She's different from anyone I've ever dated."

Zach grinned. "You mean she has class and morals?"

"You know me too well," Nick said with a chuckle. "But seriously, I don't want to screw this up."

"Just take it slow and easy. My understanding is that Taylor's family is pretty well-connected on the island. If you hurt her, you're going to have a hard time recovering."

"I don't plan on hurting her," Nick replied.

"Good."

A comfortable silence fell between them as they waited for their food. Nick thought about what Zach had said.

When the timer sounded, Zach turned back to the microwave. "Lunch is ready." He removed the dish while Nick reached for two plates.

When they sat, Zach bowed his head to pray, then they dug in, neither speaking for several minutes.

"They're loaded," Nick said, reaching for his Coke.

"Who?"

"The Murray's. They live on a huge estate, acres and acres of property, house three stories tall with porches and balconies. There are converted horse barns they now use for the landscaping business and several gigantic greenhouses. Taylor owns a Chincoteague pony, and I don't mean the ones that are still wild. She has one in her yard."

"I didn't know there were properties that big on the island."

"There are a few down that way. Theirs might be the biggest."

Zach took a drink and leveled his gaze on Nick. "What's your point?"

"How can I compete with all that? I've got nothing but a beat-up car and a house I'm renting to own."

"You don't need material things to have value, Nick. It's what's on the inside that determines a person's worth."

"Like the Cave of Wonders in Aladdin. 'Do not be fooled by its commonplace appearance…it is not what is outside, but what is inside that counts'."

Zach rolled his eyes. "Can you ever be serious?"

Nick sighed. "I am being serious. What if what I have inside isn't enough?"

"For whom? If Taylor is half the person I'm told she is, then she will see exactly the kind of person you are and what your worth is. I think the only one who doesn't see all that you have to offer, is you. Don't dwell on her wealth or your past. Concentrate on who and what you are now and what you have to offer each other, not in money or things but in kindness, support, love, faith, and all those things that truly matter. Taylor goes to Mass every Sunday, never misses. That's the kind of thing that matters to her, not the car you drive or the house you live in."

Zach stood and collected the dishes. "Let's get these cleaned up. We can get another hour of work in, and then I'm going home to my wife and kids. Now, there's the kind of wealth every man should strive to have."

Zach reached for his Chincoteague Ponies High School baseball cap. "Let's get it done."

They returned to the dock and spent the next hour hammering away, making good, steady progress on the dock and extended pier.

When Nick retreated to his bedroom to take a nap, he fell asleep with Zach's advice running through his head. He was determined to show Taylor he was worth more than his car or his bank account or his checkered past.

***

"Taylor, it's Will Cheney. How are you?"

Taylor held the phone between her chin and shoulder as she wiped her hands on her jeans and stood. She walked to the corner of the house for privacy.

"Hello, Will. I'm fine, and yourself?"

"Just fine. Taylor…" He hesitated. "I've just returned from a meeting with the higher-ups, and I've got bad news."

Taylor leaned her back against the house and closed her eyes. She waited for him to continue.

"I'm afraid they've already chosen someone to replace your father. I'm sorry."

Taylor bolted upright. "Already chosen someone? Who? How did that happen so soon?"

"Taylor, you know the swim is less than two months away. Things move quickly this time of year."

Seething, and ready to spit nails, she clenched her teeth. "I asked who it is."

"I think you'll be real pleased with the choice. I know your dad always thought of him as a son, and rumor has it that you two might even marry someday. It's Chad Nixon."

Taylor closed her eyes and saw red. The one person she thought she could trust. That son of a... He hadn't even told her.

"Thank you, Mr. Cheney. I'll be in touch." She started to disconnect but quickly raised the phone back to her ear. "And Mr. Cheney?"

"Yes, Taylor?"

"There is no way in this universe or any other I'm marrying Chad Nixon. You can tell that to the rumor mill."

With that, she hung up.

"Taylor? You okay?" Dan McGettigan, known to all as Mickey, looked at her with a wary eye.

"Just peachy." She stomped past him. "Let's get this job done. I'm tired of being behind schedule."

For the rest of the day, Taylor threw herself into the job. She used her anger to haul trees, move bricks and pavers, and shovel dirt. She had enough restraint not to bark at her employees, but internally, she called Chad every name she could think of.

Two hours past quitting time, Taylor and her crew assessed the finished project. The backyard looked like something out of a magazine, her father's vision a thing of beauty. An oversized stone firepit loomed large in the middle of the stone patio. Mossy-like greens surrounded it to give it color. A wooden swing in a matching frame provided seating in addition to several high-end patio chairs. A low brick wall enclosed most of the space but opened into gardens of tall purple sprays of Lavender and Salvia complimented by bright pink Bougainvillea and green Hosta and 'Blue Mist' Dwarf Fothergilla. Silver grasses stood in round gardens carved out of the stone patio, accompanied by dainty purple Baptisia. Rare, white Heliotrope dotted the gardens and filled the air with the fragrance of candy.

"Your dad would be proud," Mickey leaned over and said quietly.

Taylor nodded but couldn't speak. The exquisite garden stood as a testament to her father's talent, wisdom, and eye for beauty. It was a tribute to the man he was.

Taylor waited for the last man to leave before she let the tears unleash. This was the last project she would ever plan with her father, and she wept for love of him, for missing him more than she ever thought possible, for the hole he left in their lives with his absence. She wept in anger and bitterness over the disregard for his last wish. She wept with remorse over her crushed dream. When there were no more tears left to be shed, she plodded to her truck and began the forty-five-minute drive back to the ranch. Slowly, an idea began to form. By the time she pulled into the driveway, she knew what she had to do.

When I arrived on the island, my life was spinning out of control. As a child, I had traveled all over the world and lived in small huts and wide-open savannahs. I knew how to kayak down a river gorge. I knew how to climb massive mountains and find my way home by following the stars. I understood the mating rituals of primitive tribes and the burial rites of Aboriginal Peoples, but I didn't know how to navigate my own personal life. Coming to the island helped me gain focus. It allowed me to grow and mature. It taught me that one small island in the Atlantic can bring me opportunities as big and beautiful as an African sunset.

From *Discovering the World On a Barrier Island*
by Katherine Middleton Kelly

CHAPTER NINE

It had been a long week, and Nick was glad to have two days off to recuperate from the lack of sleep and the non-stop hustle and bustle of the beginning of summer on the island. He slept most of Thursday and worked on the dock in the evening after the sun sank low and the temperature decreased. It was coming along. Zach had put in a few hours earlier, before his final track practice of the year, and Nick was more than grateful for his help and their friendship.

They worked steadily on Friday until Zach left for his last meet and Nick went to get ready for his date. Taylor had texted that morning to say that they had finished the job she'd been on and that she was spending the day taking care of a personal matter. He didn't pry but thought, perhaps, she'd share more at dinner. He longed to know everything about her no matter how mundane.

Dressed in a new pair of jeans and collared shirt, Nick headed to Taylor's at five. His hands were clammy, and his heart beat just a bit faster than normal. It dawned on him that he was nervous, and he chuckled to himself. He was trained to kill anyone who threatened him, had jumped from helicopters into unknown lands, and fired at combatants in the desert, but he was nervous about spending the evening with a beautiful woman.

He stopped at the local florist and asked for help choosing a bouquet for someone who knew everything there was to know about flowers.

"Taylor Murray? I hear you two really hit it off at Zach and Kayla Middleton's wedding."

Eyes blinking and mouth agape, Nick looked at the woman behind the counter. She shrugged.

"What? It's a small island."

Shaking his head, Nick accepted and paid for the bouquet of what he was informed were white and lavender roses combined with Asiatic lilies, Lisianthus, and ferns. He was trying to impress her, and he hoped it worked.

Driving down the lane to the ranch was even more intimidating this time than the previous two times. The first time, he didn't know Taylor existed. The second, he was there out of courtesy. This time, he felt like his future was dependent upon how the night went. He reminded himself that it was too soon to think like that, but the notion remained in the back of his mind as his car came to a stop in front of the house.

Nick carried the flowers around the long, winding sidewalk from the driveway to the front door and rang the bell. He heard the same melodic chime he'd heard the last time he was there, but this time, it was accompanied by hurried footsteps. When the door opened, Jenny looked at him with big blue eyes and a welcoming smile.

"Come on in. Taylor's coming. Can I get you something to drink?"

"No, thanks, I'm fine." Nick gazed at the interior of the house. It was more modest than he imagined, but that shouldn't have surprised him. Taylor's family didn't seem to put on airs or drip with wealth. The large foyer had wood floors, not marble like he imagined, and the staircase was your normal wooden staircase, nothing like the grand spiral staircases in the movies.

"I'm going to get something. Come on. You can wait for Taylor in the kitchen. Nice choice of flowers, by the way."

"Thanks." So far, so good.

He followed Jenny to the kitchen at the back of the house, passing by a modest-sized dining room with traditional furniture. The kitchen was divided into two areas, a cooking area and a dining area, with wide glass windows that looked out onto a magnificently manicured patio and gardens overlooking the water. Along the long wall of the room were counters and cabinets with a tiled backsplash that probably cost more than his entire kitchen put together. Still, it wasn't ostentatious in the least, and he appreciated the simplicity of the rest of the rooms. Even he recognized that the room was designed to highlight the gardens and the water on the outside and not the appliances on the inside.

"Hi, Nick." He turned around to see Taylor standing in the doorway. She wore a pink, sleeveless blouse and a pair of short white pants, he couldn't remember the name, but he knew they weren't pants and not long shorts. Her muscled frame seemed petite and feminine in the white and pink outfit, and he felt his heart flutter.

"Hi, Taylor. Are you ready to go?"

"Hold on," her mother said, coming up behind her. "I don't think we've ever had a proper introduction. I'm Donna." She held out her hand, and Nick stepped forward to take it.

"Nick Black. Nice to meet you." The flowers felt awkward in the crook of his arm, and he hesitated for a moment, not sure whether it was more appropriate to give them to Taylor or her mother. He decided to go with plan A and held them out to Taylor. "I got these for you. I hope you like them."

She took the bouquet and lifted it to her nose. "Lilies are my favorite. Thank you." She smiled at him, and her cheeks suddenly matched the pink in her blouse.

"I'll take those for you, honey. Jenny and I will find the perfect vase for them." Nick noticed she said 'vase' like blaze and not like Roz. He liked that for some reason.

"Thanks, Mom. I think we're ready," Taylor said to Nick. She stood aside, so that he could pass by but gently grabbed his sleeve when he turned toward the way he came. "This is faster."

She led him in the opposite direction to a nice-sized living room with a fireplace on one wall and a large-screen tv on the other. A door just inside the room led to another section of the wrap-around, covered porch. They walked through a small garden area to the driveway.

"We almost never use the front door. Next time, you can just come through here and ring the bell. It has a different chime, so I'll know which door you're at." The only words that registered were, 'next time.'

Nick held open the door for Taylor, and she thanked him before getting in. He closed the door, thankful that he had taken the time to wash and vacuum the car earlier that day. Once they were on the way, Nick looked over at Taylor and smiled.

"I hope Ropewalk is okay with you."

"Sounds good. Have you been there before?"

"Have not. Zach recommended it."

"It's nice. Not too fancy and really good food."

"I thought, maybe, if you're not too tired or anything, we could take a walk after dinner. We can walk through the town or maybe go to Assateague and walk on the beach." He was hopeful she wouldn't be ready to ditch him by dessert.

"That sounds nice. Why don't you let me come up with where to go. We have a few hidden gems where there won't be as many tourists."

Nick glanced at her and then at the road. "I didn't wear my marsh boots."

Taylor laughed. "I promise, no marshes."

***

Though the restaurant was crowded with locals and visitors, Nick had managed to reserve a quiet table on the corner of the deck. Taylor waved to people she knew and chatted with the staff, most of whom she knew from school. A few were friends of Jenny. They ordered a crab dip appetizer and a pitcher of beer.

"Tell me about yourself," Taylor asked and immediately regretted asking.

Nick's expression hardened. He took a long swig of beer and looked out at the water. Taylor waited out the uncomfortable silence.

"Not much to tell." He avoided eye contact, and Taylor wondered what kind of dark and mysterious past he had but then realized it couldn't have been that bad since he was a police officer now.

"Okay, so let's start with the basics." She placed her hands beneath her chin and leaned forward. "Where did you grow up?"

"Here and there." He took another drink and poured himself another helping.

Taylor sat back and eyed him. "Really? You know everything there is to know about me, and you won't even tell me where you're from."

"New Jersey. I lived there until I was eighteen."

"When you joined the Marines."

"Correct."

"Do your parents still live there?"

Nick cocked his neck to one side and then the other, eliciting painful sounding pops from his joints. He inhaled and looked at Taylor. "I don't know. I never knew them."

She closed her eyes and let out a long breath before looking back at him. "I'm sorry. I didn't know."

"No big deal."

She reached her hand across the table and laid it on his. "It is a big deal. And it was insensitive of me to push you. Please, forgive me."

The crab dip arrived, and they placed their dinner orders, scallops for Taylor and rockfish for Nick.

"Do you mind if we pray?" Taylor smiled. "It's awkward, I know, but it's what we Murrays do."

"Not awkward at all. Go ahead." He bowed his head and let her say the blessing.

"Thank you. So, what would you like to talk about?"

Nick scooped a helping of dip onto his plate and spread some on a piece of bread that he popped into his mouth.

"I was raised by foster families, some good, some not so good."

Taylor thought about Trevor's upbringing and wondered if Nick's compared. "Did they...did they hurt you?"

Nick shrugged. "I got pushed around now and then. It wasn't that bad." He told her about the fight he was in, how he joined teen court and then the ROTC. Taylor was impressed with how far he had come and told him so. Nick's face reddened and he hid it with another drink.

By the time their meal arrived, Taylor understood why Nick joined the Marines and why the police department was such a good fit. She could also see that he had a kind heart and a good soul, things she already suspected about him. He cared deeply for Zach and the rest of Zach's extended family, and she got the impression that he was hoping to have his own family someday.

"You're not your past, you know."

Nick looked at her with a puzzled expression.

"I mean, look where you are now. All of that stuff that happened when you were a kid, it shaped you, but that doesn't mean it has to define you. What's that line from the *Lion King*? 'Put your past in the behind'?"

Nick laughed. "It's 'you got to put your behind in the past' but good try."

"Thank you," she said with a mock bow. "Anyway, I don't think it matters where you came from. What matters is where you're heading."

"That's a good one. You should send it to Disney."

"Maybe I'll do that."

They enjoyed their meals, making small talk as they ate.

"So," Nick said when they finished their entrees. "What's going on with the cowboy deal?"

Taylor felt her blood pressure rise and was about to tell Nick the whole saga when a shadow fell over the table.

"Hey, Taylor. I saw you over here and thought I'd say hi."

"Well, speak of the devil," she said, glaring at Chad.

"Hey, what did I do?" His smile wavered, and Taylor saw that he knew exactly what he had done.

"How can you ask me that?"

"Taylor, honey—"

"Don't you 'honey' me. She took the napkin from her lap and tossed it on the table."

"Let me explain."

Nick stood, "Look, I don't know who you are, but it doesn't look to me like Taylor wants you here. Maybe you'd better take your leave before somebody does something they'll regret."

Chad turned his gaze on Nick. "Who the heck are you?"

"Chad, Nick. Nick, Chad." Taylor motioned to the waitress. "Check, please."

"You're leaving? Don't you think we should talk?"

"No."

The waitress returned in record time and brought the manager with her. "Ms. Murray, is there a problem?"

"Yes, this man won't leave us alone."

Nick hastily handed several bills to the waitress. "Keep the change," he said as he reached for Taylor's hand and led her down the steps and onto the sandy outdoor seating area.

"This isn't over," Chad called.

"You bet it isn't," Taylor yelled back as she and Nick hurried around the building and into his car.

"Who was that?" Nick asked, putting the car in reverse. "An ex?"

Taylor guffawed. "Maybe in his dreams. No," she said, turning to Nick. "He's the SOB who took my spot as a Saltwater Cowboy."

***

Taylor gave Nick directions, and he drove to the secluded cove he had only seen in photos.

"Is this the cove Kate and Aaron like to escape to?"

"It is, but I want to take you somewhere even better."

"What could be better than this?" Nick stood on the shore and gazed across the water. A heron glided past, and a bald eagle landed in a nest high in a tree. The sun was low but not setting, and its light created a mirror image that could grace the top of a puzzle box.

"Come on. Follow me." Taylor disappeared into the trees, and Nick knew he would follow her anywhere.

They walked without talking for several minutes before the path opened onto another cove. Taylor was right; it was even better. The view of the water was another puzzle wannabe, but here, flowers of many colors dotted the landscape.

"Wow! How did all of these get here?"

"We planted them."

"We, as in you? Your company?"

Taylor nodded. "They're all *Herbaceous Emergents*, or marsh plants. We were hired to plant them because they help with the ecosystem and fight erosion. That's a big problem on the island."

Nick inhaled the scent of flowers mixed with saltwater. "That's really cool," he said, and he meant it.

She pointed to a cone-shaped purple flower. "This is a *Pontederia cordata*, or pickerelweed." She sidestepped to another flower. "A Harlequin Blueflag Iris." She hopped to another. "And these that look like little purple beads are *Scirpus cyperinus*. Woolgrass."

Nick watched as she headed toward the water and motioned for him to join her. She stepped down onto a tiny beach and out onto a hidden dock. They sat on the dock, their arms touching, and Nick desired nothing more than to stay there for the rest of his life with her beside him.

They admired the view for several minutes before Taylor began to talk. "I went to see a friend of my father's, Will Cheney. He's the president of the bank and one of the longest-standing members of the Saltwater Cowboys. He said he'd take my dad's will to the rest of the men-in-charge and get back to me." She picked at an invisible thread on her capris as she spoke. "He called me yesterday to tell me that he was too late. They'd already chosen a replacement, someone who, he said, was like a son to my dad."

"Chad."

She nodded. "Chad." She scoffed as she looked at the water. "Jenny told me that dad didn't even like Chad."

"Then why did they think that's who he would want to replace him?"

"Because Chad and I were inseparable growing up. Our mothers were friends, and we were always together." She looked at Nick. "Yes, we dated off and on, but it was never serious, at least I didn't think it was. Apparently, folks on the island think we're destined to get married someday. According to Will that was supposed to make the choice okay." She brushed her hand on her capris as if to make the invisible thread go away. Nick reached for the hand.

"I'm sorry," he said, pulling her hand to his lap. "Is there anything else you can do?"

"I already did." She stared down at their entwined hands for a moment before raising her eyes to his. "I hired an attorney."

"To do what?" he asked, though all he could think of was how close their faces were, the smell of her shampoo, how soft her skin looked, how her lips would taste. He swallowed.

"To fight for my spot on the team," she said quietly.

"Tell me how to help."

Her green eyes lowered to his lips and then back to his eyes. "Kiss me."

***

When their lips met, Taylor's stomach rolled over in a somersault. All her senses were heightened. She could taste the salt on his lips and smell the flowers just behind her on the dock. She heard birds cawing and frogs singing. She felt her heart pounding in her chest.

When they finally pulled back from one another, the tip of her tongue reached to touch the inside of her lip, and she saw his eyes flicker.

"It's getting late," she whispered. "We should find our way back before the sun goes down."

Nick simply nodded and stood. He reached for her hand and pulled her up.

"Not before this," he said, pulling her to him once more.

She wrapped her arms around his neck and enjoyed the feel of being in his arms, his lips exploring hers. They parted, and Nick leaned back, taking in her face.

"You're right," he said to her. "This cove is much better than the other one."

***

Saturday felt like the longest day of Nick's life. He couldn't wait to get off from work so that he could see

Taylor. They had agreed to a dinner again, but this time, she was packing a picnic, and they were heading to the beach. Their hope was that most of the weekenders would have left the beach for the day and headed to dinner somewhere.

Nick hummed to himself as he got dressed. In the mirror, he saw his guitar leaning against the corner of the bedroom. He went to it and picked it up, inspecting its strings. He found the case under his bed and packed up the instrument. When he pulled out of the driveway, it was in the backseat.

Music rang from the speakers, the only things in the car that were less than ten years old. The windows were rolled down, despite the humidity. Nick was used to that, and he knew it was only going to get worse as the days on the calendar ticked by. He might as well enjoy the fresh air now before air conditioning was a life-saving necessity.

Taylor stood in front of the house, picnic basket in hand. Nick jumped out to take it from her and placed it in the popped-open trunk. He didn't know whether to hug her, pull her in for a kiss, or just act cool, like nothing had ever happened. Before he could decide what to do, her mother walked out onto the front porch.

"Taylor, there's a storm predicted for later on. Make sure you're off the beach before it hits."

"Will do, Mama," she called before going around the car to the passenger side. Nick hastened over to open the door for her, and she smiled as she got inside the car. He called to her mother, wishing her a good night, and waved before getting into the car. He looked at Taylor and smiled, and his heart did that little flip it had started doing every time he thought of her. Was she as nervous as he was? She didn't look it.

"To the beach?"

"Sounds good," she said.

Nick put the car into gear and headed down the driveway. He reached for Taylor's hand and enjoyed the simple pleasure of holding it in his.

Taylor was right about the beach. Most people were gone or packing up. They picked a spot and spread their blanket. She had looked at him with a fair amount of curiosity when he'd pulled the guitar out of the backseat, but she didn't ask any questions. They ate fried chicken, potato salad, and pickles. They talked and laughed, and Nick wondered how he'd gotten there—a job he loved, a beautiful woman by his side, and a community where he felt at home.

"Okay, so what's this?" Taylor asked, reaching for the case.

"What do you think it is?"

She opened it and took out the guitar. "Do you play?"

"No, I just like bringing it to the beach with me in case I need to use it for a raft," he said sarcastically.

She rolled her eyes and handed the guitar to him. "Let's hear."

Not usually afraid of playing in front of people, Nick found himself hesitating. He hadn't played in months. What if he messed up? What if she laughed?

Taylor thrust the instrument toward him. "Come on, don't get shy with me now."

Unable to resist her smile, he took the guitar. After spending a few minutes to get it in tune, he strummed a few chords. He let himself fall into that place where the music took over, and before he knew what was happening, the melody pulled him to another dimension, one where only he and the guitar existed.

Nick played Don McLean's *American Pie*, John Mellencamp's *Jack and Diane*, and *Wanted* by Bon Jovi. He even threw in an animated rendition of *Let it Go* from *Frozen*. He was lost in the music and went from one song to another without thinking about his playlist until he heard crying. It was then that he realized he'd gone straight into Eric Clapton's *Tears in Heaven*.

Nick stopped playing, put the guitar aside, and pulled Taylor to him. "Sh, baby, it's okay. I'm so sorry." He stroked her hair as she cried.

Once her heaving slowed down, she looked up at him. "I'm sorry. I didn't mean to cry. Your playing was beautiful."

"I wasn't thinking. I was lost in the music, and I-"

A loud clap of thunder rattled the air, causing them both to jump. Nick quickly tucked the guitar into its case while Taylor began packing the picnic basket. They picked up the blanket, shook it out, and hastily folded it as another round of thunder reverberated around them. Nick tucked the blanket under the arm that held the guitar case and reached for Taylor's hand.

The sky opened, and they were pelted with rain as they ran toward the parking lot.

By the time, they reached the car, they were soaked. Thunder boomed, and lightning split the sky. Nick opened the door for Taylor and took the picnic basket from her. As the rain assaulted his back, he dropped everything in the trunk and ran to the driver's side of the car. Just as he slammed the door, he cursed.

"What's wrong?"

"I shut the keys in the trunk. He reached for the trunk release button, but Taylor laid her hand on his leg.

"We can wait it out."

"Are you sure?"

"I'm positive." She shivered, and Nick realized she was as wet as he was.

"Are you cold?"

"A little," she admitted.

Nick reached across and put his arm around her. He pulled her to him as much as he could with the center console between them.

Thunder shook the car, and the lightning reached across the sky like outstretched fingers on a bony hand. Suddenly, hail rained down on the car. The wind blew so hard, the tiny car swayed back and forth.

Taylor looked up at Nick and smiled. "I suppose I should be scared, but I'm not."

"That's good because I'm petrified."

"You make me feel safe, Nick. Safer than I've ever felt with anyone."

Nick squeezed her tighter. He prayed that the wind didn't rip the doors right off the car, but he didn't say it out loud. He just held Taylor tighter and continued to help her feel safe.

***

"Good morning, Father." Taylor greeted Father Darryl the following morning when they arrived at the church.

"Good morning, Taylor. How's everyone holding up?"

"Better than expected," she assured him.

She took her regular seat and knelt down to pray. It still felt strange to be there without her father, but she realized that what she had told Father was the truth. She was doing better than expected. Even her mother and sister seemed to be doing better with each passing day. Willing herself to concentrate on her prayers, she looked up at the crucifix above the altar.

Thank you, Lord, for all the years you allowed Daddy to be in our lives. Thank you for the love he gave and the example he showed. And thank you, for bringing Nick into my life just when I needed him the most.

She spent the rest of the day working with Stormy. Each time she rode him, he turned back into her hands more easily. He was going to be a fine breeding pony if she decided to go down that path.

At dinner that evening, Taylor felt her mother's gaze settling on her more than once. When Jenny excused herself to study for her finals, Taylor looked up at her mother.

"Is everything okay, Mama?"

"You look…different. I don't know what it is."

Taylor smiled. "It's called being happy, Mama."

"He's good to you?"

"Very much so."

"That's good. You are being… careful, aren't you?"

Taylor blushed. "Mama," she groaned. "For goodness sakes. We've only gone out twice, and you know me better than that. You and Daddy raised us right. You have no worries."

"Men can be very persuasive."

Taylor thought back to the previous evening. She and Nick, soaked to the skin, were trapped in a car during a storm. And what did he do? He held her. He held her without asking for anything more. Maybe he wanted more, but he didn't ask or push or even suggest. Perhaps it was because he was a police officer, but she believed there was more to it than that. She believed it was because he was Nick, a good person who respected her, cared for her, and wanted the best for her. She just wished all the men in her life were more like him and her father.

One of the first things I noticed, when I arrived on Chincoteague Island, was the hospitality of everyone I met. I was welcomed and accepted from the very start, as if I were a family member or an old friend returning to the fold. I witnessed this same acceptance with my brother and then with my friend from back home. Just like with many of the indigenous peoples my father studied, the islanders, no matter their relation or lack thereof, formed a tight-knit family. Woe to the man or woman who tries to come between them or hurt one of them.

From *Discovering the World On a Barrier Island*
by Katherine Middleton Kelly

CHAPTER TEN

The sun beat down on the worksite where Taylor and her crew labored. Around ten o'clock, Taylor felt her phone vibrate in her pocket. An unfamiliar number appeared on the screen. Perhaps another job.

"Hello, Murray Landscaping, this is Taylor."

"Taylor Murray?"

"Yes, may I help you?"

"Ms. Murray, this is Rebecca Adams. I was referred to you by my colleague, Martin Green."

Taylor pulled off her gloves and gripped the phone. "Yes, ma'am. Did Martin, Mr. Green, explain my situation?"

"He did, and I'm very happy to accept your case if you want me to take it."

"Should we meet?"

"Yes, I can come to you if that's easiest. I really want this, and I'm willing to work hard on your behalf."

"Okay, then. Are you close to the island?"

"No, I'm farther up on the shore, in Easton, Maryland, but I can be down there tomorrow at nine. Where would you like to meet? Somewhere in private would be best."

Taylor admired her initiative and was willing to see what she had to say.

"We have an office at our home. Is that okay?"

"Perfect. Just give me the address."

When Taylor hung up the phone, she heaved a sigh. Tomorrow at nine, she hoped to be one step closer to riding Big Red in the Pony Swim.

***

The smell of her mother's cooking awoke Kayla from her nap after a long day at school for Todd's field day. Though still a little tired, she felt much better. Spending the day outside on the athletic fields had worn her out. She rolled out of bed and made her way to the bathroom. She always kept a supply of toiletries at her mother's house and was grateful for that as she reached for her toothbrush. As she brushed, she gazed at her reflection. Her hair was almost two inches long all the way around. Soon, she'd be able to style it. The thought made her smile.

Laughter flowed down the hall from the kitchen, and Kayla found herself chuckling before she even entered the room. Ronnie looked her way with a wide grin.

"Your father is cooking steaks, and Zach is on the way."

Kayla made herself a glass of water and placed the drink on the table but didn't sit.

"I just realized I left my phone in the bedroom. Let me grab it in case Zach calls for anything."

Just as she reached for the phone on the nightstand, it began to vibrate. An unfamiliar number scrolled across the screen. 'Baltimore, Maryland' was the only recognizable information.

Probably a telemarketer.

Rather than sending the call to voicemail, Kayla slid the button across the screen and held the phone to her ear.

"Hello."

"Hi, is this Kayla Reynolds? Sorry, I mean—" There was a shuffling noise. "Kayla Middleton?"

"Who is this?" Though she still presumed it was a telemarketer, for some reason she couldn't fathom, Kayla's senses went on high alert.

Again, the voiced asked, "Kayla Middleton?"

"Who is this?" she insisted.

"My name is Cody Boteler. I'm with the Baltimore Sun. Do you have a minute? I'd like to ask you a few questions."

Kayla shook her head as if he could see her. "I'm sorry. I don't want a subscription, but thanks for calling." She started to disconnect, but she heard him on the other line ask her to wait. Reluctantly, she put the phone back to her ear. "Yes?" she said impatiently.

"I'm not calling to offer you a subscription. I'm calling to see if we can set up an interview."

"Oh!" Their publisher sure was on top of things. The book wasn't due out for over a year. "Well, of course, but I'm not at home right now. Can we set it up at a time that works for Zach and me both? I know he'd want to be part of it. After all, half the recipes in the book are his."

Kayla's heart fluttered. She'd never given an interview and had no idea how or why this was happening so long before the book's release, but she was thrilled for the publicity.

"I'm sorry. Recipes?"

Kayla froze, the phone still against her ear. "Yes," she said hesitantly. "Aren't you calling to interview me and my husband about the new cookbook we're publishing?"

"Um, no. I'm calling to see how you feel about the Lifetime movie that's coming out in a few weeks. About your husband. Your first husband, I mean. Rather, about the case he was involved in when he was killed."

Kayla's hand shook as she ended the call. She fumbled with the phone but managed to block the number.

"Kayla, what's wrong?" Ronnie said from the doorway.

Kayla looked at her mother, unable to speak. Her heart raced, and she was barely able to hold onto the phone, her hands were shaking so badly.

"Kayla." Her mother rushed into the room and eased her down onto the bed. "Who was that? What's going on?"

Kayla looked up, still unable to accept the man's words or the idea of a movie. Though she had heard rumors, a couple years back, that Lifetime had acquired the rights to a movie about the taking down of the Mayor of Baltimore, she had never dreamed it would really happen. After all, it had been almost seven years, and the attention factor of the American citizen was way shorter than that.

"It was a reporter." She looked at her mother as though Ronnie could answer all of Kayla's unasked questions.

"A reporter? About what?" her mother asked. Her confusion apparent in the crease of her brow and the tone of her voice.

Kayla answered quietly. "About Eddie."

Kayla repeated the conversation to her mother, aware that Trevor and EJ now stood in the doorway.

"Okay, let's see what they know so far," Ronnie said. She stood from the bed and went to the desk in the corner, as in control as ever. "EJ, go play with Todd." She tapped on the laptop, and the screen came to life as she took a seat.

"But Grandma, I want to—"

"EJ, listen to your Grandmother." It wasn't often that Kayla raised her voice, but her nerves got the best of her. EJ obeyed but not before sending a pleading look to Trevor who shook his head and pointed toward the living room.

Ronnie typed a few words into the browser and skimmed the page.

"It doesn't mention you and the boys, but it does mention Eddie and how his unfortunate death was the catalyst that broke the case. They've got a nice-looking guy playing his part," she remarked.

Kayla went behind her mother and looked over her shoulder. "He looks a lot like Eddie."

"He does."

"There's a cast button." Trevor pointed to the corner of the screen. "You should click on it."

Kayla looked over at her father and nodded. "Yes, mom, go ahead."

Ronnie clicked on the link and scrolled down the page. Kayla scanned the cast.

"Wow. Look who's playing the part of the computer networker, Susan. She's a big network star. Remember Susan, mom? She helped crack the case."

"I do. She put her life in danger to save those girls who witnessed, the uh…"

"Eddie's murder," Kayla finished the sentence. Her heart ached as she said the words.

"There you are," Trevor said. He pointed at the screen and put an arm protectively around his daughter.

"I don't recognize the name of the actress," Ronnie said, "but it says she's been in a lot of TV movies."

"At least she's pretty," Trevor said. Ronnie and Kayla turned to look at him. "I mean, I wouldn't want my daughter to be played by someone unattractive."

"Thanks, Dad. I guess that's something to be grateful for."

"Look at it this way," Ronnie said. "At least it's on Lifetime and not Netflix."

"True," Kayla agreed.

Ronnie turned away from the screen. "Well, what next? Reporters don't give up easily."

"And with you and Zach and the boys making a new start, the timing couldn't be worse," Trevor reminded them.

"When it rains, it pours," Ronnie said.

Indeed, it does, Kayla thought. "That always seems to be the case with our family, doesn't it?"

"It will all be fine," Ronnie assured Kayla, standing and putting her arms around her daughter. "God doesn't give us more than we can handle."

Kayla shook her head. "Yeah, but what's that other saying? I wish he didn't think I could handle so much."

***

"I'm glad you called," Taylor said, settling next to Nick on the couch. A box of half-eaten pizza was on the coffee table along with two empty and two partly-full bottles of beer.

"I thought you could use a relaxing night after spending all day, every day, in the hot sun."

"It's hot and messy work, but I love it. You've been putting in a lot of hours yourself."

"Summer has arrived. The island is crazy. Any news about the pony swim?"

"As a matter of fact, I got a call today from an attorney. She's driving down from Easton tomorrow morning to meet at the house."

"An attorney driving two hours to meet with you? Either she's an ambulance chaser or she's really serious about helping you."

"I never thought about that," Taylor said, concern arising. "I wonder if I should have checked her out first. She could be one of those attorneys who just wants to make a fast buck and doesn't care about me at all. I wonder how much she's going to charge."

"We can always do an online search and check her out."

Taylor mulled it over for a moment. "Let me meet her first and see what she says."

"Your call."

Nick pulled her toward him, and Taylor snuggled closer. She breathed in the fresh scent of his body wash. Things had turned a corner with Nick, and she was excited to see where they went.

Taylor stole a glance at Nick. His face glowed in the dim light from the television where Maui the demigod, in *Moana*, extolled his own virtues. Taylor knew Nick had the entire movie, score included, memorized, but she reached for the remote control and hit pause. Moana looked up at Maui with a stern look of disapproval.

"Nick, can I ask you a question?"

"Sure. Ask away." His tone was light, but he turned a concerned gaze on her.

"Do you think I'm doing the right thing? Do you think everyone will hate me?"

"Because you want to join them?" Taylor nodded, and Nick sighed. "Honestly, Taylor, I'm not going to sugarcoat things for you. It's going to be hard. Some people are going to be angry. They may say or do some mean and hateful things. There are those who don't accept change, and they're going to take it personally. Overall, though, I think most of the islanders, including the Cowboys, are going to support you."

"Would you? If you were in their spot?"

Nick paused before answering. "Taylor, it's like this. When women first wanted to go into combat, there was a lot of controversy. A lot of guys were angry; a lot still are. Most of us don't think women have a place in the military."

"You included?" She gathered, from his tone, that he might not be as open-minded as she gave him credit for.

"Me included." He reached for his beer and took a swig. "Here's what a lot of people don't understand. It's not about whether or not she can do the job or aim the gun or keep up with the men. It's the age-old problem of the sexes and how they react to and with each other."

"It's about sex? You all worry that you can't resist each other, so she shouldn't be there?" Taylor felt her ire rise. That was the stupidest excuse she'd ever heard.

"You misunderstand. It's not about *sex*, it's even more basic than that. Let's say I'm in Afghanistan, and we're in close combat with an enemy force. Not only do I have to think about myself and my brothers, but I have to pay extra attention to the woman in our ranks. She's a special target. If the enemy gets me, he'll use any number of ways to torture, humiliate, and rattle me. But her? We all know what he's going to do first. And then he'll do worse things than that. Before I can even think about myself or any of the men I'm with, I've got to make darn sure that she's safe. It's a whole different level of reasoning. And it's not sexist. It's human nature."

"So, you're saying that women are the weaker sex and need to be coddled or rescued all the time?" She tried to maintain some calm in her voice as she spoke.

"Not at all. I'm saying that men think differently in high-stress situations when there's a woman involved. We feel the need to protect her. Blame it on the cavemen if you want. It's stressful and frustrating. I'm not saying that's a good reason for them to keep women off the team. I'm saying that may be part of the mentality that has allowed them to stick to the status quo."

Taylor sat back and thought about what Nick was saying. "Okay. I get it. The question is, how do I get around it?"

Nick laced his fingers and stretched them out in front of him, drawing out a series of cracks from his joints. "I'm glad you asked because I've been thinking about this a lot."

"And you didn't bother sharing your theory sooner?"

"Not until I thought the time was right." He stood and paced the floor as if gathering his thoughts. "I've given this a lot of thought, and here's how I think you should handle it."

Taylor listened as Nick outlined his idea. The more he talked, the more she knew he was right. By the time he finished, she felt like she had a much better handle on what the men were thinking and what she needed to do to change that way of thinking. She had a lot to discuss with Ms. Adams in the morning.

***

The screen on Nick's phone displayed the time as 7:15. Nick put the phone down on the nightstand and contemplated getting up and going for a quick run before starting his nine o'clock shift and decided it was probably a good idea. He needed to expend some energy, and too many of his meals lately consisted of pizza and beer. As he reached to pull back the covers, he heard his phone vibrate and reached for it.

"Can you talk? My wife's in trouble."

Nick flipped onto his back and propped himself up on a pillow to listen to Zach.

"What's up, man?"

"You know about Kayla's first husband, right?"

"The one who was murdered?"

"Yeah. Lifetime is apparently making a movie about the takedown of the Baltimore mayor who had him killed. Some reporter just called and wants to interview her."

Nick sat up on the edge of the bed. "What do you need from me?" Nick asked.

"Just that you keep an eye open. Obviously, I'll be doing the same. But maybe you could spread the word at the station. If anyone from the Sun comes around asking questions, don't let him know where we live."

"No problem, Zach. Keep her out of sight for a while, and I'll get the word out."

When they finished, Nick recalled the little bit of information he knew about Kayla's past and about her husband, a murdered FBI informant.

He shook his head.

Does every woman have some kind of traumatic situation from her past that she has to deal with?

As soon as the thought entered his mind, Nick was reminded of the answer. At the academy, he'd learned that, yes, most women did. Nick and his classmates had been taught that a woman in America is assaulted every ninety-eight seconds and that one in every six American women has been the victim of a sexual assault. Nearly twenty people per minute, in the US, are assaulted by an intimate partner. He supposed Kayla and Kate were lucky that their stories weren't worse.

Nick brushed his teeth and wondered what kind of person could hurt, rape, murder, or abuse another person. It has to take an extremely strong person to get over something like that. Kayla and Kate were two of the strongest people he knew. What Taylor was going through was completely different, but he wondered, in her mind, did it feel like abuse? He hoped that the talk the night before helped her to understand that not all men took advantage of women. Some of them wanted, more than anything, to protect them even if their efforts were misplaced and misconstrued.

***

Taylor nervously walked into the foyer in answer to the chime. She was completely shocked by what she saw when she opened the door.

Rebecca Adams was of average height but rail-thin. She had straight, brown hair that was pulled back into a ponytail. She wore a grey pantsuit without heels, by which Taylor was surprised. What was most surprising, though, was her age. Rebecca looked to be just a few years older than Taylor, and Taylor couldn't help but wonder if the woman had ever even tried a case before.

Forcing a smile, Taylor reached her hand out and introduced herself. "Won't you, please, come in. We have an office just down the hall."

Rebecca, as she asked to be called, followed Taylor through the first floor to the office her father had added to the design of the house. Over the past couple weeks, Taylor had slowly grown to think of the space as hers. On the few rainy days they'd had, she replaced her father's degree with her own and began the process of boxing up his things and bringing in hers. It was a bittersweet move—one they had planned on making once Pete was ready to retire many years in the future.

"Please excuse the disarray. I'm doing a bit of updating. Would you like some water? Coffee perhaps?"

"Water would be nice, thank you."

Taylor opened a small refrigerator behind the desk and took out two bottles of water while Rebecca pulled a file from her leather briefcase.

"Let's sit over there." Taylor directed Rebecca toward a pair of overstuffed chairs in the corner of the room. "It's more comfortable than leaning across the desk."

They each took a seat, and Taylor studied the attorney, looking for any signs that she was at all competent or perhaps older than she appeared. Rebecca got straight to the point.

"Taylor, first, let me say that I want this case. It's important to me, and I want you to know that I mean that. So, I'd like to do it pro bono."

Taylor was pretty sure she knew what that meant, but she wanted to clarify. "You want to take it on for free?"

"Yes, one-hundred-percent." She sat up, and her eyes brightened. "When I was a little girl, my parents often brought me to Chincoteague in late July for our summer vacations—not every year, but many, many years. They knew how much I loved horses, but we lived in a neighborhood in Easton, so every year, when I asked for a horse or pony for Christmas, I got a new bike instead. Believe me when I say, I never care if I see another bike for as long as I live."

Taylor smiled. Rebecca was quite likable.

"Anyway, we would rent a boat and go out into the channel around four in the morning. I'm sure you've done the same."

"I've been out there earlier than that every year for my entire life," Taylor said.

"I figured. I loved the feel of those mornings; you could inhale the anticipation. It had a smell, a taste, a tangible quality that filled me with joy. I remember one year, we were close enough to Assateague to hear the pounding of the hooves when they neared the shore. I would watch as the ponies walked to the water, and I held my breath as they swam the channel with their noses above the water like alligators swimming in haste to the other side. I worried for the little ones and cheered them on. When they reached the opposite shore, it was all I could do to contain my excitement. It was as if I had made the swim with them, felt their fear and their excitement in a surge of adrenaline that propelled us all to the dry land that awaited."

Though she had experienced the swim many times, Taylor found herself captivated by Rebecca's account.

This woman must be able to hold a jury in the palm of her hand.

"I used to dream of riding beside the ponies, protecting them, herding them to safety on the far shore. I wanted to be part of the pony parade when they made their way down the street toward the fairgrounds." She stopped and smiled. "Of course, I also wanted to be Elle Woods in *Legally Blonde*. I guess she won."

Taylor laughed. "I can see that. But you still have that same girlish love for the ponies."

Rebecca nodded. "I do. And even though I won't be riding alongside them, I don't see any reason why you shouldn't. So, your turn. Tell me why you want to be a Saltwater Cowboy."

Taylor's feelings were much the same as Rebecca's, but on a more personal level. Her father and grandfather had both ridden with the ponies. The women spent the next hour discussing the details of the filing. Taylor shared Nick's opinion and Rebecca agreed with his assessment and his advice.

"You don't want to be the enemy," she told Taylor. "You need them to trust you, not resent you. When all is said and done, you'll have to work together."

"Do you really think it will happen?"

Rebecca leaned forward. "I know it will."

Later that day, Taylor shared her news over lunch with her closest friend, Holly. They sat on the front porch of the farmhouse. Holly looked over at Stormy.

"So, tell me why the ponies are such a big deal around here. Where did they come from?"

"Nobody knows for sure. Many believe that they were the lone survivors of a Spanish shipwreck in the 1750s. There have been some who claim that the shipwreck was only a legend and that the ponies belonged to the area's earliest settlers and were released. There have been books written and studies that have been done that strongly suggest that they came here by shipwreck." Taylor picked up a potato chip and popped it in her mouth.

"How did the pony penning begin?"

"It's been done since the 1700s, almost as long as the ponies have been here. It started as a way for local livestock farmers to assess and brand their herds after foaling season."

"But now, it's the firemen that round them up?"

"Well, yes, mostly firemen. The Saltwater Cowboys are comprised of firemen as well as other men and teenaged boys from the island and surrounding parts. The auction is the fire company's biggest fundraiser. They've been running the show for almost a hundred years. In 1947, they started buying back ponies from bidders in order to preserve the herd."

"Hi, Holly." Clay walked up behind them.

"Hey, Clay. How's work?"

He nodded toward Taylor. "The boss lady is keeping me pretty busy.

"It's that time of year." Taylor smiled at her greenhouse manager. "And better busy than out of work." She loved the relationship they had and the way they were able to tease each other. Her father had chosen a good man in Clay.

"Taylor, how do you know that exact date off the top of your head?" Holly asked.

"We're all tested on the history of the ponies in order to graduate."

Holly looked at Taylor with her mouth wide open. "Really?"

Taylor laughed. "Of course, not. Coincidentally, that was the year that *Misty of Chincoteague* was written and became an international bestseller. I read that book at least a dozen times when I was growing up."

"Then she started saving her money to buy a pony and set her sights on becoming a Cowgirl," Clay said.

"Aren't you supposed to be working?" Taylor teased.

"Aren't you?"

Laughing, Taylor nodded. "I suppose so."

Holly stood. "I've got to get ready to head into work myself. I'll talk to you later, Taylor. Let me know what happens with the suit."

"Will do."

"You think it will work?" Clay asked.

"I have no idea, but at this point, what have I got to lose?"

I always thought my life would turn out differently than it had by the time I arrived on the island. I couldn't imagine how I would ever pick up the pieces. Even though I had a strong family unit, I felt utterly alone, as cold and desolate as the shoreline on a winter day. I had no idea how to move forward, how to pull myself from the waves that kept smacking me down and find safety and security on solid ground. I only survived thanks to the love and support of the islanders and the path they led me on that reacquainted me with God.

From *Discovering the World On a Barrier Island*
by Katherine Middleton Kelly

CHAPTER ELEVEN

Taylor was wide awake at four-thirty the next morning when the newspaper was delivered to the house. She slipped on a pair of flip flops and made her way down the driveway. With trembling hands, she unfolded the newspaper. As Rebecca expected it would be, the story of the filing of the lawsuit was the top story. Taylor's stomach knotted as she looked at the old high school yearbook photo they had dug up to run with the story.

Local business owner and horse trainer, Taylor Murray, has filed suit in the Accomack Circuit Court, 2nd Judicial Circuit of Virginia, alleging sexual discrimination on the part of the Saltwater Cowboys, the organization that herds the Chincoteague ponies from Assateague Island to the fairgrounds every July. Murray is suing both the association and the

Chincoteague Fireman's Company. Murray, 23, was born and raised on Chincoteague. Her late father, Peter Murray, participated in the pony swim as a Saltwater Cowboy for the past thirty-two years. In his Last Will and Testament, Murray left his spot in the organization to his daughter, Taylor, an unprecedented move in the history of the pony penning. According to a spokesman for the group, before the matter was brought to their attention, they had already replaced the older Murray with Chad Nixon, a close friend of the Murray family. "Chad was like a son to Pete," the spokesman contended. "Pete would be pleased to know that such a fine replacement had been chosen for him."

In a statement released by Murray's attorney, Rebecca Adams, Murray said she understands the concern of the men and praises all the work they've done with the ponies. "I feel that I am just as qualified as any man and can pull my weight on the team. I'm not looking for a battle of the sexes. I know that we can all work together for the good of the ponies and the island."

The article went on to give the history of the pony swim and an outline of events during the annual week in late July. Taylor skimmed the rest, looking for more information about the case but didn't read any. Nowhere did the article state that Taylor was not the first woman to ask to join. Neither did it state any reasons why she should not be allowed to do so.

It was one of those days for Taylor, the kind when she preferred to work alone. While the rest of the crew planted trees in a new development off-island, Taylor worked on a flower garden in front of the community center. She listened to music via earphones and enjoyed the solitary work. As she hummed along with Kacey Musgraves, someone tapped on her shoulder.

When Taylor turned around, Chad was standing behind her, arms crossed over his chest, and a smoldering expression on his face. She slowly popped out her earphones and offered what she hoped resembled a sincere smile.

"Hi, Chad," she said as she stood.

"Don't 'Hi, Chad' me. What the heck, Taylor?"

Taylor bit her lips together, not sure how to respond.

"Cat got your tongue? It looks like you were able to say plenty to an attorney and to the newspaper."

"I didn't actually talk to the newspaper."

"Save it. I don't want to hear it. I want to know why you're trying to steal my spot. A spot I earned."

Taylor breathed deeply through her nose and balled her hands into fists. "And what about the spot I earned, Chad? I've been on the list and have been working with the ponies just as long as you have. Don't you think I should be the one to replace my father?"

Chad released his arms and shook his head. "It doesn't work that way, Taylor."

Taylor put her hands on her hips and set her jaw as she met his gaze. "And why not, Chad? Why can't it work that way?"

"It just doesn't. It's a man's job."

Taylor closed her eyes and mustered all her will not to scream or propel herself at him and tear his hair out. She looked him in the eye and spoke in a steady, confident tone. "I know more about horses than you'll ever know in your lifetime, and you know it. If anyone deserves to ride alongside those ponies, it's me. Now, I have a job to do, and I assume you do, too. Go back to the marina and leave me alone."

She turned her back on him and reached for the earphones that dangled around her neck.

"I should have known you wouldn't listen to reason. You never did. Just like when I tried to tell you that you were making a mistake breaking things off with me."

She whirled around. "Enough! There was never anything to break off. I told you that back then. Yes, we went out a few times, but that's all it was. There was never anything more between us. We're friends, Chad. Or so I thought we were. And if you ever cared about me, in the least, you would know how much this means to me." Tears threatened, but she refused to let him see her cry. She put the earphones in her ears and turned back to her work.

Seconds ticked by while she worked in his shadow, but eventually, Chad walked away. Taylor breathed a sigh of relief and collapsed into the grass. Her gloved hands left streaks of dirt across her cheek after she wiped away her tears.

***

"Zach, I'm off on Saturday. What do you say we put the boat in the water and find a nice fishing hole?"

Nick held the phone under his chin and reached into the department refrigerator for the peanut butter and jelly sandwich he had packed himself for lunch.

"Kayla and I planned on taking the boys to the beach. She's tired of hiding out."

"Bring them along. I plan on bringing Taylor. I'm thinking she could use a day away from other people."

"I saw the newspaper this morning. Have you talked to her today?"

"Just a quick text early this morning. We're both working."

As if on cue, Steve stuck his head in the door. "Nick, we've got a call on Cleveland Street. Gotta roll."

"Zach, I have to run. Saturday at eight?"

"I'll text you and let you know."

Nick disconnected the call and headed out to Steve's squad car. "What's the call?"

"Fist fight at the grocery store?"

"Seriously? About what?"

"Guess we'll find out."

When they reached the store, they found two young men with swollen faces, one with a bloody nose, and the other holding up a swelling hand.

"What's the problem, gentlemen?" Steve asked.

"Ask him." The one with the bloody nose pointed to the other man.

"That Neanderthal says Taylor's got no place in the pony swim. I told him my cousin's got more horse know-how than anyone I know."

Steve looked at Nick. "You want to handle this?"

"Isn't that a conflict of interest?" Nick hoped this wasn't an omen of things to come.

"Look, here, guys," Steve said. "You're both old enough to know… hey, how old are you anyway?"

"I'm seventeen," said Taylor's cousin before spitting a mouthful of blood.

"Sixteen," said the swollen-hand guy.

"Okay, look, I really don't want to have to haul you two in for fighting. If we let you go, do you promise to go home, clean up, and stay away from each other?"

"That's going to be hard to do," swollen hand answered. "He's my brother."

"For heaven's sake," Nick said. "Taylor's your cousin, too?"

The kid grinned. "I believe that's how it works."

"Go home," Nick told them. "And grow up. Taylor has enough on her plate without her own family taking sides against her."

"You the officer she's seeing?" Bloody nose asked.

"None of your business," Nick sneered. "Just do what I say and knock off this BS. You got it?"

By then, both boys were grinning at each other. They got up and walked toward the parking lot together, each complimenting the other on their boxing skills.

"It's not going to be the last time," Steve said. "Right or wrong, she's started something too big to contain."

"As long as she isn't the one who ends up hurt."

***

Taylor stood back and assessed the gardens. The job had taken the better part of the day, but she was pleased with the work she had done.

"Excuse me."

Taylor heard a small voice behind her and turned around to find a little girl, maybe about eight or nine, in a Girl Scout uniform.

"Are you Taylor? Mommy showed me your picture in the newspaper this morning."

Taylor licked her lips. She didn't know whether to lie or tell the truth. "I am," she admitted.

The little girl smiled. "See this?" The girl proudly held out one side of her vest and pointed to a patch with a horse on it. "I got my horse care badge last month. Someday, I'm going to be a Saltwater Cowgirl, like you."

Taylor didn't know what to say. She felt a lump form in her throat. "Wow! That's a pretty neat badge. I earned one like that back when I was your age."

The girl's eyes widened. "You did?"

"I sure did."

"Lauren, what are you doing?" An older version of Lauren came around the corner of the building. "I'm sorry. Was she bothering you?"

"Mommy." Lauren tugged on her mother's t-shirt. "It's *Taylor*."

"I know, honey," she said to the little girl before looking at Taylor. "I'm sorry. She recognized you when we arrived for her meeting. I didn't know she'd come over here."

"It's okay. I told her I used to have a badge just like hers."

"You're her new hero, you know. You're an inspiration to all the girls on the island. I'm Alicia Ward, by the way. Jenny babysits for Lauren sometimes."

Taylor removed a glove and shook the outstretched hand. "Taylor Murray. Nice to meet you."

"Keep up the fight, Taylor. A lot of people are behind you."

"Thanks, Alicia. I appreciate it. And nice to meet you, Lauren."

The little girl waved as she skipped back to her troop, her mother following behind.

No matter what Chad thought; no matter how many glares or stares or angry words are thrown her way,

Taylor would remember all the Laurens of the world who wore their horse badges with pride. They all deserved the chance to cross the channel beside a pony.

***

"How's she holding up?" Nick peeked around Zach from the bow of the boat and watched Kayla, Taylor, and the boys get settled on the stern.

"Which one?"

"Good question. Taylor's okay. Keeping busy and out of the public eye. She reads every letter to the editor. Some make her cry. Others remind her why she's doing this. How about Kayla?"

"She's hanging in there. No more calls since the other night. Kayla blocked the number, but I'm sure that won't be enough to deter him."

Nick nodded and smiled at Taylor as she looked up at the men. He asked the group, "Everyone have their life-jackets on?"

"Aye, aye, Captain!" Todd's grin stretched from ear to ear. He held onto the side of the boat and giggled when EJ reached into the water and splashed his younger brother.

Admittedly, the boat was too big for a single man, but it was the perfect size for taking a family out for a day of fishing. Aaron was at work, and Kate, nearing her sixth month, thanked Nick for the invitation but said she and Miren would pass. She wasn't sure her legs would be sea-worthy, and she had errands to run.

Amid the cawing of the gulls and the humming of the motor, the crew set off toward the open waters. As they glided through the channel, they could see Anne and Paul's house and Veteran's Memorial Park on one side of the channel and the Assateague Lighthouse on the other. After they passed through Tom's Cove and out into the ocean, they were greeted by a blue sky that seemed to go on into eternity. The air was heavy with the scents of salt and sea, and the water was reasonably calm. Nick felt like Leonardo DiCaprio's character as he set sail from Belfast to New York. Nick was ready to jump onto the bow of the boat, throw out his arms, and declare himself the 'King of the World.' Hopefully, his vessel was more seaworthy than the ill-fated Titanic that DiCaprio's character, Jack, sailed upon.

Taylor made her way up to the cockpit and wrapped her arms around Nick. He took her arm and pulled her around so that she was nestled between him and the steering wheel. She wore a bright pink bikini under a flowy cover-up, tied in front, that didn't cover up much. Nick breathed in the smell of the salt air and the scent of her, a lethal combination.

"So, you've done this before, I take it." He placed his chin on the top of her head, liking the way her shorter body fit so perfectly into his own.

"A time or two," she said.

"No fear of slimy worms and scaly fish?"

"Fish fear me," Taylor said.

"Oh, is that so?"

"You'd better believe it."

Nick loved that Taylor enjoyed the outdoors and was willing to do just about anything. She had a spirit almost as wild and carefree as the ponies she loved so much.

"The fish finder says this spot looks good." Nick stopped the boat and cut the engine. "Time to put your money where your mouth is."

"Oh, really? Is that a challenge, Officer Black?"

Nick looked her in the eye. "Maybe it is."

"Put my money where my mouth is, huh? Care to make a friendly wager?"

"What's your ante?"

"The first one to catch a fish chooses the restaurant for our next night out. Smallest fish has to pay."

"I'll take those wagers and raise you."

She arched a brow. "The one who catches the most fish gets to watch the other one clean all the fish."

"You're on," she said, her green eyes sparkling.

Nick bent down and placed a loud kiss on her succulent lips. "The game is on," he said before walking away.

"That was gross, Nick," Todd said.

"You just wait, kid. You just wait. Zach, throw out the anchor. I've got a line to bait."

"Aye, aye, Captain." Zach raised his hand in a salute and turned to drop the anchor as Todd giggled and EJ grinned.

"Did anyone get a picture of the officer saluting a subordinate?" Nick looked around at the group with his hands on his hips.

"It's your ship, right?" Zach asked. "In my limited boating experience, I'd say that makes you the commanding officer."

"I'll take it," Nick said. "At least as long as Aaron isn't on board. The real commanding officer might take offense at that."

"But he's in the Coast Guard. You were a Marine." EJ looked at Nick with his brow furrowed in confusion. "How can he outrank you?"

"Doesn't matter, EJ. And I will always be a Marine." He winked at Zach and saw Kayla and Taylor look at each other and roll their eyes. With more than their fair share of military men in their lives, both women were oblivious to any military bravado.

Nick, Taylor, and Zach went to work on the fishing gear while Kayla took pictures with her fancy camera.

"Okay, who's ready to cast their line?" Nick asked.

"I am." EJ picked up the rod he baited on the ride out and chose a spot on the boat. "Can I go ahead?"

"Be my guest," Nick said. "Todd, do you need help?"

"Dad's gonna help."

Maybe it was just the salt in the air, but Nick was sure he saw Zach's eyes mist over a little. Zach had been 'dad' for a few short months, and he relished every minute. Taking his sons fishing was just one of the many things Nick knew Zach looked forward to doing with the boys over the summer.

Once everyone else was settled, Nick turned to Taylor. "Ready?"

"Ready to win," she answered.

"Just watch the pro at work." Nick demonstrated while Taylor shook her head.

Nick positioned himself next to Taylor. They both cast their lines and watched as they soared out into the blue sky and dropped down to be gobbled up by the waves. The boat ebbed and flowed beneath them, and Nick felt Taylor looking at him now and then. He concentrated on his line, slowly releasing and tugging on it a few times before tightening it with the reel. He felt for the small twinges on the line indicating he had a bite.

Though Todd and EJ laughed and hollered as they each reeled in a speckled trout, and Kayla danced around taking photos, all of the sounds and movement faded away until only Nick and Taylor stood in the boat, casting and reeling, casting and reeling, over and over again.

Suddenly, Nick saw Taylor's line go taut. "You got one!"

Taylor squealed as Nick felt a tug on his own line. He began reeling in at a frantic pace, stealing glances at Taylor as she did the same.

"Come on, baby. Come to papa." Nick felt his anticipation escalating as he reeled in the line.

Taylor fought to reel in the fish. Nick wondered how big it was and imagined her reeling in a bluefin tuna or a white marlin, its sword-nose pointing into the air as he and Zach hauled it into the boat. He ground his teeth and yanked hard at his line. He had to be first.

"I see it!" Todd yelled. "Taylor's got the first fish!"

Nick pulled his catch into the boat a split second after Taylor pulled in hers. She held out her fish and wrinkled her nose. Nick looked from his nice, big fish to Taylor's small fish, flipping its fins to and fro, trying to disengage from the hook.

"Well, I guess I caught the first fish." Taylor's smirk made Nick laugh.

"You call that a fish?"

"It was the first one, Nick. Hers beat yours to the boat." Todd reminded him.

"Yeah, well…" Nick reached out and pulled his catch closer to him so he could remove the hook and throw the fish into their cooler. "I caught the biggest one."

"So far," Taylor said with a mischievous grin.

"What kind of fish is it, Taylor?" Todd asked.

"A flounder," EJ said. "Right, Mom?"

"That's right, EJ." Kayla looked at Taylor and shrugged her shoulders. "Unfortunately, it's a bit small."

"It's too small to keep," EJ supplied. "But it's a nice-looking fish."

"I'm just warming up," Taylor said. She freed the fish from the hook and started to toss it back.

"Wait," Kayla said. "We have to take a picture of you with the first fish."

Nick shook his head. "It's barely a fish."

Taylor grabbed his arm before he put his fish in the cooler. "You heard the lady, picture time." She looked at Kayla. "Just be sure to remember who got theirs in the boat first."

"Be careful," Todd said. "Fish scales are prickly."

After the picture, Taylor tossed her fish back into the water.

"Ready to try again?" she asked Nick.

"You bet." Nick replaced his bait and cast his line while wondering how he had gotten so lucky.

***

Zach didn't think the day could get any better. He helped Todd with his fish, talked with EJ about the fall track season, and watched as Kayla's short, curly hair fluttered in the wind. It was a picture-perfect day spent on the water with his family and one of his closest friends.

Sometime in the early afternoon, they ate their picnic lunch as the sun sent down searing waves of heat more powerful than the caressing waves under the boat. Zach saw Todd yawn.

"He's going to sleep like a rock tonight," Zach whispered to Kayla.

"Not if he falls asleep on the way back in."

"We'll have to play a game or something to keep him awake."

Kayla smiled. "Hey, you're pretty good at this dad thing."

His heart swelled as he wrapped his arm around her and pulled her close to him. He leaned over to lay a gentle kiss on the top of her head and was momentarily blinded by a ray of sunlight reflecting off something in another boat.

Zach squinted as he looked across the water at the other vessel, a good fifty yards away. As his gaze focused, his blood turned to ice. He released Kayla and stood, walking toward Nick.

"I think it's time to go."

Nick swallowed his bite and looked up at Zach. "What? We haven't gotten our limit yet."

Zach tilted his head to motion toward the boat. "We've got all we need for now. Let's get the women and the boys home."

Taylor and Nick both turned to the right and looked at the anchored boat across the water. There was one man on board. The man held up a camera but, when his lens focused on Zach's stare, he quickly put it down and turned away.

"Who's he after?" Nick asked Zach. "Your date or mine?"

"Either way, let's get them both out of here."

***

Taylor waited patiently as the men tied up the boat. She and Nick said goodbye to Zach, Kayla, and the boys, and she mulled over the situation as they walked up the steps to the stilted house.

Once in the living room, Taylor dropped her bag inside the front door of Nick's house and crossed her arms across her chest. She waited for Nick to close the door behind them.

"What's the deal? You and Zach hurried us out of there faster than you could reel in a fish. Who was that guy?"

"No clue, but we weren't taking any chances. You and Kayla both need to watch your backs right now." Nick retreated to the kitchen for a Coke and Taylor followed, accepting the bottle of water Nick held out to her.

"You think he was some kind of reporter?"

"Could've been. Either way, he had no business tracking us down and taking pictures like that."

"I guess it's something I may have to get used to, at least for the time being. I just hope he was spying on me and not Kayla. She's been through enough already."

"You're right about that." Nick shook his head. "I can't believe Lifetime is making a movie about the case. I don't blame her for not wanting anything to do with it. She doesn't need anyone poking into her life, past or present, or disrupting the boys' lives."

"Boy, how I understand and appreciate that. I can't even work without people coming up to me and asking about the suit."

"Is anyone harassing you? Chad hasn't been back around, has he?"

"No, he hasn't, and no, I'm not being harassed. Most of the people have been pretty supportive."

"Good. Let me know if anyone threatens you or won't leave you alone."

"You don't think that will happen, do you?"

"I think anything is possible." Nick stood and tossed his can into the recycling bin. "Speaking of work, I could use a nap before I head in for the late shift."

"No problem." Taylor stood and tossed her bottle on top of Nick's can. "Just make sure you clean those fish before you go to bed. It's going to take you the rest of the afternoon to go through all the ones I caught."

"Ha ha. At least you're paying for dinner."

"Yep, and you get to choose where. How's the deli sound?" She grinned with delight.

Nick grabbed her and pulled her to him. Taylor squealed and put her arms around his neck.

"Don't even think about it," he said quietly as he held her. "I want to make sure you get your money's worth."

"Oh, is that so?" She felt her pulse quickening and her breathing becoming shallow. "So, we aren't going to the least expensive place on the island?"

"No, and if you protest, I'll have to arrest you for insubordination." Nick kept his eyes locked on her lips.

"I promise not to resist," she whispered.

When his lips found hers, an explosion of fireworks went off behind her closed eyes. The kiss was full of emotion and desire and the promise of everything Taylor was hoping for.

I never thought any of my father's research would interest me, but the older I get, the more I recall about my youth and our time spent among indigenous peoples who still live in remote villages on the plains and in the forests. To many, their lives seem primitive, perhaps barbaric. I've come to believe that they are living life the way we were meant to. It's the presumed civilized people who often turn out to be barbaric. I prefer a quiet, simple way of life, and that's what I've found here on the island.

From *Discovering the World On a Barrier Island*
by Katherine Middleton Kelly

CHAPTER TWELVE

"Do you really think it was him?" Kayla kept her voice low as she peeked out the kitchen window that faced the water.

"I do."

"Not someone after Taylor?"

"For what purpose? She filed a public suit. Anyone who wants to interview her can just ask. This guy was being sneaky. And he wasn't local. He was in one of the marina's rental boats."

"And he was taking pictures of us." Kayla was relieved that there were no strangers outside the house or on the water, but she hated the idea of someone taking pictures of her and her kids. Releasing a long breath, she let go of the curtain so that it fell back into place. "What can we do about it?"

"I'm not sure we can do anything about it. I don't think we can prove he was spying on us unless we get a warrant for the camera."

"I hate this." Kayla collapsed into a kitchen chair and pulled the hat off her head. She ran her fingers through her hair and thought about all they had been through. "Every time I think all of that mess is truly behind me, it rears its ugly head."

Zach took the seat next to her and reached across the table to hold her hand. "I'm sorry this is happening. I know how hard you've tried to protect the boys from the truth." He hesitated, and Kayla felt his hand squeeze hers tighter. "But I think, perhaps, it's time to tell them what really happened."

Kayla felt her heart lurch. She had spent the past seven years telling her boys how much their father loved them, how he was looking down on them from Heaven, protecting them. She had never once let on about how angry she was with Eddie for years, how she blamed him for getting himself killed, or how she blamed herself for thinking the worst of him—that the secrets he was keeping were due to an affair. She hadn't given her husband, the love of her life for five years, the father of her children, the benefit of the doubt.

"I don't know how to do that," Kayla admitted. "There's so much more to it than just the facts."

"Of course, there is, honey." Zach gently caressed her hand as he held it. "But you don't have to go into all those details. And there's a big difference between the past seven years and now."

Kayla looked up at Zach, love flowing from her heart. She knew exactly what he meant even before he said it.

"Now, you all have me."

Kayla felt a solitary tear escape her eye. Zach let go of her hand and lovingly wiped away the tear with his thumb.

"When do you want to do this?"

Never?

Kayla knew that wasn't an option. She sighed and took a hold of Zach's hand that was still on her cheek. "I guess now is as good a time as ever."

Zach offered to get the boys while Kayla gathered her thoughts. She felt the need to look outside once again and checked the kitchen window as well as the front window in the living room. She was thankful when she didn't see anyone but Nick. He stood on the top step of his house and watched Taylor back out of his driveway. Kayla smiled. Those two had a future together, she was sure of it.

"Mom, what's up?"

Kayla turned to see EJ and Todd standing in the living room. Zach was behind them with a hand on each boy's shoulder.

"Boys, come sit." Kayla sat on the couch and patted the cushions on each side of her. Todd and EJ looked at each other and then took a seat next to their mother.

It took less than five minutes for Kayla to tell the boys about their father's death, but to her, it felt like five hours. Not since the day she told them about her cancer had she been so nervous about talking to her boys and about their reactions.

As usual, EJ surprised her with his knowledge. "Mom, you know this is all online, right?"

Kayla looked at her son and blinked. "Well, yes, but did *you* know?"

"Mom, everyone googles himself. And my name is Edward Reynolds…or was." He nodded at his adoptive father who was sitting in a chair across from them.

Kayla turned her gaze to Zach. He was trying hard to suppress a grin, and she couldn't help but laugh. Taking a deep breath, she looked back at EJ.

"So, you already knew about your dad?"

EJ shrugged. "Sure."

"For how long?"

He shrugged again. "I don't know. A while. Since Zach first came around…" He looked away, his face reddening.

There are times in a mother's life when she realizes that her children are much older and wiser than she ever gave them credit for. For Kayla, those times began the previous year when she realized how protective EJ was of her, how it took him a while to trust Zach, how he tried to shield his family, especially his brother, from everything evil and harmful. Despite all those times, all those moments of realization, despite the knowledge that EJ was wise beyond his years, like most mothers, Kayla had never stopped to consider just how much her son knew, how adept he was at finding information for himself, and how being a parent got even harder as the children got older.

"EJ, does that mean you also know about..." She looked toward Zach and swallowed. EJ cast a quick glance at Zach and then at the floor at his feet. He nodded and swallowed, his Adam's apple bobbing up and then down.

Zach's past, too, could easily be found online, but it had taken Kayla months to realize it. How had EJ so easily discovered it?

"Mommy, I don't understand." Todd interrupted her thoughts, reverting back to the baby voice he used when he was hurting or confused. He looked up at Kayla. "Was daddy a bad guy?"

Kayla wrapped her arms around Todd, her baby, who had been through so much in nine years but was still such a little boy. "No, honey, your dad was one of the good guys, one of the very best guys. He helped put a very bad man in jail, and by telling the truth, he saved two little girls who were just a little younger than you boys are now."

"If daddy wasn't a bad guy, why did he get shot? Don't only bad people have guns?"

Kayla bit her lip and looked at Zach for help. Before he could answer, EJ spoke up.

"No, Todd," he said softly. He raised his eyes toward Zach. "Sometimes good guys have to use guns, too. That's how we stay safe, by having police officers and," he swallowed again, "soldiers who use guns to protect us."

Zach nodded. "He's right, Todd. And your daddy was a hero. He didn't shoot anyone. He only had the gun in case he needed to protect you or himself. When he went to the house that day, he thought he might get hurt, but he knew that he had to stop that man from trying to hurt you or EJ or your mom. He didn't know that the man was going to take the gun away and hurt your dad instead."

Todd sniffled as he nodded. "Okay, I understand." His eyes went back to Kayla. "Is that bad man going to come find us? Is that why you're telling us this?"

Kayla sucked in her breath. "Oh, no, Todd, he's never going to come after us. The man who shot your father is dead, and the man he worked for will be in jail for a very long time."

"It's about the movie, isn't it?" Once again, Kayla was astonished by her son's knowledge.

"EJ, if you don't grow up to be an investigative reporter or a detective, you will have missed your calling." She looked at Todd. "Sweetie, there's a television channel that makes movies about real crimes. They're making a movie about the men who killed your father. There's a reporter who is asking questions about us, and he might try to talk to you."

Todd's eyes widened and a gap-toothed grin appeared on his face. "You mean, I might be in a movie?"

Kayla gritted her teeth. She should have thought that through a bit more. "No, Todd. You are not going to be in a movie, and neither are the rest of us." She sighed. "I've worked very hard not to make what happened to your father affect you boys or your lives. We moved back here to get away from all that and to be near Grandma and Granddad and Uncle Aaron. Uncle Aaron did his very best to be a father to you until Zach came along and became your dad. And now, we're going to keep living our lives and not let this movie interfere."

"But don't you want everyone to know that daddy was a hero like Zach, I mean Dad, said he was?" Todd looked at Zach for encouragement.

Zach raised his brow and looked to Kayla for an answer. She sat back on the couch, a cyclone of thoughts racing through her mind, swirling everything she thought she knew and felt into a funnel of confusion and chaos.

"Well, I guess I hadn't thought of it that way."

Todd stood and looked from one person to another. When he spoke, Kayla thought he suddenly looked every bit like a nine-year-old and maybe older. "I think the whole world should know that our first dad was a hero who died because he was trying to help the FBI and keep us safe. When Mr. Palmer took me, I was afraid I was going to die, but Nick and Mr. Paul and the FBI found me. They were good guys, like dad, and I think everyone should know that he was working with people like them to keep us safe."

EJ made a clicking noise with his tongue. "He's got a point there."

After a moment, Kayla realized everyone was looking at her for an answer. She forced her mouth closed, swallowed, and blinked.

"Well, I guess that settles that." She turned to Zach. "Maybe we need to call a family meeting and let everyone know how we're going to handle this. If anyone asks us about Eddie, we're going to tell them that he died a hero."

"You know," EJ said, "I think Todd and I are pretty lucky kids. In spite of all the sh—stuff that has happened to us, we get to have two heroes as dads. Not many people can say that."

Kayla lifted her eyes to Zach's and smiled. Once again, EJ had proven that he was the wisest of them all.

Just then, Zach pulled his phone from his pocket. "This thing's been going off since we started talking." He looked at the screen and jumped up from the chair. "It's Kate. I've got to call Aaron."

Kayla watched as he ran from the room. She lifted her eyes toward the ceiling and thought,

Please, you've made your point, but I think enough is enough. We've already got all we can handle.

***

Something bothered Taylor as she drove down the lane toward the house. The paddocks didn't look right. They looked…Her breath caught in her throat, and her heart began to pound. They looked empty.

She ground the truck to a halt in front of the open gate and raced into the barn. It was empty, too.

How had this happened? She was certain she had closed the gate after her morning ride. Hadn't she? Of course, she had! She washed down Big Red and fed him, worked for a little while with Stormy and fed him, then she made sure they were secure in their own paddocks and closed the gate. There was no way she could have left all of the gates open.

"Taylor, get a grip," she told herself. "What's important is finding Stormy and Big Red."

She looked around at the expanse of the property. Where would they go? If they were spooked, they might have blindly taken off at top speeds. She searched the ground for hoofprints. Both animals seemed to head in the same direction. She stood and looked toward the north. All that was in that direction was marsh, miles and miles of marsh, and then the Chincoteague Bay. From this side of the island, there wasn't any land close enough for them to swim to if they ended up in the water.

Her panic increased. She looked around for help. Clay was off on Saturdays. Her mother's car was gone. Was Jenny home? Taylor ran toward the house while reaching into her pocket for her phone. She sprinted up the steps as she dialed 911. She relayed the information as she searched the house. There was no sign of Jenny.

Taylor knew she couldn't take the truck to search for them, and a bikini wasn't going to cut it as far as clothes. She raced up the stairs to her room to change while punching the button to call her sister.

"Jenny, did you see Stormy or Big Red this morning?"

"No, I wasn't there. I stayed at Monica's, remember? What's wrong?"

"They're gone. The gates were open. All of them. Where's Mom?"

"I don't know. What can I do to help?"

"Can you call the Windsors and the Leves? See if they've seen them? That would save me the time of going there if they aren't there."

"I'll call now. I'm sure they're fine," Jenny assured her, though the worry in her voice gave her away.

"Thanks. I hear the police. Gotta go."

She threw on a light-weight long-sleeved shirt with her jeans and ran down the steps to the mudroom. She was still pulling on a boot as she hopped onto the porch and hurried to the waiting car.

"Taylor," Paul said as he exited the car. "Two horses are missing?"

"My dad's horse, Big Red, and my pony, Stormy. Both were here this morning. I closed the gates when I left. I'm sure of it. There are three of them. Even if I missed one, the others would still be closed." She looked around him, knowing that time was wasting. She had to find them.

"Where would they go?"

Her phone vibrated. It was Jenny. "Hold on, Mr. Parker. Jenny, what's up?" Taylor listened and closed her eyes. She thanked her sister and disconnected the call. "They're not at either of the neighbors' houses. I'm afraid…" She looked in the direction she feared they had gone.

"I called Will Cheney. He's rounding up a few others. They'll be here soon."

Before he finished speaking, Taylor heard the truck and trailer coming down the lane. Will leapt from his truck and went around to open the trailer. He led his horse out and climbed onto his back.

"Point me where we should go," he said to Taylor.

She indicated the way. "The hoofprints lead off that way. Beyond our property, there's nothing but marsh and then the Bay."

"Understood. Rebel and I will head that way. I brought Gypsy." His eyes conveyed compassion when he looked down at her. "I knew you'd want to help, and I trust you with her, have since the day we got her. You know that. You work magic with the ponies."

She wondered if there was a hidden meaning in his words, but she didn't have time to ponder them. She nodded and went into the trailer and took out the pony she knew meant the world to Will. It had belonged to his late wife. Taylor spoke gently to the horse she had trained. Gypsy was Taylor's first, and they shared a bond as deep as the one Gypsy shared with her late owner.

Once mounted, Taylor called to Paul. "When the others show up, point them in the right direction." She spurred the horse into action and rode off after Will.

It didn't take long for Hank to join them or for them to find Big Red. He stood in the marsh, chomping down on the tall grass. He looked up at Taylor as if to say, "It's about time."

"I'll lead him back," Hank said. "You can keep looking." Taylor nodded and put her hand over her eyes, scanning the rest of the marsh.

"Taylor! Over here!" Will's panicked call sent Taylor and Gypsy flying through the marsh, sending mud and grass into the air behind them.

She was still several yards from Will when she heard the braying and the thrashing. Stormy's worn-out voice was weak and muffled by the slosh of the marsh. She looked at Taylor, and Taylor felt sure Stormy was asking for help.

Will was already standing beside the pony. Taylor climbed down and went to her.

"She'll kick the tar out of us if we try to pull her with our hands," Will warned.

"I've got a rope." The voice came from behind them. Taylor turned to see Chad. She didn't know whose horse he rode—he didn't own one himself—but Taylor was grateful to see him. He threw the rope to Will. "If you can get it around her, I can ease her out."

"You go on one side, and I'll go on the other," Taylor said. She thought she sounded calmer and more confident than she felt. Will tossed the rope over the pony, but it slid off her backside. He tossed it twice more before it stayed on the pony's shoulders long enough for Taylor to grab it.

"How are you going to get it around her?" Will asked.

Without answering, Taylor moved closer to Stormy. Her boots sunk deeper into the marsh, and she felt a slimy rush of silt spill over the top and into the boots. "Sh, baby, sh. It's okay." She crooned to the pony in a low, soothing voice. "I'm here. We've got you." The pony's dark eyes followed her movement. She stopped thrashing, and their eyes met. Taylor continued to talk to Stormy. "We're going to pull you out. It's all going to be okay."

Taylor was as close as she could get without sinking down into the same pit as Stormy. She balanced on outstretched legs and reached as far as she could with the rope until she felt Will's hand grasp it on the other side. Stormy stayed still, her eyes never leaving Taylor's. Within minutes Will had the rope secured.

"Pull her up," he said to Chad. "Slowly and gently."

Taylor coaxed Stormy with her soothing words, walking alongside the pony until she was safely out of the pit. Only then did Taylor allow herself to breathe.

Once they were back at the ranch and the horses were secure, Taylor thanked Will, Chad, and Hank. She invited Paul into the house to fill out a report but asked for a minute to speak with Chad while Will and Hank loaded their horses.

"Thank you for coming. I know things aren't great between us right now."

"Taylor, stop." Chad took both her hands in his. "It's okay. I'm glad I was able to help. Look…" He stopped and looked toward the other men. Paul cleared his throat and went to see if he could assist Will. "I love you. I always have. But I think I get that it isn't the kind of love we're both looking for. I'm sorry for getting angry with you. And I'm sorry for taking your spot. What you did out there. That was amazing. I don't think I could have done it." He let out a breath and shook his head. "You're the one who truly deserves to be part of the swim, not me."

"Chad." Taylor squeezed his hands. "I love you, too. You're the brother I never had. And I think Dad would want us both out there."

"Ahem, Taylor?"

She looked over at Will. He nodded and said, "I'm fighting for you. I just want you to know that."

Taylor nodded, thanked them again, and said her goodbyes. She might have a few of the men in her corner, but somebody was clearly trying to send her a message. She'd have to trust that Paul could find out who.

The indigenous peoples of the Yukon believe that all life is connected. There is a direct relationship between people and animals. Thus, all animals are respected and revered. They see no difference between the spirit of a human and the spirit of an animal. Like with the wild ponies that roam the shore on the barrier islands, animals and humans are seen as partners, co-inheritors of the earth, who work together to maintain a worldly balance.

From *Discovering the World On a Barrier Island*
by Katherine Middleton Kelly

CHAPTER THIRTEEN

Sunday morning's newspaper had a second above-the-fold article about Taylor's case. This time, the story was a history of the pony swim and a scathing account of the number of women who had applied to become Cowboys. The reporter did not name her source but said that 'an insider' supplied the list of well-qualified, sometimes over-qualified women, who had been turned away from the pony committee. The insider said that no explanation was ever given.

Taylor wondered who the source was and what others on the island thought about the article. While she was reading, her phone vibrated.

"Hello?" The voice belonged to an unfamiliar female.

"Is this Taylor Murray?"

"Yes, it is."

"You ought to be ashamed of yourself. You are tarnishing the reputation of our community. You're nothing but a selfish, self-serving—"

Taylor disconnected the call and blocked the number. It was not the first call she had received since Friday. She feared it would not be the last.

***

Nick hit the ball over the net, and Aaron spiked it back. A cheer went up, and Nick nodded to Aaron.

"Nice play."

"Thanks. You, too."

"Anyone want to step in?" Nick called to the onlookers. "I'm going to go find Taylor."

"I'll play," EJ said.

Nick looked at Zach. "Sure, why not? You're big enough to join the game."

A wide grin spread across EJ's face. Nick tussled his hair. "Good luck, kid. Your uncle is brutal."

"I can handle him."

Nick grinned. "I bet you can. Just play well and work with your team." Nick put his hands on EJ's shoulders and looked him in the eyes. In his most serious voice, he said. "Remember, 'the strength of the Pack is the Wolf, and the strength of the Wolf is the Pack.'"

"What does that mean?"

Nick widened his eyes. "Haven't you ever seen *The Jungle Book*?" EJ shook his head.

"Zach, this kid's never seen *The Jungle Book*. What's up with that?"

"Nick, not everybody bases all of their life choices on Disney movies. Now, get out of the way."

Nick shook his head as he made his way through the hedge. He opened the cooler, took out a beer, and looked around for Taylor.

"She's inside with Anne." Kate walked down from the patio.

"Taylor?"

"Yeah. She's helping with dessert." Kate winced. "Oh!" Her hand flew to her stomach and she smiled.

"Kate?" Nick grabbed her arm, intending to lead her to someplace she could sit down. "Are you okay? You're not going to pass out, are you?"

Kate laughed. "No, no. I'm sorry if I scared you. I guess Zach told you I was feeling faint the other day, but everything is fine. That kick was just harder than usual."

"He's kicking?" Nick looked at her belly in wonder.

"Is he ever." Kate smiled. "Aaron says he's going to be the star punter on the high school team."

"If it's a boy," Nick said.

"Or a girl." Kate shrugged. "I'm an equal opportunity mom."

"There's no way in he—, no way any daughter of mine would play football."

"The world is changing, Nick. Just look at what Taylor's doing."

Kate shifted so that she was looking past him. A frown formed on her face, and Nick turned to see what she was staring at. A man in jeans and a polo shirt was talking to Anne on the front walkway. She was shaking her head and pointing like she was telling him to go away.

"Who's that?" Nick asked.

"I have a feeling I know. I'm getting Zach." Kate hurried to the hedge to get her brother.

"You go ahead, but I think I can handle this." Nick reached into his back pocket and retrieved his wallet, opening it to reveal his badge. He walked over to Anne and the stranger.

"Excuse me, Anne, everything okay here?"

"Nick, this man wants to crash our party. I've asked him to leave, but he refuses to go."

Nick held up his badge. "Nick Black, Chincoteague Police. And you are?"

"Cody Boteler, with the Baltimore Sun. I'd just like to have one minute or two with Kayla Middleton."

"I'm told Kayla doesn't want to talk to you." Nick looked the man over and sized him up. He was in his late twenties with thick, dirty blonde hair and sunburned skin that made him look more like a surfer than a reporter.

A deep, angry voice spoke from behind Nick.

"You get that sunburn when you were spying on my family yesterday?"

Nick saw Cody's eyes flicker to Zach as the color drained from his burnt face. Zach had the power to intimidate the Terminator himself.

"Uh, Mister, I mean Captain Middleton, Sir—"

"What do you want?" Zach demanded.

"I just want to have a few minutes with Kayla, I mean Mrs. Middleton. I don't want to cause any problems."

Nick heard shuffling behind him and turned to see the entire party joining them in the front yard. Paul and Steve, both wearing CPD t-shirts, pushed their way to the front. Taylor, Tammi, Anne, Kate, Marian, and Debbie began forming a protective circle around Kayla behind the rest of the men.

"My sister doesn't want to talk to you."

"Respectfully, Mister, uh…"

"Commander Kelly," Aaron firmly said.

Cody swallowed and nodded. "Yes, Sir, Commander Kelly. As I told the officer here, I don't want to cause any trouble."

Nick watched Cody move his eyes from Aaron. He scanned the crowd until his gaze settled on Kayla. "Please, ma'am, just a few minutes."

Nick looked at Kayla and then Zach, who looked at each other. He saw an unspoken agreement pass between them before Zach spoke.

"Five minutes, and I'll be there, too."

"So, will I," Nick added. "Just to make sure you stay within the confines of the law."

"Yes, sir, five minutes."

"We're good, Nick, but thanks."

"You sure?" Nick asked Zach.

"I'm sure."

Nick nodded to Zach and then watched as Zach, Kayla, and Cody headed one way, and the rest of the crowd headed the other. Taylor waited for him on the sidewalk.

"What do you think?" she asked.

"I think that guy's going to have to get through Zach to talk to Kayla."

"Is it wrong of me to say that I'm glad he wasn't looking for me? After what happened yesterday, I really don't want any more publicity."

Nick put his arm around Taylor. "It's not wrong at all. You had a major scare yesterday. I can only imagine how you feel."

"You all aren't going to be able to figure out who did it, are you?"

Nick sighed. "Probably not. There were no prints on the gate, so they probably wore gloves. Any footprints were destroyed by the hoofprints, and there were too many vehicles in and out that day to identify tire prints."

"I guess I just have to hope that it was a meaningless prank."

Nick took her chin in his hand and forced her to look at him. "It was only meaningless because nobody got hurt. If something had happened to one of the horses or to you…" He looked away, loathing and disgust churning in his stomach. "I just hope nothing like that happens again."

"Me, too," she whispered, and all he wanted to do was take her in his arms and shield her from ever being hurt or frightened again.

"Hey, you've been in the house all afternoon. How about joining me outside for a while?"

"Actually, would you be upset if I left? I know Mom and Jenny encouraged me to come and said they'd keep an eye on things, but…"

"You're worried about Big Red and Stormy."

She nodded.

Nick pulled out his phone and checked the time. "To tell the truth, I'd better get going, too. I've got to shower, and I'd like a short nap before I go in. You okay driving home?"

"I'll be fine." She tried to smile, but he knew she wasn't feeling it.

He kissed her goodbye and watched her walk toward her car, her long, blonde hair shining in the sunlight. He smiled as he thought of the words of the Emperor in Mulan, "The flower that blooms in adversity is the most rare and beautiful of all." Nick couldn't agree more.

***

Zach and Kayla dropped the boys off at Ronnie and Trevor's house, telling them they wouldn't be long. As agreed, Zach, Kayla, and Cody met at the deli at five o'clock. Kayla surveyed the room. Though still moderately crowded, the deli had cleared out with the Sunday afternoon exodus of the weekenders.

They ordered drinks and a basket of fries so that they weren't just taking up space. Kayla had no desire to eat anything. Her stomach felt like a novice handcrafter had crocheted it into one of those long loopy chains that had no purpose at all except to perfect the skill.

"So, what do you want to ask my wife?" Zach gazed intently at Cody.

As nervous as the young man had seemed just an hour earlier, he displayed marked confidence as he pulled out his notebook and pen. Kayla surmised that Cody was much more at ease surrounded by strangers than when confronted with caring friends and family of the person he was pursuing.

"Mrs. Middleton, may I call you Kayla?"

"No."

"Yes."

Zach and Kayla answered in unison, and Kayla gave Zach a slight shake of her head as she laid a hand gently on his arm. She turned to Cody.

"Yes, you may, but only as a courtesy. I don't want this to come off as a hostile exchange."

Zach regarded Cody with a cool stare as the man thanked Kayla for her cooperation.

"I'm not here to cause any trouble."

Kayla felt Zach tense, and she squeezed his arm, assuring him that she was okay. She reminded him on the drive that this was what they had agreed upon—to tell the truth and let the world know that Eddie had died an American hero. Zach agreed but said there was something about the reporter that he didn't trust. Kayla chalked it up to Zach's past. There were few people outside of his former military command whom he did trust.

"Now, I'm sure you know about the movie."

"I didn't until you told me on the phone, but I've looked into it since then, yes."

Cody nodded. "As I'm sure you're well aware, the arrest of the mayor and his chief of staff came as quite a shock to the city. Even more shocking was the revelation that they had been running a human trafficking ring through the auspices of the city government."

"Yes, I'm aware," Kayla said, her nerves having settled as her curiosity piqued. "But I didn't know anything about any of that. I had no idea my husband was working with the FBI, and I never met Mr. Moore or Mayor Simpson."

Cody made a few short notes before asking his first question. "Did you know Susan Russell? Her name was Susan O'Neil at the time."

"I did not."

"Jim Russell?"

"No." Kayla sighed. "Mr. Boteler—"

"Cody, please."

"Cody, we did not live in the city, nor did we live in Lakespring. I had no connection to anyone involved. My husband was simply an office worker. We didn't socialize with any of the men he worked for. As I'm sure *you* know, I didn't even testify at the trial."

"Yes, that was interesting." Cody tapped his pen on the table as he observed Kayla, leaving her to wonder what he meant by that.

Letting his eyes wander to his notepad, Cody flipped through the pages until he came to one that seemed to interest him. He looked back at Kayla, and she saw a spark kindle in his eyes that burned a hole right through her chest. "Kayla, did you know that Eddie had embezzled half a million dollars from the state, and that's why he agreed to cooperate with the FBI? To keep his theft a secret and to shorten his jail time?"

The room began to spin. Kayla's hand squeezed Zach's arm so tightly, she could feel the blood pulsing through his veins. No, it was her blood, pulsing so fast and furiously, her heart felt like it would explode. Cody continued to talk, but his words made no sense.

"Kayla, did you know that Eddie was looking at, even with a reduced sentence, at least twenty-five years in prison?"

Kayla felt Zach rise to his feet.

Cody's voice became rushed as he leaned across the table toward her, their eyes locked on each other's. "Do you believe he went to Moore's house that day with the hopes that he wouldn't make it out alive?"

"That's enough," she heard Zach say from somewhere very far away.

"Do you think your husband was on a suicide mission? That he hoped if he lived through his confrontation with Moore, that someone else would take him out under Moore or Simpson's orders?"

"I said that's enough," Zach growled, leaning down into Cody's face.

Kayla watched as if she were seeing a movie play out in front of her, not a real-life scene in which such hateful and untrue things were being said about Eddie. She felt Zach take her arm and lift her from her seat.

"Do you think your husband planned to die rather than go to prison?" Cody was practically shouting as he stood, never taking his eyes from hers.

Kayla started to shake her head over and over, the room becoming a blur.

"We've heard enough," Zach barked, and somewhere in her conscious mind, Kayla felt the stares of the other customers. "He's paying," Zach called to Jane as he dragged Kayla from the restaurant. She could still hear Cody Boteler calling to her as the door slammed behind them. Or were his words just echoes in her head?

Do you think your husband planned to die rather than go to prison?

***

A wave a relief washed over Taylor when she spotted Big Red and Stormy standing under the shade canopies. It was hard enough to join her family at Mass that morning but agreeing to go to the cookout with Nick was more than she could handle. She needed to be home, needed to see for herself that everything was okay.

Once in the house, Taylor went to the office to look over the work calendar for the week. July would be here before she knew it, and the jobs would shift from planting and pruning to hydrating, weeding, composting, and feeding. There would be a good deal of spraying, too, to combat beetles, lawn pests, and mites. July was the only time Taylor wasn't crazy about her job. It was more about maintenance and prevention than about design and creation.

She looked at the calendar, made some notes, decided who was best on which job, and sent a few emails. Taylor skipped several emails, sending them straight to the trash. She had already read others like them. They warned her to stop her suit, called her names that would make a sailor blush, and warned her that she was going to regret 'going after' the Cowboys. Taylor didn't think she was going after anybody. She just wanted what was rightfully hers. She pictured the little girl with the pony badge. She was doing this for girls like Lauren, for all little girls who just wanted to be a part of the island's special heritage. She loved her hometown. She only wanted good things for her community. Why didn't they understand that?

Taylor was getting up from the desk when her phone vibrated. She recognized the number and answered right away, settling back into the chair.

"Ms. Adams, hello."

"Hello, Taylor, and it's Rebecca."

"Rebecca, I didn't expect to be hearing from you over the weekend, especially on a Sunday."

"I didn't expect to be calling, but I got a call a little while ago. I hear you had some excitement yesterday. Why didn't you call me?"

Taylor raked her bottom lip through her teeth. "I guess I didn't think about it. I mean, we don't know for sure that it was related to the suit."

"Maybe you can't prove it, but somebody thinks it's related."

Taylor sat up in the chair. "Who?"

"A Mr. William Cheney."

"Will. He's the longest standing Saltwater Cowboy and a friend of my dad's."

"Well, he's also a friend of yours. He says a group of them want to meet with us as soon as possible. What's your schedule like this week?"

Taylor only briefly considered all the planning she had done for the past hour. "I can be free any time. Just say when."

"I'll get back to Mr. Cheney and let him know."

When they hung up, Taylor sat back in her father's chair. Was this going to be good news or bad? She was afraid to get her hopes up, but a glimmer of hope pushed itself into her mind, and she clung to it with all her might.

***

After Nick left the party, he went home, changed into his uniform, and drove toward the station for his late shift, figuring he might as well go in early. As he neared the station, the dispatcher's voice came across the radio. 911 had received a call from a customer at the deli about a provocation taking place in the restaurant.

"Officer Black responding," Nick relayed back.

When Nick strolled into the deli, he saw the reporter, Cody somebody, being cornered by several locals. Nick asked a few questions and then ordered Cody to turn around. Nick read him his rights as he fastened the man's hands together behind his back.

"Are you really doing this? Ever heard of freedom of the press? The Sun has a good attorney, you know."

"Glad to hear it. You can call him as soon as we get to the station."

"Why am I under arrest?"

"Disorderly conduct." Nick turned from Cody and looked for Jane among the onlookers in the deli. He spotted her behind the counter. "Jane, I've heard from these fine people, now can I get a statement from you?"

"You sure can." Jane raised the hinged counter and slid under the upright arm. She made her way through the parting crowd, shoulders back and head held high. "This man was disturbing the peace in my restaurant." She pointed toward Cody. "He verbally attacked one of my customers and yelled repeatedly when she and her husband walked out."

Something clicked in Nick's mind. He glared at Cody before turning back to Jane. "Jane, who were the customers he verbally attacked?"

"Kayla and Zach Middleton." She shook her head. "To think of that poor girl being attacked after everything she's been through." Jane snarled at Cody. "You should be ashamed of yourself."

"Thank you, Jane. We'll let you know if we need to follow up." Nick took Cody's arm and led him from the store.

"This is bogus, and you know it. Charges will never stick."

"Maybe not," Nick said as he gently pushed Cody into the backseat of his shiny new squad car. "But they'll keep you away from Kayla for the night."

Nick slammed the door and radioed back to the station that he was bringing Cody in. Before opening his door and getting into the car, he pulled out his phone.

Your reporter friend was just arrested for disorderly conduct and disturbing the peace at the deli. This should cool the guy off for the evening.

Nick watched the screen for a moment, but he saw no indication that Zach had read his text. He hoped things were calm with the Middleton family. Jane was right. Kayla didn't need more heartache in her life.

I remember my father telling me that the Métis and Inuit Peoples of Canada believe that all pain and evil is caused by Malsum, a Transformer who unleashes hardship on the world. By praying to his brother, Glooscap, they can overcome the hardship and experience good. I often wondered if there are still civilizations today where people still believe in praying when they need help. Not long after arriving on the island, I learned that there are people who pray, who believe that there is a God, and who still believe that all things will work for the good.

From *Discovering the World On a Barrier Island*
by Katherine Middleton Kelly

CHAPTER FOURTEEN

On Tuesday afternoon, at precisely one-thirty, Taylor and Rebecca Adams were escorted into the boardroom at the bank. Will stood from his seat at the head of the table when they walked in.

"Welcome, ladies. We're glad you could join us."

Taylor scanned the room and saw several familiar faces. There was Hank, who helped with the search on Saturday, and Mr. Becker, a local teacher and Cowboy for many years. There was Mr. Windsor, her neighbor, and Alan Floyd, a retired police officer. There were several firemen in CVFC shirts; some she knew, others she did not.

"Thank you for having us," Rebecca said.

"Please, have a seat." Will gestured toward two empty chairs to his right.

The women made their way around the table and took their seats.

"First," Will began, "I want to offer my sincere apologies for what happened at the ranch on Saturday.

Though we have no way of knowing who was involved or why they did what they did, I know that I can speak for everyone when I say that no good could come from any harm to your horses or you personally."

There was a general nod and murmur of agreement from the men around the table.

"Having said that, we do hope that Taylor sees fit to not hold the fire department or the Saltwater Cowboys collectively responsible for what happened."

"So, you're saying that, if a perpetrator is found, you want him or her held responsible for his own actions and that the fire department and Saltwater Cowboys claim no knowledge or responsibility for what happened. Is that correct Mr. Cheney?" Rebecca regarded him with a gaze of steel, and Taylor again saw a woman of great poise and strength who must be fierce in a courtroom.

Will cleared his throat. "Yes, that's what I'm saying. I hope that nobody from either organization is found to be associated with the incident at the ranch, but if he is, we want to be clear that the conduct was not approved or condoned by any of the ranking members."

Rebecca made a note on her legal pad and nodded. "Could we, please, get that in writing, Mr. Cheney? So that we have it on record as an official statement." She smiled demurely, but Taylor knew it was not meant to be friendly. She wasn't totally sure why it mattered, but she knew Rebecca had her reasons for everything.

"Yes, ma'am. That can be arranged."

"Very good. Anything else?"

"Yes, um, we, the members of the pony committee would like to invite Ms. Taylor Murray to become a rider in the Annual Chincoteague Island Pony Swim."

Taylor's heart began to race. She wanted to jump from her seat and give Will a hug, but Rebecca's hand reached for hers under the table and signaled her to stay put.

"Mr. Cheney, does that mean that Ms. Murray will officially join the ranks of the Saltwater Cowboys with all duties, responsibilities, and notoriety as such?"

Will looked around the room as if he expected an objection before settling his gaze on Taylor. "Yes, it does." He shifted his eyes to Rebecca. "Do you want that in writing, too?"

Rebecca squeezed Taylor's hand before letting go. She smiled and nodded, "Yes, please. And one other thing."

Will raised an eyebrow. "Yes?"

"Send word out among your members and to anyone else who matters and tell them to stop harassing my client. She's one of you now. Show her the dignity and respect she deserves."

"Harassing?"

"Yes. The incident at the ranch was just the most egregious of the actions, but the phone calls, the emails, the threats and warnings, they have to stop."

"I wasn't aware that anything like that was happening. Taylor, you should have told me."

"They need to stop, and there needs to be a public declaration, a newspaper article, community email, however you all do things here, that announces Taylor has been accepted with enthusiasm as a Saltwater Cowboy and that you are all looking forward to having her work beside you. You don't have to mention that she's the first woman. That shouldn't be necessary. Her gender should have no bearing on her membership and never should have."

Though Taylor detected a ruffle of disapproval on the part of a few of the men, Will agreed to the terms. Again, Rebecca insisted that the agreement be put in writing.

Before they left the office, Will pulled Taylor aside. He lowered his voice as he spoke. "My Ginnie, she would have been tickled to see this day. You know, she always wanted to ride with us. I…" His voice cracked. "I was always afraid she'd get hurt. Now, I wonder if I was the one doing the hurting by not letting her ride."

"Will, I'm sure she's looking down on you and smiling. You did the right thing, and she knows it."

Taylor had managed to maintain her composure through the meeting, but as soon as she and Rebecca exited the building, she jumped in the air and hollered.

"You did it! Thank you! I can't believe they said yes."

"I think you did it, Taylor. I was just the catalyst that helped bring about the inevitable."

Taylor hugged her. "I can't wait to tell my family and Nick. He's a police officer. And my friend, Holly. She works at the deli. And Uncle Trevor and Aunt Ronnie."

"Whoa, Taylor, slow down. You can tell everyone you want, but I wouldn't throw a parade in your own honor. There may be some very unhappy people. Be proud of yourself. Hold your head high, but don't gloat."

"I wouldn't do that," Taylor assured her.

"Good. I don't want to see any other incidents take place like what happened this past weekend."

"Speaking of incidents this past weekend, can I talk to you about another issue my family is having? I think my cousin could use your advice."

***

The pain hit her like a shot in the chest. Kate's memories came flooding back from the first time she felt pain like this. She grabbed at the counter that separated the tellers from the bank customers, seeking some kind of support.

"Kate!" Tammi yelled, reaching for her friend across the counter. "Someone help! Call 911."

Kate felt arms around her as she blacked out. Her last thought was of little Miren, whose cries began to fade as the world went silent.

***

"It never ends," Taylor said to Nick while they waited for their dinner to arrive. "As soon as someone gets good news, something bad happens."

Nick had heard the 911 call and immediately texted Taylor, taking some of the air out of her balloon.

"I'm sure everything is okay. Isn't it normal for pregnant women to faint?"

Taylor frowned. "Only on soap operas." She took a sip of her water. "I'm just worried because of her heart condition. Hopefully, there's nothing wrong."

"She seemed just fine on Sunday. I'm sure she's okay."

The waiter approached with their plates as the door opened, and Chad walked in with Holly on his arm.

Taylor smiled and waved them over. Most of Taylor's friends from high school had moved away and started lives in other towns and other cities, so she was thrilled when she and Holly hit it off after Holly arrived in town. Taylor had never thought of her and Chad as a protentional couple but seeing them together made sense.

Nick and Chad shook hands, a much more congenial greeting than the first time they met.

"How are my two best friends?" Taylor asked, giving Chad a wink.

"We're doing great, and I hear congratulations are in order." Chad pulled her up from the booth and gave her a hug.

Holly followed suit. "We're so happy for you. You're going to put those men in their places."

Taylor shook her head. "No, I'm sure I have a lot to learn from them, and it was never about that. It was only about me and others like me who want to be part of the roundup, the swim, and the penning. I don't have anything against any of the men and look forward to working with them."

"That's big of you, Taylor," Chad said.

She shrugged. "Not at all. I don't blame any of the members. It was the system that was wrong. Hopefully, that ended today."

"Well, we won't keep you two from eating," Chad said. "Again, Taylor, congratulations."

She thanked him and watched them take their seats across the room.

"Everything seems to be good between you two," Nick said.

"I think everything is better than good." She beamed. "I think Chad and I finally know where we stand and what we mean to each other. Now, let's say grace. I'm starving."

***

When Kayla's friend, Dr. Debbie Swann, entered the exam room, Aaron shot to his feet.

"Debbie, what the heck is going on? Dr. Sprance said it was safe." Aaron charged at the woman he had known his entire life, a woman he trusted. "He said her heart could handle another pregnancy."

"He did, and I concur." Dr. Swann responded in her naturally calm and collected way. "I conferred with Dr. Sprance and with Kate's heart surgeon, Dr. Carter, and none of us believe that Kate's mitral stenosis is the cause of her fainting spell." Dr. Swann leaned against the counter and began to smile. "Kate's having an ordinary, run-of-the mill pregnancy. No problems with her heart or anything else."

"Then what made her black out?" Aaron asked, his own heart feeling as though it was being ripped from his chest. He glanced at Kate who looked pale even next to the sterile white walls and bedding. She seemed to relax at the doctor's words.

"I think it was an anxiety attack."

"Anxiety attack? I'm not anxious." Kate gazed at Dr. Swann.

"How about I ask you some questions, then, and we'll see if we can get to the bottom of this. First, Kate, when was the last time you ate?"

"I ate breakfast. I haven't had a chance to get lunch yet."

"Maybe you should start having some light snacks between meals." Dr. Swann glanced at Kate's chart. "What about your anticoagulation medications? Are you taking them as prescribed?"

"Absolutely," Kate assured her. "But…"

"No buts. Without that medication, we can't guarantee that your heart will continue functioning properly."

"I know, and I'm taking them." Kate bit her bottom lip. "But I'm afraid. I can't watch another baby from a window, hold her in the palm of my hand while wearing gloves and a mask, spend months praying that she gains an ounce. I need to bring this baby to term, full-term."

"Miren is healthy," Aaron reminded her. "She gained weight, she's growing, she's on target with her development. There's nothing wrong with her." He shook his head. "I mean, even if she was behind or disabled in some way, there would still be nothing wrong with her, but she's *not*."

"I know. It's just that—"

"Kate," Dr. Swann began. "I think we've discovered the source of your anxiety, but if you have any thoughts, whatsoever, about stopping the meds, get them out of your head. Do you understand?"

Kate nodded. "Okay, but I did some research and read some studies. There have been women who went off the meds and carried their babies to term without incident. Of the ones who stayed on the meds, most had pre-term babies, and many had miscarriages. I was thinking that maybe I'm healthy enough to be one of the ones who could go without meds." She looked at them with hope in her eyes, and Aaron's anger dissipated. As frightened as he was, he couldn't imagine how she felt.

"Kate," Dr. Swann said, standing and walking toward her. "We will monitor you very closely. There are things we can do to prolong gestation. There's nothing that guarantees that you will go into pre-term labor just as there's nothing that leads me to believe you won't carry to full-term. You were doing well the last time, before you even had surgery, and might have gone full-term, or near-term, if not for the, ah, incident."

"If Mark hadn't shown up and tried to kidnap her," Aaron supplied.

"Yes," the doctor agreed. She spread her hands wide in front of her. "I'm going to do everything I can to make sure this baby stays inside where he or she belongs for as long as possible. So will Dr. Sprance if we need him. Will you agree to do the same?"

"Yes." Kate looked contrite, and Aaron wanted to scoop her in his arms and promise her that everything was going to be okay.

Dr. Swann put her hand on Kate's shoulder. "Keep taking your meds and eat regularly. No skipping meals. Eat some healthy snacks. And continue your regular check-ups. Kate, you're still young and strong. You should have no trouble carrying this baby to term."

Kate inhaled and closed her eyes, nodding her agreement.

"Good." Dr. Swann clapped her hands together. "Come back and see me in two weeks."

"Thank you, Doctor," Aaron said.

"Just promise me one thing, Kate." Kate looked at the doctor. "Stay off of the Internet. No more reading studies and trying to be the doctor. Let me do my job." She turned and left, closing the door behind them.

Once they were alone, Aaron wrapped his arms around her. "You're my whole world, Princess. You and Miren." He pulled back and looked her in the eye. "I know you're stressed. And I know it was hard when Miren was in the hospital all those months, but if the alternative is losing you, I'm willing to do it over again. Please, don't let your fears get in the way of us spending a long, happy life together."

"I'm so afraid I'll lose the baby."

"You won't. Everything is different now. You've had surgery. You're on medication. You're healthy. Mark's not a threat. It's all going to be okay." He gently took her face in his hand. "I promise."

Kate swallowed and nodded. "I love you," she whispered.

"I love you, too. More than you'll ever know. Now, let's get to Tammi's and pick up Miren. I'm taking the rest of the day off to spend it with my favorite girls."

***

"How's Kate?" Zach anxiously answered his phone. He'd been calling his sister and Aaron for over an hour, but neither had answered. As soon as Zach read the text from Aaron and relayed the information to Kayla, they said a prayer. The ride home from

Kayla's appointment in Baltimore had felt painfully long.

"She's fine. Stressed but fine."

Zach gripped the wheel and listened as Aaron relayed what the doctor said. He gritted his teeth as he thought of his hard-headed sister.

"Thanks, Aaron. You tell her that I'm not dropping everything to sit by her bedside this time. She better listen to the doctor."

After saying goodbye, Zach repeated Aaron's rundown of the situation to Kayla.

"Thank heaven she's okay. But don't try to convince me that you wouldn't give everything up to take care of your sister again."

Zach sighed. "You know I would, and so does she. I just wish she wasn't so worried. The baby is fine, and everything else is just stuff. It will all come together. But I don't like that she's worried about her meds."

He ran his hand over his face as he pictured Kate in the ambulance that horrible night over a year ago. He glanced at Kayla and saw a strange look on her face. "What?"

"I get it," she said, leaning back in her seat and pushing her short hair from her face. It had started growing in faster and was covering her head in wispy curls that made her look ten years younger. Zach loved it, but Kayla wasn't so sure. She told him that she had wanted naturally curly hair all her life, but now that she had it, she had no idea what to do with it.

"Kate's scared," Kayla said. "She's not sure if the medicine is safe for the baby, and she can't help but think of what she can do to increase the odds in favor of the child."

"How would it increase the odds if she risks killing herself?"

"I didn't say it was rational. I said, I get where she's coming from. If we decided to have a baby, I would be worried to death about the cocktail of drugs I take every day."

"Kayla, sweetheart." He glanced at her, wishing he wasn't driving so he could take her in his arms. "You know that I'm okay with not having a baby, right? EJ and Todd are mine, and I'm proud to be their dad."

"I know. And I'm no spring chicken anymore. Between my age and the cancer, it would be difficult to say the least, especially with the possibility of going into chemo-induced menopause, but if we did decide to try, I wouldn't want to be taking any meds either."

Zach glanced over and tried to read her expression. "First, you're not old, menopause or not. Second, you're healthy now, and we don't need to jeopardize that in any way, including doing something that would mean you have to stop taking meds." He frowned. "I mean, you are healthy, right? Everything is good with…?" He raised his brow and gestured to her breasts.

"Everything is fine." She swallowed, and her breasts tingled as if they could sense that they were the topic of conversation. "I just hope that everything is fine with us." She rolled her lips, and he saw the same old question in her eyes.

"I just told you, didn't I? I love you, and I love the boys. We're the perfect family. I don't want it any other way."

He saw the tear glistening in her eye and longed to wipe it away.

"Besides," he said with a lopsided grin, "I like having you all to myself when the boys are at school."

"Zach, hush." She blushed and looked out the window but started laughing. "You're incorrigible."

"Yes, but you love me anyway."

"I do." She frowned. "I just…"

"Hey." He reached for her hand and gave it a squeeze. "I love you. We have a great life. I will never hide anything from you or lie to you, and I will do everything in my power to make sure that Eddie's secrets and lies don't hurt you anymore either."

Kayla blinked away a tear and gave him a loving smile. "Thank you," she whispered. "For being here. For being you."

"Always." He squeezed her hand again and locked his eyes on the road ahead.

Zach's heart tugged. He would do anything to protect her, to protect his family. It was who he was, and that would never change.

***

Will Cheney must have had some big connections at the newspaper because the article was in the next day's edition. Taylor smiled as she read the news under the title, *Chincoteague's Saltwater Cowgirl*. She finished her coffee, cleaned up her breakfast dishes, and hummed as she went to brush her teeth. When she reached the barn to help load the day's equipment, she was met with an eerie silence. Where was everyone? She called out names as she walked to the back part of the building where the crew kept their personal gear. Their trucks were all there. Where were they?

She didn't hear a sound when she entered the room and didn't sense the movement behind her. She let out a scream when two sets of strong arms grabbed her and hoisted her into the air.

"Hip, hip, hurray!" went up the cheer as Mickey and Clay lifted her again and again to the chant. As the men whistled and clapped, she was carried around the room like the Queen of Sheba.

Taylor laughed and told them to put her down. They had scared the daylights out of her, but it was worth the few minutes they shaved off her life. She laughed as the men all took turns shaking her hand.

"I knew they'd come to their senses," Clay said. "We all did."

She watched as Joey and Earl carried a cake from the make-shift breakroom that used to hold equestrian tack. The cake showed a cowgirl on a horse, twirling a lasso over her head and read, *Congratulations Saltwater Cowgirl.*

Taylor didn't try to stop the tears that flowed down her cheeks. She may have lost her father, but she had this ragtag group of men in her life who were there for her, and she loved every one of them.

There wasn't a cloud in the sky when Taylor spread the blanket on the warm Assateague sand. The beach was crowded, but she didn't care. The guys had insisted she take the day off, and though she'd missed more time in the past month than she had in the past two years, she was looking forward to a day with no stress and no commitments. Nick would be on the schedule for the next several days, but he was off today, and they were going to enjoy themselves.

Children waded in the water, teens rode boogie boards in the surf, and women sat in beach chairs with books perched on their thighs. Assateague and Chincoteague were both teeming with tourists, and they couldn't have asked for a more perfect day. It was hot but not blistering hot, and a salty breeze blew off the ocean. Taylor asked Nick to rub sunscreen on her back.

"It's going to be crazy on the island for the next month. I'm glad we've got today to relax before I start working double shifts," Nick said. His hands caressed her shoulders, more of a massage than an application of lotion. She wondered if he could feel the tension that she'd built up over the past few weeks and if he knew how good his hands felt on her skin.

"Me, too." She closed her eyes and allowed herself to relax into his touch. "We're switching into July mode, and we'll have long, hot days, cutting grass, irrigating, and weeding."

She felt Nick's hands kneading her shoulders and wanted to moan.

"I thought you just did specialty designing and planting. I didn't know you were a full-service lawn care business."

"Something has to pay the bills when it's too hot to plant. I've got six men who depend on those paychecks. And I'd get bored if I didn't have a full-time job."

"Did you always want to go into landscape design?"

She shrugged. "Yeah, pretty much. I mean, I really wanted to be a barrel racer, but my mother said, no way."

Nick chuckled. "I can understand that. But why don't you work with horses full time?"

She turned around and sat facing him on the blanket. Without his hands on her back, she shivered. The heat of the sun couldn't compare to the heat of his hands. "I don't know. There's not much need for that on the island. The most I get to work with them is after the pony auction when people hire me to break their ponies."

"Why do they call it that? It seems so harsh."

"You're right, but it's not harsh. The term goes back to the days of cattle drives when trainers were under pressure to tame horses quickly so that they could be useful. Back then, it was harsh, and many say the goal was to 'break' the horse's spirit. Today, though, most of us use a much gentler approach. I like to get to know the pony, convince her to trust me, and work together as a team to train her to do as she's told. It's not unlike training a dog."

"So, people buy ponies and ask you to break them?"

"Sometimes. If they live close enough. Every now and then, they will leave the pony with me until it's ready to go to its new home. I'm not a fan of that though," she said honestly. "It causes the horse to bond with me and not the owner, and it makes it hard for him when it's time to leave. I'd rather work on their farm with the primary rider or caregiver nearby."

"So, you're content here on the island?"

Taylor scrutinized his face, trying to figure out where he was going with the question. "I am. It's home. There's not really any other place I've ever wanted to live. Living in Blacksburg was nice when I was at Virginia Tech, but I prefer the beach to the mountains."

He pulled her to him. "Well, I'm sure as heck glad you're here." He looked in her eyes. "Because I'm not planning on going anywhere either."

"Wanna take a walk?" She asked.

Nodding, Nick stood and reached for her hand. Taylor accepted and let him pull her up.

For several minutes, they silently walked down the beach, hand-in-hand, until they stopped to watch someone reel in a nice trout.

"That day on your boat was a lot of fun. We'll have to do that again after the July crazy days are over."

"I'd like that." Nick pulled her to him and wrapped his arm around her. They continued walking. "After all, I have to outdo you next time."

Taylor expelled a laugh. "Oh, really? We'll see about that."

Nick was silent for a moment before he stopped walking. He took hold of her shoulders and turned her to face him. "Taylor, I just want you to know that the past month…it's been the best month of my life.

She turned her gaze up to meet his eyes. "You know, that day Daddy had his heart attack, was the worst day of my entire life. Riding to the hospital in the back of your car, I was so scared. I knew that, if Daddy died, nothing would ever be the same, and I would never be able to smile or laugh or enjoy anything ever again. You changed that, Nick. You showed me that it was okay to keep going, to keep living. You have no idea how much that means to me."

"Taylor, I hope to spend a very long time making you happy."

With the sun shining down upon them, and the foamy waves lapping at their feet, Taylor and Nick stood in each other's arms. When Nick leaned down and pressed his lips to hers, Taylor felt a surge of energy course through her veins. She knew she was falling hard and fast, and she welcomed the thrill of it all.

I learned a long time ago that family isn't always those people to whom we are related by blood and marriage. Sometimes, those people aren't family at all. Real families are the made up of people who are there for each other, care about each other's welfare, and would do anything to help one another through life's most difficult moments. God has blessed me with two families—my real family and my island family. The indigenous people of Hawaii understand this wider concept of family. 'Ohana' doesn't just mean close relatives; it encompasses extended family and neighbors. Perhaps that's what living on an island is all about—creating ohanas.

From *Discovering the World On a Barrier Island*
by Katherine Middleton Kelly

CHAPTER FIFTEEN

"Surprise!"

Kate held back tears as she looked around the room. Since this was her second pregnancy, she hadn't even considered that her friends would give her a shower.

At the forefront of the group, stood Kayla. Kate rushed to her sister-in-law and embraced her.

"You did this, didn't you?"

"Your first shower wasn't exactly traditional."

"What? Not all pregnant women have a baby shower in their bedroom while on strict bedrest?"

Kayla laughed. "Only you, Kate."

Kate wiped away more tears as she greeted the other party-goers. Over a crab cake and salad lunch, the women discussed all that was happening in their lives. They were all thrilled for Taylor, but she refused to steal any of Kate's thunder.

Before they cut the cake, Kate opened presents. Once again, Tammi outdid herself with a magnificent baby blanket. This time, rather than a crocheted blanket, she made a lightweight quilt with delicate, machine-embroidered doves and olive branches adorning the corners.

"It's a prayer sewn into a quilt—that your baby may be blessed with all the fruits of the Holy Spirit and live a life of peace and prosperity."

Kate wept at the thought of the prayer and hugged Tammi, knowing she could never adequately thank her for the gift of the quilt and the gift of her friendship.

Anne's gift was a simple but stunning mosaic of an angel. "It's a replica of one of the mosaics discovered at the Church of the Nativity in Bethlehem. I thought your baby could use an angel to watch over him or her."

Shannon gave a collection of children's books for both the new baby and for Miren. Among them were some of Kate's childhood favorites.

"How did you know?" Kate asked as she blinked away more tears.

"Your mother told me about all the books she read to you and Zach when you were children, living in remote places around the world. I thought you might like to share those books with your own children."

An avid traveler, Marian gave Kate a print with a traditional Irish prayer,

> *May God give you...*
> *For every storm, a rainbow,*
> *For every tear, a smile,*
> *For every care, a promise,*
> *And a blessing in each trial.*

For every problem life sends,
A faithful friend to share,
For every sigh, a sweet song,
And an answer for each prayer.

Kate shed more tears as she read the prayer. She hugged Marian.

Kate was in awe of how far she had come in the past two years and how many wonderful friends she now had.

Donna handed Kate a large box that was covered with pastel-colored bows and ribbons.

"It's from the three of us," she said.

Kate gently lifted the lid of the box and gasped. "Oh, Donna. They're magnificent." She lifted the delicately crocheted baby sweater for everyone to see. Next to the sweater was a delicate little hat, and beneath them was a blanket.

"I'm glad you like them. The girls picked the colors. Jenny so wanted to be here when you opened it, but work got in the way."

"I love the colors, Taylor. They're all my favorites. Thank you, Donna."

Every gift was special, but the most special one of all was from Kayla. She and Zach had managed to get a hold of the antique baby cradle that was in the attic of the Middleton home in Georgetown, which Kate's parents had recently sold. The cradle, now lovingly restored, was used by Kate's mother and her mother before her. Though Kate was born in a hospital in

Africa, Zach had lain in the cradle as an infant. Kate couldn't help but wonder if it pained her brother to know that he would probably never put his own baby to sleep in the family heirloom, but she quickly dismissed the thought. Zach was no longer a man of regret, and she knew that he loved the family he now had with all of his heart.

Kate looked around at the women, the food, and the decorations and felt enormously blessed. She marveled at what Kayla could accomplish. Despite recovering from cancer, throwing a recent wedding reception, trying her best to avoid that pesky reporter, and reeling from the discovery about her late husband, Kayla had managed to pull off a surprise shower for Kate. Some women truly are Wonder Women.

***

Taylor watched the other women and felt inspired by them. They had true friends, loving families, and good lives. Despite losing her father, Taylor knew that she was one lucky woman.

As she listened to the conversations and watched Kate packing up her presents, Taylor had a thought. All of these women had something in common—their unwavering faith in God and participation in their church community.

Sitting in that room, surrounded by those women, seeing their happiness despite all that each of them had gone through at some point in their lives—Tammi who had lost a son, Kayla who had lost a husband, Marian who had struggled with infertility, Kate who had almost lost her life to her ex, she and her mother losing her father—Taylor realized they all knew something that she had been taught but had never really given any thought to. Having the perfect life wasn't what mattered. It was having the faith that joy could be found even during the trials, the heartache, and the fears that are inevitable throughout life. No matter what these women went through, they had faith that God would see them through it and that there was greater joy waiting for them when their earthly trials were over.

***

"You look happy," Nick told Taylor after they put in their drink order at Etta's. The temperature outside was scorching, but the view of the Channel through the restaurant windows was spectacular. The Assateague Lighthouse was visible, and Taylor could make out two ponies grazing in the marsh.

"I am happy." She looked like she was on top of the world. "You know what I realized today?"

"Tell me." Nick bent closer and gazed at her across the table, his heart bursting with happiness as well.

"I realized that I'm pretty darn lucky."

Chuckling, Nick sat back in his seat. "Well, you're with me, aren't you?"

Taylor shook her head. "You're incorrigible. But yes, that's part of it. At the shower today, I was thinking about how blessed we all are—me, Kayla, Kate, Tammi, everyone. Even though life hasn't been easy for everyone, and has been downright tragic for some, we're all really blessed."

Nick looked at her and wondered where this was leading. "And?"

Taylor lifted and released her shoulders. "I don't know. I was just thinking about how good God has been to all of us."

"You put a lot of faith in something you've never seen."

Taylor sat up straighter. "Don't you? I mean, I thought you believed in God."

"I do. I even went to church quite often when I was overseas. In a place like that, you had to have something to believe in."

"But not here?"

The waitress stopped by with their drinks and asked if they would like to order.

"Fried pickles, please." Nick looked at Taylor. "Anything else to start?"

"No, that sounds good. Thanks." After the waitress left, Taylor looked back at Nick. "So, you believed in God when you were fighting a war, but you don't believe now?"

"No, it's not that. I don't know. I guess, when things are this good, I don't feel like I need to think about God. I mean, he's still there, but I don't really need his help right now."

Taylor slowly nodded. "So, your philosophy is, you only think about God when you need him."

Nick squirmed in his seat. He wasn't sure how to answer that. "I guess I never really thought about it before."

Taylor leaned across the table. "Well, how about you think about this…You're off tomorrow morning. I'm going to Mass. You should go with me." She sat back and studied him, waiting for an answer.

Nick reached up and scratched an itch above his ear. "I could do that."

"It's settled then," Taylor said triumphantly.

The waitress placed the fried pickles on the table. "Are you ready to order your meals?"

"We are," Taylor said. She proceeded to place her order.

Nick wasn't sure he was ready to order. He wasn't sure he was ready for anything. Taylor was the perfect woman for him, but maybe he wasn't perfect for her. Maybe she was looking for something he didn't know how to provide and wasn't completely sure he wanted to.

***

"It's been a long time, Nick. Welcome back." Nick wasn't sure how to take the words of the priest, Father Darryl. Was he admonishing Nick for not being at

Mass for a while, or was he genuinely pleased that Nick was there?

"Thanks, Father." Nick ducked quickly through the doors and scanned the church. He spotted Taylor, her mother, and her sister near the front of the church, on the opposite side from Zach, Kayla, and all of the Kelly crew. He made his way up the aisle, genuflected, and sat in the pew beside Taylor. He'd been to Mass many times, but he felt anxious. He'd barely slept, kept awake by the thought that he wasn't the man Taylor was looking for. Was he even good enough for her? For the first time since they'd met, he wondered if their upbringings were too different.

Taylor came from obvious wealth, even if she didn't flaunt it and really didn't seem to care about it. Nick grew up without two pennies to rub together. She was college educated and ran her own business. He earned his GED and served in the military. He would probably spend the rest of his life working as a police officer, advancing only so far due to his lack of education.

When Taylor reached for his hand, his grip felt stiff, and he wondered if she noticed. He swallowed and looked down. Was it his imagination, or did their hands look strange together? Her strong, tanned, firm hand in his pale, somewhat stubby fingers with nails bitten so far down they sometimes hurt. As the music began to play, and they stood for the entrance procession, Nick couldn't help but wonder if he'd been living a fantasy for the past several weeks and if it was time to face reality.

***

Taylor watched Nick walk away. A thick feeling of discomfort filled her stomach as though it had been poured into her like a can of paint, coating her insides with a nearly impossible-to-remove stain. When Ronnie had invited them back to the house for Sunday dinner, Nick suddenly remembered an errand he had to run before work. When they hugged, his embrace felt rigid and cold, and he didn't kiss her, or even meet her eyes, when he let go and said goodbye.

"Everything okay?" Jenny asked.

"I'm not sure." She frowned as Nick's car pulled out of the parking lot. There was no glance her way, no wave or smile.

"Did something happen?"

"Not that I know of. Maybe I pushed too hard." Was that it? Had she forced him to go to church? Had she pressured him about his belief in God? They had such an easy, open relationship. There had never been anything they couldn't say or share, no subjects off-limits.

"How did you push him? What happened?"

Taylor needed time to think. "I, uh, I…" She forced a smile. "I'm sure it's nothing. Let's go. I want to take Big Red to the island today to start warming up for the swim. It's only a couple weeks away."

Though Jenny didn't press her, Taylor felt her sister's questioning gaze as they walked to Donna's car. If Nick was that uncomfortable about going to church, maybe he wasn't the man she'd been waiting for after all. The thought made her heart ache.

***

Nick paced the deck of the boat. He had a few hours before he needed to report to the station, but he couldn't decide how to spend them. Ordinarily, he wouldn't hesitate. There was only one person he wanted to spend any off-duty time with, but he was having a hard time giving her a call. He was afraid that he had let himself get caught up in a Disney-proportion fairy tale of his own making. What could Taylor possibly see in him? How soon would it be before she realized they just weren't cut from the same cloth?

"You going fishing or just testing the sturdiness of those boards?"

Nick squinted as he turned toward Zach, the late-afternoon sun dazzling overhead.

"Just thinking."

"Mind if I board?"

"Be my guest."

Zach hopped on board and took a seat on the side of the boat.

"What's up?"

Nick sighed and took a seat next to him. "Nothing. Just have some stuff on my mind."

"Care to talk about it?"

"I don't know." Nick looked out at the water for a moment then shook his head. "You wouldn't understand."

"Try me."

"Taylor and me, I just don't think it's going to work between us."

"Why? I thought things were going great."

Nick lifted his shoulders and let them drop back down, feeling as though they were weighed down with worry and regret. "I thought so, too, but the reality is, we come from such different worlds. If we stayed together, the day would come, sooner rather than later, when she would realize I'm just not the man for her."

"Why would you say that?"

"Oh, I don't know. Maybe because she's beautiful and smart and talented in so many ways, and I'm just me. I didn't actually graduate from high school. I never went to college. I enlisted because I didn't know what else to do with my life. I'll never make enough to keep her in the lifestyle she's used to. And about a hundred other reasons."

Zach eyed Nick. A muscle in his jaw twitched, and Nick recognized it as a sign that Zach was weighing his options, trying to find the right thing to say. So, even Zach knew Nick was right.

"I'm not sure you know Taylor as well as you think you do."

Nick squinted his eyes as he studied his friend. "Meaning what?"

"Meaning, you're not giving Taylor enough credit. From what I've been told, she worshipped her father. She thought he could do no wrong. But he enlisted right out of high school. When he got out, he busted his butt to get his degree and build a business. He was an honest, hard-working man who made something of himself, but he started with nothing. Do you think Taylor loves him any less for that?"

Nick shook his head. "It's not the same."

"It's not? What about Trevor? Kayla told me he had a past worse than yours. Did you know that his father killed his mother?

Nick's eyes widened. "He did?"

"He did. Apparently, he beat her to death. He beat Trevor, too. Trevor had nothing. It was Taylor's grandparents who took him in and treated him like a son. Do you think Taylor would look down on you when her family has always thought the world of Trevor?"

Nick gazed across the horizon. He watched an osprey swoop down low, glide across the water—it's talons scraping the surface—and rise back up with a shiny fish in its grasp.

"I don't know, man. She's just out of my league. And she's all about going to church and all. I don't know if that's for me."

"You're the one who got me going back to church, remember?"

"Yeah, but that was different. We were facing death every day. It seemed like the right thing to do at the time."

"And you don't think you're still facing death every day?" Zach looked intently at Nick. "You don't think you could leave here tonight and get shot by some idiot with a concealed weapon?"

"Here? I hardly think so."

"Yeah, and I'm sure that's what Kate thought when Mark showed up on the island. And how about Todd? You think he went to school that day thinking, 'Today, I might get kidnapped and be left for dead in the marsh'? You don't think you could get caught in a sudden storm, lose control of your car, and end up wrapped around a tree? My wife could have died last winter. None of us knows when our number is going to be called."

Nick considered Zach's words. "I guess you're right, but still...Taylor expects me to be something I'm not."

"And just what does she expect you to be, Nick? A good person? A caring individual who looks out for the people he loves? A man who works hard to make a good, honest living? Because that's what I see when I look at you."

Nick stood and walked to the other side of the boat. He took a deep breath before turning around. "I love her, man. I don't know how or when that happened, but I love her. What if she takes a good, hard look at me and realizes she doesn't love me back?"

Zach stood. "There's only one way to find out, my friend. Be the man you are, not the man you think someone else wants you to be, and continue to treat her well. Show her you love her. When the time is right, tell her you love her. Then just let things unfold. You don't need to rush into anything. Let it happen naturally."

Nick looked at Zach and grinned. "I can't believe I just told you that I love her. God help me. I really love her."

Zach laughed and clapped Nick on the back. "No, Nick, God help her. I'll see you later. I've got to get to dinner at Ronnie and Trevor's" He climbed back up onto the dock, looking at the new boards that extended the pier. "You know, you did a pretty good job with this dock."

"I had help."

"Yes, you did. Life's funny like that. Often, we think we can tackle things on our own, and most of the time, we end up making out pretty well, but sometimes, we need to rely on others to help us out. Asking for that help can be the hardest part; but seeing when help is needed and being there when the time comes to lend a hand, that's what really counts. And sometimes, it's the man upstairs you need to ask. Try it, Nick. You might get more answers than you expected. You might even find that you like what he has to say."

Nick watched Zach head toward his house and thought about what he said.

"You know," Nick yelled, "you're becoming quite the philosopher in your old age."

Zach kept walking down the long stretch of the newly extended pier until he made his way, over the marsh, to the dry land. He raised his hand in a silent wave, and Nick smiled. The second-best thing he ever did was track Zach down on this island. The best thing? Well, that was responding to that call all those weeks back that led him to Taylor's ranch.

***

Taylor closed the back of the trailer and climbed into her truck. The sun was setting, but the air was still broiling and saturated with humidity. She and Big Red had had a good ride. Her dad would be pleased. She smiled as she thought of him looking down on her and Big Red, both now and on the big day.

When Taylor passed by the police department, she wondered what Nick was doing. Was he out on patrol somewhere? And what was going on with him that morning? What was she missing?

She turned onto the long road that led to the ranch. It was getting dark fast. A black cloud hung low over the trees ahead. Out of nowhere, a long, white streak raced across the sky, cracking it open like a dropped flower pot.

Without warning, the trailer swerved, causing Taylor to nearly lose control of the truck. She glanced in her rearview mirror and saw that the trailer was sagging on one side, pulling hard on the truck. It caused her to swerve again as the clouds released a sudden, violent cascade of rain. It was all she could do to keep the vehicle on the road. She tried to brake without losing control. The trailer began to tilt, and her heart raced.

Please, God, no. Don't let it go over.

She gripped the wheel and fought the pull of the horse-filled trailer. Another crack in the sky caused her to lose focus. She looked back as the trailer began to go over, and she held on tight, knowing the truck was going to go with it.

***

Kate began feeling the pains not long after the early dinner at Ronnie's. She tried to convince herself that it was nothing, but as time went on, there was no denying what was happening. Willing herself not to panic, she called 911, Debbie, and Aaron, in that order.

Please no, not again. Please, God. It's too soon.

"It's going to be okay," Aaron assured her. She heard him tell his co-workers that he was leaving. He continued to reassure her as the background sounds changed from office sounds to whistling winds and distant thunder as he hurried to his truck.

Kate made her way to the back of the house and gently nudged her sleeping child.

"Sweetie, it's time to wake up. I think the baby's coming." Kate tried to smile, but she feared that it was more of a grimace; her worry plagued her. She hastily packed the diaper bag and heard Aaron's truck engine start through the phone. Kate held the phone with her shoulder and reached down to pick up Miren but was gripped with pain.

"I've got her," Zach said from behind. He lifted the little girl up and put his hand on Kate's back. "Aaron texted me. Let's go." Kate could hear sirens growing closer.

Suddenly, Kate felt a gush of fluid down her legs. She looked at her brother as she spoke to Aaron over the phone.

"My water just broke." Her voice trembled. It was too soon. Her worse fears about this pregnancy were coming to fruition.

"Okay, don't worry. It's going to be okay. Is Zach there?"

She nodded, wondering how he could sound so calm.

"Princess?"

"Sorry. Yes, he has Miren."

"Very good. I'm almost there."

She followed Zach to the front door. He opened the door as the paramedics rushed up the steps to the house. They popped open the stretcher and helped Kate position herself so that they could carry her outside. She heard the growing rumble of thunder and prayed it wasn't a bad sign.

"Where will you take her?" Zach asked as Tori wrapped a blood pressure cuff around her arm.

"You tell us," Tori said, looking at Kate. "Riverside or Norfolk?" Tori and Jimmy had been the paramedics who responded to all of Kate's prior emergencies. They knew her case, but they would need her to give them some direction this time. She had to think.

"I don't know." Kate tried to remember the plan that she and her doctors had put together. "I think you need to check my heart first. Yes, that's right. Here's the plan."

She relayed the plan that she and Debbie had gone over several times. Unless the paramedics detected anything abnormal, she would go to the island hospital and attempt natural labor. If her heart showed any signs of distress, she would be sent by helicopter to Norfolk where Dr. Sprance would be waiting.

"Okay. Let's check you out," Tori said, pumping air into the cuff. She listened to Kate's heart.

"Blood pressure and heart sounds are normal."

"Aaron, did you hear that?" Kate's normal heart fluttered with relief.

"I did, and I'm pulling up."

Knowing Aaron was there, and her heart was stable, Kate no longer held back the tears. Still holding a sleepy Miren, her brother grabbed her hand and squeezed it as she was rolled out onto the porch.

"Kate, I'm going to take Miren to your dad and get your mom. We'll follow you. Do you need anything?"

"Prayers?"

"Of course." Zach let her go as they reached the bottom of the steps where Aaron was waiting in the rain. "I'll see you there."

Kate saw Aaron nod toward Zach before she was lifted into the ambulance. Once she was settled and Aaron was on board, the doors slammed shut. Kate, who was unconscious during Miren's emergency birth, prayed as she had never prayed before.

In the jungles of South America, I witnessed the birth of a child. I was a child myself, frightened but awed by the sight. I watched from behind some bushes, knowing I was intruding, fearing my parents' wrath if they found out. But I couldn't look away, couldn't move, couldn't contain my emotions. Though I was very young, I understood in that moment that what I was seeing was much more than a mother giving birth. As my gaze moved from one member of the tribe to another, I felt the bond they shared, the closeness that held them all together, the miracle that they all participated in as one. It remains one of the most intimate and moving experiences of my life. The only other time I felt anything close to that was when I gave birth to Miren, and I knew that half the island was nearby—hoping, praying, and sending life-giving love.

From *Discovering the World On a Barrier Island*
by Katherine Middleton Kelly

CHAPTER SIXTEEN

Taylor opened her eyes to the sound of loud braying and kicking. Big Red. He needed her. The truck was on its side, and she was wet. Rain seeped in through the cracked windshield. She took a minute to assess her pain and decided it was minor. She ran her hand around her head, neck, and arms and felt for blood. She was okay. What about her horse?

She undid the seatbelt and tried to open the door. It was too heavy. She moved away from the steering wheel and kicked the already cracked windshield. Nothing. She opened the glove box and searched for something, anything. She reached under the seat, felt something hard, and pulled out a crowbar. She had no idea why it was there but thanked God for it. Taylor remembered the sweatshirt that had been in the backseat for weeks, months maybe, and managed to reach it. Another miracle on top of many she had experienced so far in that short span of time since the vehicle rolled. She pulled it over her face for protection and slammed the crowbar against the glass window.

After several attempts, it shattered, and she used the crowbar to push away the glass as rain drenched her. Laying out the sweatshirt, hoping it would provide some defense against the jagged glass, she felt only one rip in her shirt and the skin beneath it as she pushed herself over the hood and onto the fender of the truck. Carefully, Taylor eased herself to the wet ground.

Barely catching her breath, she jumped up and ran to the trailer. She called to the horse as she fumbled with the door. Just as she was about to give up, headlights reflected off the metal door. She turned and waved frantically at the approaching vehicle.

Her neighbor, Dan Leve, jumped from the vehicle. "Taylor, are you okay?" He yelled over the roar of the storm.

"I'm okay. But Big Red is in the trailer."

It took both of them several minutes and strength that Taylor never imagined she could muster to fight the rain and wind and gravity that held the door closed. Once the door was open, they found the horse worn out from desperation and fear. There were dents where he had tried to kick himself free, but the harnesses had done their job and held him in place during the fall. From what Taylor could see, the horse looked unharmed.

Dan helped her undo the harnesses and ease the horse out into the rain. Taylor didn't know how they managed to get him out without any one of the three of them getting seriously hurt. The rain was just beginning to let up when Taylor stood beside Big Red and ran her hands over his body, assessing any damage. Dan called 911, and man, woman, and horse waited in the road for help to arrive, under a clearing sky.

***

"Breathe, Kate, breathe." Debbie was positioned between her legs, and Aaron stood by her head, brushing her hair back from her face.

"You can do this, Princess. It's almost over."

Kate shot Aaron a look of disdain, and he bit his tongue. He knew she was in pain, but he didn't know how to help her other than by offering words of support and encouragement.

"I see the head, Kate. You're doing great. Take a break, and then we're going to give it one good push when I say. Okay?"

"We? There's no 'we' doing the pushing."

Aaron held back a smile. He wondered if there was something wrong with him, but man, was she sexy when she was feisty. Even with sweat pouring down her beet-red face, her feet up in stirrups, and her hair matted to the top of her head, she was beautiful.

Kate collapsed on the bed, her head thrown back on the pillow, her eyes closed. Aaron rubbed an ice chip on her lips. With the force of an express train, Kate sat up in the bed. Her hands gripped the bed rails, the red in her face deepened, and she let out a blood-curdling scream.

"This is it, Kate," Debbie yelled. "Push, push hard!"

Kate was the one who screamed, but Aaron felt as if he were the one being ripped apart. There is no pain that compares to that which is felt when a loved one is beyond your help. If he could, Aaron would take all of her pain upon himself.

He held her hand, losing feeling in his fingers as she squeezed harder than he would have thought possible.

When the cry broke out, and Kate collapsed back onto the pillow, Aaron felt a release that made him weak in his knees.

***

For the second time that evening, the call went out for an ambulance. Nick half-listened to the exchange between the caller and the dispatcher.

"911, what is your emergency?"

"There's been an accident. An overturned truck and horse trailer on Wildcat Lane"

Nick's head shot up, and the hair on the back of his neck stood.

"Are there injuries on the scene?"

"I don't know. She seems okay, but it may be adrenaline. You should send an ambulance. We're going to need help with the truck and trailer, too."

Nick met Paul's eyes on the other side of the room.

"Let's go," Paul said. "I'm driving."

Over the course of the short drive, Nick found himself praying more than he'd ever prayed in his life. He knew in his gut that it was Taylor, and all he could think of was, *how would I go on without her?*

When they pulled up to the scene, Nick had his seatbelt off and door opened before Paul put the vehicle in Park.

"Taylor!" He yelled as he ran past Dan's truck.

She looked up and ran to him, throwing her arms around his neck. Nick pulled back, holding her forearms in his hands so that he could get a good look. They heard the approaching ambulance behind them.

"Are you okay?"

Taylor nodded. "I think so. I don't know what happened. I remember knowing something was wrong with the trailer, feeling it pulling the truck over, and then I woke up with everything on its side and rain coming in through the cracked windshield."

Nick looked down and saw the blood seeping through her shirt. "You're bleeding." His heart raced as he lifted her shirt to assess the wound.

"I did it when I climbed through the windshield. I'd forgotten about it until now."

"She's got a gash in her gut," Nick yelled to one of the EMTs. A stretcher was brought over, but Taylor shook her head.

"Oh, no, I'm not going anywhere."

"We've got to get you checked out," one of the EMTs said. Taylor did not recognize him and wondered where her high school friend, Tori, was.

"I can't leave my horse."

"Seth's bringing my trailer," Dan said. "I'll get him to Doctor Peterson and have him checked out."

Taylor grabbed Nick's shirt and locked eyes on him. "Please, don't let them take me. I have to know he's okay."

"Taylor, don't get me wrong. I know you love that horse, but dammit, I love you, and you've probably lost a pint of blood. I'm not letting you lose more."

The pleading in her eyes turned to surprise, and then tears began to flow. She nodded and let him pick her up and lay her gently on the stretcher.

Nick looked at Paul.

"Go with her. I'll stay with Dan and the horse. I'll call Steve and Chris to help secure the scene."

As they walked toward the ambulance, Nick heard Dan say to Paul. "You might want to call in a forensics team. That tire has a horseshoe nail it, and I don't think it got there by accident. I think someone was trying to send a message."

***

"You have another baby girl, Aaron. Come cut the cord, Dad."

A lump formed in his throat as Aaron moved toward his new daughter. Miren's birth was filled with a whirlwind of emotions. As soon as she was born, Kate had been rushed into heart surgery, and Miren was whisked away to the NICU. Now, he was gazing at a baby who looked completely healthy, not the size that his nephews were at birth, but bigger than her palm-sized sister had been.

The baby let out a loud wail, nothing like the quiet mewing that Miren did at birth, and Aaron felt a warm tear run down his face.

"Is she…?"

Debbie quickly explained the care that the baby would be given before turning and looking at her patient. "Ready to finish up, Kate?"

"Can I hold her?"

"As soon as she's checked out. Let's get things finished down here." Debbie glanced toward the monitor. "How's she looking?"

"Her vitals are good. Heartbeat's normal. Breathing is as expected."

"Good." Debbie nodded. "Let's get it done, Kate. Your baby is waiting for you."

Aaron went to the other side of the room and watched the nurses attending to his daughter. He thought her color looked good, but he didn't really know what to look for.

"APGAR is a solid 9," the nurse called out with a smile.

"Is that good?" Aaron thought it was good, but everything he and Kate had been taught in class went right out the window hours earlier, the moment Kate called him.

"It's almost perfect. Your baby is a fighter, Dad."

Another wave of emotions hit him, and Aaron found it difficult to maintain his composure. He went to Kate's side. He could read the questions in her expression.

"She's a 9 on the APGAR test. She has good color, and did you hear her cry?"

For the first time since they arrived, he saw Kate smile. "She's okay?"

"Better than okay," a nurse said as she slid between them and placed the baby in Kate's arms. "You can hold her for a minute, but she needs to be checked out and probably put on CPAP. Don't worry. It's what she needs to make sure she knows how to breathe. That doesn't mean anything is wrong."

Aaron recalled their first few days with Miren. Kate was so weak, she couldn't go see her, and Miren was in the NICU for months. The CPAP had been one of dozens of things she was hooked up to. Seeing his wife holding their baby so soon after this birth was the happiest moment of his life. Whatever they needed to do to keep her healthy was okay with him.

"Name for the birth certificate?" another nurse called to them.

Aaron looked at Kate and smiled. "Sarah Hope."

"Did you hear that, Sarah? You have a beautiful name." The nurse holding Sarah smiled.

"It means 'Princess' in Irish," Kate told her.

Aaron winked at his wife. "A princess for my princess."

A few minutes later, Aaron was in the NICU with his daughter when the pediatrician came in. Aaron watched and listened attentively and was overjoyed when the doctor said that all that was needed was the continuous positive air pressure for a couple days. The baby would remain in the NICU for a few weeks, but there was no reason to believe that she wouldn't be a completely healthy child.

Aaron was beside himself with joy when he went to the family waiting room to see his mother. Kayla was there with their mother as well as Zach.

"It's a girl," was all Aaron could say before a flood of joyful tears was unleashed.

***

Nick was surprised to see Trevor walking into the hospital carrying Miren. "Trevor, what are you doing here? Is Miren okay?"

"She's fine. I'm here to see my granddaughter. My *other* granddaughter." Trevor's smile was radiant.

"Your other granddaughter? Kate had the baby?"

"She did. During that storm."

"Is she okay?"

"Better than okay, from what I hear." Trevor's smile morphed into a frown as he took in Nick's appearance and the blood on his shirt. "Nick, why are you here? Is someone hurt?"

"Taylor was in an accident. She's fine. She needed stitches and some blood, but she's okay. I'm just getting some coffee while she's sleeping. They're keeping her overnight as a precaution."

"Was it caused by the storm?"

"She was on her way back from riding her horse, and the trailer got a flat tire. She lost control in the rain, and it rolled. Took the truck with it."

"My goodness. And she only needed stitches?"

"She said it was a miracle." Nick looked around and bent close to Trevor. He lowered his voice. "It might have been a miracle, but it was no accident. Paul said that a horseshoe nail was embedded in the tire."

"How does that happen? Taylor would never be so careless as to leave one of those lying around."

"Exactly," Nick said. "Someone wanted that tire to go flat."

Trevor straightened and blew out his breath. "Thank God she's okay."

"You're telling me," Nick agreed.

***

Taylor ran her hands along every inch of her father's horse. She knew that the vet had given him a clean bill of health, but she still couldn't quite believe it. There was no excuse for either of them making it out virtually unscathed, and Taylor thanked God several times a day for taking care of her and the horse.

"How many times are you going to check him out?" Nick asked. He was leaning against the door jamb of the open barn.

"As many times as it takes to convince myself that he's really okay." Taylor gave Big Red an apple and walked over to Nick. "I still can't get over it."

"That you weren't seriously hurt?"

"No, that someone purposely did that to us. Who would want to hurt my horse?"

Nick tilted his head back and forth, cracking his neck, in a gesture she had come to recognize as stalling. "Someone who didn't want you to be able to ride him. Or someone who wanted to hurt the horse and you at the same time."

"I refuse to believe it, Nick. I told you that. It's not the way we do things around here, not the way we treat people."

"You upset a lot of people, Taylor. You said yourself that you've received threats."

She shook her head. "It's just not possible."

Nick took her by the arms and forced her to look at him. "Someone let the horses out of the yard. You know that was done on purpose. Why can't you see that the same person could have put that nail in the tire?"

"Because letting horses out of the yard is a heck of a lot different than almost getting someone killed." She took a deep breath and blinked away tears. If anything had happened to her father's horse, she never would have forgiven herself. Maybe the naysayers were right. Maybe she should have walked away, just let things go, and let the status quo continue.

"I see those wheels turning," Nick said quietly. "Don't go there. You did the right thing."

"Are you sure about that?"

"I'm positive."

Taylor moved closer until Nick wrapped his arms around her and pulled her to him. She melted into his chest.

"Thank you," she breathed.

"For what?"

Taylor raised her eyes to his. "For being here at every moment I've needed you the most."

"I'll always be here. I meant what I said that night. I love you, Taylor."

"I love you, too, Nick."

***

Kayla was nervous as she and Zach waited for the attorneys to finish their closed-door meeting. When the door finally opened, Rebecca Adams motioned for them to enter.

A representative of Lifetime Television welcomed them to the room. "We have the paperwork for you to sign."

Kayla looked at Rebecca. "And this agreement covers all the terms we discussed?"

"It does. It's all in writing." Kayla saw the woman send a smile toward a scowling man in a dark suit. He looked familiar to her.

Rebecca continued. "You and the boys will never be mentioned by name. The woman who plays you in the movie will have her scenes cut. It will be as if the three of you never existed."

"I don't look forward to that call," said one of the executives seated at the table.

"It's either that, or we sue. You do not have the authorization to use Kayla's name or likeness in the movie. I believe the agreement makes that perfectly clear."

"It does." The man glowered at Rebecca. "Let's get this over with." The man extended the pen to Kayla, and something in her mind clicked. He reminded her of Richard Gere's character in *Pretty Woman*—an older, distinguished-looking man with wavy gray hair, blue eyes, and, she assumed, a killer smile, though, under the circumstances, she had yet to see him smile.

Kayla looked at Zach. Should she trust these men? Would they keep their word? Was this truly legally binding? As if reading her thoughts, Rebecca nodded to her. "Go ahead. You will finally be able to put this chapter behind you."

Though Kayla doubted that would ever be the case, she reached for the pen. She signed with a shaky hand and handed the pen back to the Richard Gere look alike.

***

"Kate, dear, she's beautiful." Walter Middleton beamed as he looked at his granddaughter. "She has her grandmother's eyes."

"Dad, she can't open her eyes long enough for us to get a look at them yet."

He leaned down and lowered his voice conspiratorially. "I mean the wrinkles in the corners."

"I heard that," Mitzi said, playfully punching him in the arm.

"Eyes open or not, she's the prettiest baby in here."

"Dad, I'm not sure the other moms would agree."

"Not out loud maybe."

Kate shook her head, but she silently agreed. Sarah was gaining weight every day. She had been on the CPAP for the first 48 hours, but she hadn't needed the ventilators. She was breathing just fine on her own and was taken off the precautionary machine as soon as the doctor was confident she didn't need it. Once again, Kate and Aaron had been blessed with a miracle baby. She prayed that Sarah would only have to remain in the hospital for a couple more weeks, and so far, she was right on track.

***

Steve stuck his head into the breakroom. "Nick, Zach's here to see you. He says it's important."

Nick headed toward his desk where Zach waited. As he neared his friend and saw his face, Nick's pleasure faded. He noticed EJ sitting in the chair beside Nick's desk and glanced at Zach.

"Hey, Zach, what's going on?"

"EJ has something he thinks you ought to know."

Nick took a seat and looked at the boy.

"What it is, EJ? Is everything okay?"

EJ shook his head. "No, it's not okay." He exhaled and looked up at Zach.

"Go ahead, son, tell him."

EJ looked at Nick. "I was at work today. You know, in the produce department. And I heard some kids talking. They didn't know I was around the corner. One of them said he was sorry Taylor and her horse weren't hurt, but the other said he didn't want them hurt. He only wanted to scare her into dropping out." EJ paused and took another deep breath. "That's all I heard, but I think we both know what they were talking about."

Nick just looked at the kid. Was he sure about this? Heck, this was EJ. He was always sure. He wouldn't be here if he wasn't.

"EJ, do you know who the kids were?"

He nodded. "Yeah, they're high schoolers, but I know them. One of them is Mark Fields, and the other…" He swallowed and looked up at Zach.

"Go ahead, EJ. Tell him."

With trepidation in his eyes, EJ looked at Zach and whispered. "The other one was Billy Hill."

Nick sat back and closed his eyes. Shannon and Lou were prominent members of the community. Shannon ran the local library and was close friends with Kayla and Kate. Shannon and Paul's wife, Anne, were very close friends.

"Okay, EJ, thanks for telling me. I'll talk to Chief Parker, and we'll figure out what we're going to do."

EJ stood and looked at Nick. "I'm real sorry about what happened to Taylor. I wish I had known sooner."

"There's no use worrying about that. We know now, and we can stop them from doing anything else."

"Good luck, Nick," Zach said.

"Thanks. And congrats to Kayla."

"Thanks. Tell Taylor the attorney was great and we're very thankful."

"Will do."

Nick watched them leave before heading to Paul's office. He did not look forward to the rest of the day.

***

Taylor spotted Nick right away when she exited the clinic. He was leaning against his police car. She made her way over to him, happy to see him, but there was something in his expression that caught her off guard. She hugged him and gave him a quick kiss before scrutinizing his gaze.

"What's wrong?"

"Nothing. What did Debbie say?"

She regarded him with suspicion. "I'm cleared. The stitches will be out in time for the swim, and I'm still showing no signs of a concussion though I honestly don't know how I was so lucky. I just wish I knew who did it."

"Well, it looks like we have an answer to that. Can you sit for a few minutes?"

So, that's what this is about. She nodded and waited for him to open the passenger door. Once inside the car, she found herself unsure about whether she really wanted to know the truth. Her mouth was dry, and she could feel her heart beating faster than normal.

Nick closed his door and turned to face her. "It was just a couple kids. They wanted to scare you. It was stupid, but they weren't trying to hurt you."

"Why were they trying to scare me?"

Nick frowned. "They thought they were standing up for an island tradition."

"Who are they?"

"One was Mark Fields. The other was Billy Hill."

"No!" She gasped. "They're such good kids. They're both friends with Jenny. What would make them do that?" A thought struck her. "Did they open the gates at the ranch?"

Nick nodded. "I'm afraid so. Again, they weren't trying to hurt anyone. They just wanted you to quit the Pony Committee."

Taylor sat back and stared through the windshield. She didn't know how she felt. She hated that she caused such division within her community and that there were those who were willing to put her and her animals in harm's way just to make her back down.

"None of this was what I wanted." She continued to stare ahead, not really focusing on anything. "I just wanted to be part of it all. I wanted to ride alongside the ponies and bring them to the island and escort them down Main Street. Was I being selfish?" She looked at Nick, hoping he could offer her some peace of mind.

"Do you remember what you told me about that little girl who said you were her hero? How that made you feel like you were doing this for her, even more than yourself?"

Taylor felt a sharp pain in her lip and realized she'd been biting it hard enough to cause a bruise. "Yes, I meant that. As much as I wanted this for me, I really want to make it so that any little girl who dreams of riding in the pony swim knows she has a good chance of being able to."

"Then you did the right thing. But I have to ask, do you want to press charges against the kids? Nobody was seriously hurt, so it's in your hands."

Taylor considered the implications. If she didn't press charges, the boys would think what they did was no big deal. On the other hand, if she did, was she prolonging the division? Would she feel bad every time she walked into the library and had to face Billy's mother? Mrs. Hill was such a sweet person.

"I don't know what to do. Can I sit on it for a day? Pray about it?"

"Sure. I'll let Paul know you need some time. We can hold them for a bit, make 'em squirm."

"No. I'm sure they're freaked out enough. Let their parents take them home. I'm going to take some time to figure it out. I just wish this wasn't so hard."

"Remember this, just because it's hard doesn't mean it isn't right. As Grandmother Willow said, 'sometimes the right path isn't the easiest one'."

"Nick, how is it you always have a Disney quote for every occasion?"

"I've told you. Disney movies have all the best advice you'll ever need."

"You do make me smile; you know that?"

"That's my job, ma'am."

They kissed goodbye, and Taylor smirked as she watched him drive away. She got in her truck and headed to the one place she knew she could find peace and hopefully some answers.

Taylor sat on the hard, wooden seat and wrung her hands. Candles glowed, casting a soft light on the statues that peered down at her. She silently implored God for direction.

Even with the suit decided, people were still angry. Despite Will giving his word that he would tell them to stop, she continued to receive calls and emails that made her doubt everything.

"I'm sorry to bother you, but you look like you could use some help."

Taylor looked into the smiling face of the young, red-bearded priest.

"Father Darryl, hello. I was hoping to find some answers, but I'm not sure God is listening today."

The priest sat down next to her.

"Nonsense. God is always listening. We're the ones who usually aren't paying attention to what he's trying to tell us."

"Then I'm in real trouble because I think he may be trying to tell me what I don't want to hear."

"Do you want to talk about it?"

Taylor took a long breath and let it out. She started with her dream to ride with the ponies, told him about her father's will, explained the legal suit, and recounted the incidents, emails, phone calls, and conversations that had taken place. Father nodded, smiled kindly, and asked a few questions here and there.

"Some of the letters in the paper were quite harsh," he told her.

"You saw them?"

His blue eyes conveyed compassion. "I did. I prayed that you would be strong and not take them to heart, and I prayed that those who wrote them would develop empathy. It's hard fighting the system, especially when it seems like so many are against you. But it's also hard letting go of the past and being open to change."

"So, what do I do now? I have to decide whether to punish these boys, who truly do deserve to be punished, or let it go so that I'm not seen as a vengeful person."

"I hardly think anyone would see you as vengeful. Those boys could have caused real harm to your animals, and they could have killed you."

"But you wouldn't press charges, would you?"

Father was quiet as he looked toward the altar. "Jesus said, 'If your brother or sister sins against you, rebuke them; and if they repent, forgive them. Even if they sin against you seven times in a day and seven times come back to you saying, 'I repent,' you must forgive them'."

"Then what do I do? Just let it go?"

"No, not let it go. Even after making a confession, the sinner is expected to do penance. If it were me, I would find another way to make them see the error of their ways. I'm sure you can think of a compassionate way to force them to repent while not subjecting them to too much publicity, criticism, or lasting judgement."

An idea began to brew within her brain. "Father, I think I understand what you're getting at. Yes, I can find a way to let them know they were wrong without causing them to have a criminal record. They're just kids. They were stupid and reckless, and I want to teach them a lesson but not make it something that haunts them as they grow up." She leaned over and hugged him. "Thank you, Father. Thank you."

"You're welcome, Taylor. God be with you."

Taylor left the church with a better sense of how to handle things. She just had some homework to do first.

Have you ever seen the sun rise over an island in the Atlantic? I've seen amazing sunrises in some of the most picturesque places in the world, and they've all been spectacular. But imagine seeing the sun peek over the horizon, surrounded by pink and purple clouds, a golden glow sending a radiant beam across the water, creating a picture-perfect reflection. A boat slowly moves across the mirror-like surface, sending ripples in the reflected beam. Add to that a brown and white speckled pony, standing in the marsh grass, looking off into the distance. This is what he witnesses every morning. It's his world, and he welcomes us to it. It's breathtaking, and it's where I call home.

From *Discovering the World On a Barrier Island*
by Katherine Middleton Kelly

CHAPTER SEVENTEEN

The end of July came in a hurry, and the entire island was abuzz with everything ponies. Try as she may, Taylor wasn't able to fall asleep the night before the pony swim. At two in the morning, she got out of bed and dressed. She tiptoed downstairs to the office. Almost all of her father's personal belongings were now packed away. All the framed pictures on the walls had been replaced by ones that Taylor picked out, except for one. By the light of a lamp, she stood and gazed at the photograph of her father, at the age of nineteen, sitting on a horse beside the herd of ponies on the beaches of Assateague. His grin was as wide as the crescent moon that hung over his head. The photographer had perfectly captured his excitement as he prepared for his first pony swim.

"Thank you, Dad," Taylor whispered. "For teaching me about the ponies, for making me love them as much as you did, and for making everyone finally stand up and do the right thing."

Taylor wiped away a tear and headed to the kitchen for a cup of coffee. She knew her father would be riding with her today. He always knew she would take his place, and she knew she was blessed to have him in her life, guiding her, protecting her, teaching her, loving her, and supporting her, for twenty-three years.

Hours later, as the sun rose over the Channel, Taylor secured the hat on her head and spurred her horse down the beach, surrounded by a beautiful herd of ponies. Everything felt surreal. The weather was perfect, warm with an ocean breeze gently blowing across the sand, and dolphins swam near the shore as if coming to witness the more than decades-old event. When they neared the shoreline of the Assateague Channel, Taylor and the rest of the riders waited for the signal that the tide was slack, which would give them a thirty-minute window to get the ponies safely across.

The current was strong. At times, Taylor struggled to hold her horse steady and keep the ponies together, but she knew what she was doing and managed to drive the herd toward shore. Before long, she saw the first ponies hit the dry land and heard the roar of the crowd that awaited them.

The ponies were herded onto the shore, and Taylor waited for word that they should begin their procession down Main Street. When Big Red stepped onto the street, Taylor heard the sound of little girls and grown women calling her name. She held back tears as she waved to friends, neighbors, and strangers. She saw more than one photographer take her picture but tried to ignore the reporters calling to her. This was not her day. She did not want to be the story. This was a day of celebration for all horse lovers, no matter their gender.

***

Nick loaded his jet ski onto the back of the truck. He only glimpsed Taylor once when they were on the water, but the picture would forever be imprinted in his mind. She looked like she was born to sit on top of a horse. Her braided hair hung down her back beneath a white cowboy hat. Her face was set with determination as she glided through the water, cracking her whip on the waves to spur the ponies on.

Many of the police rode nearby, keeping the scores of boats and kayaks at a safe distance. Nick felt the enthusiasm of the crowd and thanked God for allowing him to be part of the day. He'd been doing that a lot lately, thanking God, and he felt like it actually made a difference in his life. He no longer worried about his upbringing or any baggage he once carried. Zach and Taylor were right. Once he relented and let the Man Upstairs take charge, he felt like a new man. He felt worthy of Taylor, but more important, he felt worthy of himself, of the man he had become. And for the first time in his entire life, he knew he had found a home—

a place to live, to love, to worship, and to become all that he was meant to be.

***

Mark and Billy were covered in mud. They smelled like sweat and dirt and horse dung. When the boys appeared before a local judge after their arrest, they were told that their victim advocated that their crimes not become part of their permanent record. Instead, they were to do community service. As commiserate with the law, the service needed to be connected to the crime and benefit the public.

For the entire twenty-four hours that the ponies would be on Chincoteague, the boys would be responsible for cleaning up after them. They followed the procession down the street, scooping and shoveling droppings into a wheelbarrow. Once the ponies were penned, the boys were to perform cleanup duties for the rest of that day and each day, between the hours of seven in the morning until five in the afternoon, until every pony was not only purchased but released.

Grateful to not have a more stringent punishment, the boys accepted the terms. They knew that the sentences they were going to be handed at home would be far worse.

***

Taylor hurried through the carnival grounds, scanning the crowd for a particular police officer. Now and then, a little girl would stop and ask for an autograph. Taylor tried to be as inconspicuous as possible when granting the request. She didn't need everybody on the island talking about her as if the attention and accolades were all that mattered to her. She was uncomfortable with her sudden celebrity status, but she also recognized that she was an inspiration for many little girls. As she walked the grounds, she smiled and waved at people she knew. She stopped briefly to lavish love and kisses on baby Sarah, and she accepted hugs and congratulatory remarks from her Uncle Trevor and Aunt Ronnie. When she ran into Steve and Chris, she inquired about Nick, but they had not seen him since they parted ways after loading their jet skis.

Taylor couldn't think of a single place she hadn't looked and was about to give up when she ran into Zach, Kayla, and the boys. "Have you seen Nick anywhere?"

Zach responded no, but Taylor saw a look pass between Todd and EJ.

"OK, spill it. You boys know something you're not telling me."

"Oh, look," Kayla said, pointing to the other side of the carnival grounds. "I see my parents. We shouldn't keep them waiting. We'll see you later Taylor. Congratulations again. I can't tell you what a thrill it was to see you coming onto the shore with the ponies."

Before Taylor could respond or question them further, the family headed off in the direction where she had seen her aunt and uncle. Keenly aware that she was missing something, Taylor continued searching for Nick.

Once she covered the entire carnival grounds and never ran into him, Taylor gave up looking, knowing she needed to get Big Red home. She went back to the corral where the horses were, found her steed, and began the long, hot ride back to Assateague where her truck and trailer waited. Disappointed that she had not been able to find Nick anywhere, Taylor loaded up the horse and started for the ranch.

There were hundreds of cars and thousands of people on the island, and it took Taylor twice as long to get back home as it normally would have. She was exhausted by the time she got the horse settled and checked on Stormy. All she could think of was a soothing bath and a long nap.

When Taylor walked into the house, an enormous bouquet of flowers sat in the middle of the table that was the centerpiece of the foyer. There were sprays of greenery, lilies, white delphinium, and three dozen roses in an array of colors. The bouquet was magnificent in color, quality, and design. Lying on the table, in front of the flowers, was a small envelope with her name on it. Taylor opened the envelope and pulled out the card that was tucked inside. As she read the card, tears began to flow down her cheeks. By the time she was finished, her tears had turned into sobs, and she could barely stand on her own two feet. Her father's final words to her made everything else that happened that day pale by comparison.

My dearest, Taylor. If you are reading this, then I am no longer there, but my final wish was granted. Starting from the time you were five-years-old, I watched you with the ponies, and I knew it was your destiny to cross the Channel with them. When you turned fourteen, I began courting the Pony Committee. I implored them to consider you as a member. I told them I would never give up, and I never did.

Taylor, I know that you will be a fine Cowgirl and an example to every child, boy or girl, who dares to follow his or her dreams and go where it wasn't thought possible. You and Jenny are, and always will be, the most prized flowers in my garden. I love you and know that you will make me proud.

Love, Dad

***

When Nick's shift ended, he hurried home, showered, and stood in front of his open closet. He selected his best dress shirt and a pair of slacks. He checked the time and figured Taylor would have had plenty of time to get some rest. He made several quick phone calls to ensure that all his plans were in place.

As planned, he went to the front door of the big white house rather than the side door he had been using since Taylor showed him the alternate entrance the night of their first date. He listened to the chime and the footsteps that hastened to the door.

"She's almost ready," Jenny told him. "I made sure she wore a dress even though she said it was too hot for it and she didn't feel like going out." Jenny grinned conspiratorially. "She looks beautiful."

Nick had no doubt about that, but when he looked past Jenny to where Taylor stood inside the doorway, his heart skipped a beat.

She stood next to the biggest flower arrangement he had ever seen, but the beauty of the flowers was nothing compared to the woman next to them. Wearing a yellow sundress, with her blonde hair pulled back in her classic braid and a smile on her face, Taylor made the flowers look like weeds.

"What's going on? Jenny wouldn't tell me anything."

"And what fun would that have been?" Nick asked, holding his hand out for hers.

Taylor accepted Nick's hand, and he led her to his car. "You're not telling me anything, are you?" she asked as he opened the door and waited for her to get in.

"Not a thing."

As they drove, Nick asked about the ride. He swelled with pride and happiness as he listened to her recount the morning. She had to pause several times as her emotions got the better of her. When she told him what greeted her when she arrived at home, he wished, for the first time in his life, that he owned one of those old-fashioned handkerchiefs so he could hand it to her to dry her tears.

By the time she finished telling Nick about her day, he brought the car to a stop under a canopy of trees.

"We'll walk from here. I think you know the way."

Taylor shot him a quizzical look. "When Jenny told me to dress up, this was not what I pictured us doing."

Nick shrugged but didn't say a word. He hoped that his vision was as good in real life as it had been in his imagination. With Kayla in charge, he was sure it would be.

Nick opened Taylor's door and reached for her hand. He closed the door behind her and led her through the trees to the secluded cove she had taken him to months back.

"Oh, Nick," she gasped. "How did you do this?"

Centered in the cove was a table covered with a pink tablecloth. Candles glowed from silver candlesticks, and two places had been set with white china. A bottle of champagne was buried in ice in a holder next to the table. Nick took his phone out of his pocket and hit play, and the air was filled with songs from a collection of Disney movie love ballads played by the Boston Symphony Orchestra. Taylor laughed. "Only you, Nick."

"If you'll take a seat, dinner can be served."

Taylor's brow knit together as she looked around. "Dinner? How…?"

Without a word, EJ and his girlfriend, Lizzie, materialized from the trees, each holding a tray with a covered dish. Taylor's laughter spilled from her, and Nick saw her bite down on her lip to stop herself. "Now I know what you and your brother were hiding."

Nick led Taylor to her seat, pulled out the chair, and waited for her to get settled before taking his own seat. The kids put the trays in front of Taylor and Nick. Nick handed EJ a roll of money, winked, and said, "Okay, your dad should be back by now." After they were gone, he said to Taylor, "Zach's been with them. Your sister texted him to tell him to hide the car. After we got here, he moved it back. He didn't want to leave the two of them down here alone."

"I should say not." Taylor grinned, and her eyes twinkled in the moonlight. "So, what's on the menu?"

"Let's find out." Nick lifted the cover from his dish, and Taylor followed suit.

"Fried chicken, cole slaw, and biscuits?"

Nick shrugged. "I figured, it's good hot or cold."

"Good point."

They put the lids on the ground beneath their chairs, and Taylor reached for both of his hands. They bowed their heads while Taylor prayed.

"So, what's this all about?" Taylor asked before they began their meal.

Nick lifted the bottle of champagne from the wine chiller and poured some in each of their glasses.

"A toast, to the first Saltwater Cowgirl and the success of her first ride."

They sipped their drinks, and then Taylor held her glass up again. "And to the man who made it happen, my father."

"To Pete Murray, may he be riding winged horses for eternity."

Taylor took a drink and set down her glass. "Thank you, Nick, for believing in me and supporting me. And for doing this."

"This was nothing. I wanted to celebrate your ride with just the two of us, but I wanted it to be more special than eating pizza at my place."

Taylor held up a drumstick. "Fried chicken is definitely more special than pizza."

"I figured you would have had enough of crowds and onlookers and kids asking for your autograph."

"How did you...? Wait, you saw me? At the carnival grounds? I looked everywhere for you."

"I didn't want to take away from your moment. It was sweet, the way those girls looked up to you, and the embarrassment on your face. You kept trying to hide the papers as you signed them."

"I didn't want people to get the wrong impression. I was never in this for any kind of fame or glory."

"Taylor, anyone who knows you, knows that already."

They talked and laughed; they ate and drank champagne, and Nick knew without a doubt that he never wanted this feeling to end.

***

On a warm Saturday in October, Nick, Taylor, Chad, and Holly went out for a boat ride. The crowds were gone, town was quiet, and the foursome all had a rare day off at the same time.

"Anyone want to fish?"

Taylor glanced behind her to see Nick holding a fishing line. "I thought this was a pleasure ride. I didn't know we were turning it into a fishing party."

"I'm always in favor of a fishing party," Chad said.

Taylor looked around. "I only see one rod. Why didn't you bring enough for everyone?"

"Didn't think of it. We can take turns. Can you grab me a drink while I bait the hook?"

Taylor walked to the cooler in the bow of the boat and pulled out a beer.

"Nick, why is there a bottle of champagne in the cooler?" Taylor lost her train of thought when she turned around and saw Nick, on bended knee, extending a fishing line toward her. On the hook, instead of bait, was a diamond ring. Her breath caught in her throat as she looked up at Nick.

"Taylor Corrine Murray, I love you, and I don't want you to be the one that got away. Will you be my keeper?"

Taylor's grin widened. She felt a laugh coming all the way from her belly. "Nick, that is the corniest thing I've ever heard." Still laughing, she took hold of the end of the line and let him reel her toward him. "But it's also the most beautiful." She kissed him while Chad and Holly cheered.

Blushing, Taylor looked at her friends. "Did you all know about this?"

"We might have known something," Holly told her.

"But if I had known what he was going to say, I would have intervened." Chad smiled as he punched Nick in the arm.

Taylor took the ring off the hook and handed it to Nick. "I think I know of a better place for this." She held out her left hand, and Nick slid the ring into place.

"Look, there's a pony!" Holly pointed toward Assateague. "I've never seen one this close to an anchoring boat. It's like he's watching us."

The sun reflected off the water as Angel, the first horse Taylor and her father bought, stood in the water. Nick pulled Taylor to him so that her back was against his chest. He leaned down and whispered in her ear. "I think he knows it's you."

"I think he wanted to check you out, to make sure you're the right guy for me."

"Well, I know you're the right woman for me." He paused and pulled her even tighter against him. "You know, Taylor, coming to this island was the smartest thing I'd ever done. Until today."

"There's something special about this place isn't there?" Her gaze stayed on the pony as it turned and walked lazily back to the sandy shoreline. Taylor turned her head so that her eyes locked with Nick's. "It's the place that made all my dreams come true."

Nick wrapped his arms around her. "That's all anyone could ever hope for."

The following July

Nick stood in the patrol boat he now commanded. He loved his job as a police officer, but it was even better now that he headed the marine police division. On hot summer days, he had the perfect job. And today, his job gave him the best vantage point to watch the show.

One-hundred ponies began their stampede into the Channel. White droplets filled the air as the horses ran into the water and slipped beneath the waves with only their noses visible. Dozens of men on horseback crossed the Channel with the ponies, along with two women. Sitting high on top of Big Red, Taylor commanded the horse into the water. Her boots skimmed the surface, but the horse stood a good two feet taller than the swimming ponies.

Nick held his breath as the black, brown, and tan noses glided across the water. It was a magnificent sight, and he felt blessed to be a part of it. In fact, he was blessed in too many ways to count. There was his best friend who lived next door, the island he called home, a job he loved, the family and community that adopted him, and the woman who, in a few weeks, would become his wife.

He thought back to the day he was carried into the desert clinic on a stretcher. He was told that he was lucky he hadn't broken his back, but the agonizing pain made him wish he had died in the fall. His life changed that day when he met the soldier in the bed next to him, a sniper who feared his vision, and his career, would be taken from him. The two men bonded and never lost touch. That bond is what led Nick to the island. He marveled at how his life had changed since then.

Like everyone in his adopted family, Nick had prayed for and witnessed miracles, made promises that were broken and promises that were kept, and learned that nothing is impossible with hope. In the end, love was woven with miracles, promises, and hope; Nick was finally a believer in all three.

The End

A Note From the Author

Over the past few years, I have grown to love this little island in the Atlantic Ocean. The messages and letters I've received from residents of Chincoteague, Virginia, warm my heart. I hope that I captured just a piece of what it feels like to live in a small town where everyone watches out for one another, and newcomers are welcomed as friends and family. Sending person after person to live on the island brought me joy and, in a way, allowed me to be a part of the welcoming community.

A few years back, I promised someone very special that I would write a book about him. Though all of the characters in *Island of Hope* are fictional, the young man in this story is the closest to a real person I've ever depicted. His background is not at all like the one described in the book, but I believe I came close to portraying his personality, his mannerisms, and his boyish charm. He is like a son to me, and I felt like he was in the room with me each time I sat down and created a new story for his life. Our Nick is getting married next year, and I welcome his beautiful fiancé, Corrine, to our family.

A book is never complete without thanking those who made it possible. Thank you, Shannon Dolgos, for your honesty after reading the first couple drafts. Thank you, Judith Reveal, my editor, for going back and forth with me as I revised and revised and revised. Thank you, Cheryl Baummer, Debbie Nisson, and Diane Swan, for helping me with the final draft. Thank you, Mom and Dad, for your never-ending support and for reading and critiquing one version after another. Thank you, Ken, Rebecca, Katie Ann, and Morgan, my life and my loves.

A final word about the Chincoteague Island Trilogy…

throughout books one and two, Ronnie was the wise sage to whom everyone turned for advice. You may have noticed, in this book, that several other characters stepped up and took on the roles of mentor and guide. To my real-life Ronnie, I didn't forget or diminish the Ronnie in book three on purpose. I came to understand, as I was writing, that some people are so skilled at departing wisdom, so steadfast in their support, and so strong in their faith, that everything they do and say becomes a part of those around them. People like Ronnie leave an indelible mark on others that reaches to the depths of their very souls. The Ronnies of the world impart wisdom, offer solace and assistance, share their faith, and then quietly sit back and let God do the rest. Ronnie, your humble advice, comfort, and faith have not gone unnoticed. All who know you are better because you are in their lives.

With love and gratitude to all who have touched my heart, I am ever faithfully yours,

About the Author

Amy began writing as a child and never stopped. She wrote articles for magazines and newspapers before writing children's books and adult fiction. A graduate of the University of Maryland with a Master of Library and Information Science, Amy worked as a librarian for fifteen years and, in 2010, began writing full time.

Amy Schisler writes inspirational women's fiction for people of all ages. She has published two children's books and numerous novels, including the award-winning Picture Me, Whispering Vines, and the Chincoteague Island Trilogy. A former librarian, Amy enjoys a busy life on the Eastern Shore of Maryland.

The recipient of numerous national literary awards, including the Illumination Award, LYRA award, Independent Publisher Book Award, International Digital Award, and the Golden Quill Award as well as honors from the Catholic Press Association and the Eric Hoffer Book Award, Amy's writing has been hailed "a verbal masterpiece of art" (author Alexa Jacobs) and "Everything you want in a book" (Amazon reviewer). Amy's books are available internationally, wherever books are sold, in print and eBook formats.

Follow Amy at:
http://amyschislerauthor.com
https://amyschisler.wordpress.com
http://facebook.com/amyschislerauthor
https://twitter.com/AmySchislerAuth
https://www.goodreads.com/amyschisler

<u>Book Club Discussion Questions</u>

1. All Nick really wanted in life was a family of his own. Though Nick was drawn to Zach and his relationship with his family, he was afraid to admit how much he wanted the same. Why do you think that was?

2. Taylor had a comfortable life, a thriving business, and good friends, but she longed for something more. Why do you think it meant so much to her to join the Saltwater Cowboys? Do you think she was trying to prove something to herself or others?

3. Once news broke that Taylor was suing the Pony Committee and Fire Company, she began to receive calls and emails from people, accusing her trying to bring bad publicity to Chincoteague. Have you ever been in a similar situation? How did people react to your actions? Was it felt that your actions were justified in the end?

4. Even after the suit was settled, Taylor continued to be harassed, and she was put in harm's way. Why do you think that there were such strong feelings associated with her fight to be part of the pony swim?

5. Kate feared that she would lose her baby because of the medication she was taking. Have you ever had to make the choice between your own health and someone else's? How did you handle that?

6. Like all mothers, Kayla had to accept that her son, EJ, was no longer a child. Why is it so hard for parents to see that in their own children? What were some of your own experiences with your children that opened your eyes to how much they had grown and matured? How did it make you feel?

7. Trevor overcame a past very similar to Nick's. I've known people with less-than-perfect childhoods who continued to flounder as adults, and I've known some who used those experiences to become better people with fulfilling lives. How do you think Trevor managed to build himself a life so drastically different from the one of his youth? How have you seen this play out in the lives of people you know.

9. Nick came to realize that he needed God in his life. Has there ever been a time when you had that realization? Did you change anything about your life in order to make God a larger part of it?

10. What do you see happening in the future for the Kelly, Middleton, and Black families?